Visit to Iceland - and the Scandinavian North

Ida Pfeiffer

Contents

VISIT TO ICELAND - AND THE SCANDINAVIAN NORTH

BY

Ida Pfeiffer

AUTHOR'S PREFACE

"Another journey--a journey, moreover, in regions which every one would rather avoid than seek. This woman only undertakes these journeys to attract attention."

"The first journey, for a woman ALONE, was certainly rather a bold proceeding. Yet in that instance she might still have been excused. Religious motives may perhaps have actuated her; and when this is the case, people often go through incredible things. At present, however, we can see no just reason which could excuse an undertaking of this description."

Thus, and perhaps more harshly still, will the majority judge me. And yet they will do me a grievous wrong. I am surely simple and harmless enough, and should have fancied any thing in the world rather than that it would ever be my fate to draw upon myself in any degree the notice of the public. I will merely indicate, as briefly as may be, my character and circumstances, and then I have no doubt my conduct will lose its appearance of eccentricity, and seem perfectly natural.

When I was but a little child, I had already a strong desire to see the world. Whenever I met a travelling-carriage, I would stop involuntarily, and gaze after it until it had disappeared; I used even to envy the postilion, for I thought he also must have accomplished the whole long journey.

As I grew to the age of from ten to twelve years, nothing gave me so much pleasure as the perusal of voyages and travels. I ceased, indeed, to envy the postilions, but envied the more every navigator and naturalist.

Frequently my eyes would fill with tears when, having ascended a mountain, I saw others towering before me, and could not gain the summit.

I made several journeys with my parents, and, after my marriage, with my husband; and only settled down when it became necessary that my two boys should visit particular schools. My husband's affairs demanded his entire attention, partly in Lemberg, partly in Vienna. He therefore confided the education and culture of the two boys entirely to my care; for he knew my firmness and perseverance in all I undertook, and doubted not that I would be both father and mother to his children.

When my sons' education had been completed, and I was living in peaceful retirement, the dreams and aspirations of my youth gradually awoke once more. I thought of strange manners and customs, of distant regions, where a new sky would be above me, and new ground beneath my feet. I pictured to myself the supreme happiness of treading the land once hallowed by the presence of our Saviour, and at length made up my mind to travel thither.

As dangers and difficulties rose before my mind, I endeavoured to wean myself from the idea I had formed--but in vain. For privation I cared but little; my health was good and my frame hardy: I did not fear death. And moreover, as I was born in the last century, I could travel ALONE. Thus every objection was overcome; every thing had been duly weighed and considered. I commenced my journey to Palestine with a feeling of perfect rapture; and behold, I returned in safety. I now feel persuaded that I am neither tempting Providence, nor justly incurring the imputation of wishing to be talked about, in following the bent of my inclinations, and looking still further about me in the world I chose Iceland for my destination, because I hoped there to find Nature in a garb such as she wears nowhere else. I feel so completely happy, so brought into communion with my Maker, when I contemplate sublime natural phenomena, that in my eyes no degree of toil or difficulty is too great a price at which to purchase such perfect enjoyment.

And should death overtake me sooner or later during my wanderings, I shall await his approach in all resignation, and be deeply grateful to the Almighty for the hours of holy beauty in which I have lived and gazed upon His wonders.

And now, dear reader, I would beg thee not to be angry with me for speaking so much of myself; it is only because this love of travelling does not, according to established notions, seem proper for one of my sex, that I have allowed my feelings to speak in my defence.

Judge me, therefore, not too harshly; but rather grant me the enjoyment of a pleasure which hurts no one, while it makes me happy.

THE AUTHOR.

CHAPTER I

In the year 1845 I undertook another journey; {2} a journey, moreover, to the far North. Iceland was one of those regions towards which, from the earliest period of my consciousness, I had felt myself impelled. In this country, stamped as it is by Nature with features so peculiar, as probably to have no counterpart on the face of the globe, I hoped to see things which should fill me with new and inexpressible astonishment. How deeply grateful do I feel to Thee, O Thou that hast vouchsafed to me to behold the fulfilment of these my cherished dreams!

The parting from all my dear ones had this time far less bitterness; I had found by experience, that a woman of an energetic mind can find her way through the world as well as a man, and that good people are to be met with every where. To this was added the reflection, that the hardships of my present voyage would be of short duration, and that five or six months might see me restored to my family.

I left Vienna at five o'clock on the morning of the tenth of April. As the Danube had lately caused some devastations, on which occasion the railroad had not entirely escaped, we rode for the first four miles, as far as Florisdorf, in an omnibus--not the most agreeable mode of travelling. Our omnibuses are so small and narrow, that one would suppose they were built for the exclusive accommodation of consumptive subjects, and not for healthy, and in some cases portly individuals, whose bulk is further increased by a goodly assemblage of cloaks, furs, and overcoats.

At the barriers a new difficulty arose. We delivered up our pass-warrants (*passirscheine*) in turn, with the exception of one young man, who was quite astounded at the demand. He had provided nothing but his passport and testimonials, being totally unaware that a pass-warrant is more indispensable than all the rest. In vain did he hasten into the bureau to expostulate with the officials,--we were forced to continue our journey without him.

We were informed that he was a student, who, at the conclusion of term, was about to make holiday for a few weeks at his parents' house near Prague. Alas, poor youth! he had studied so much, and yet knew so little. He had not even an idea of the overwhelming importance of the document in question. For this trifling omission he forfeited the fare to Prague, which had been paid in advance.

But to proceed with my journey.

At Florisdorf a joyful surprise awaited me. I met my brother and my son, who had, it appears, preceded me. We entered the train to proceed in company to Stockerau, a place between twelve and thirteen miles off; but were obliged to alight halfway, and walk a short distance. The Embankment had given way. Luckily the weather was favourable, inasmuch as we had only a violent storm of wind. Had it rained, we should have been wetted to the skin, besides being compelled to wade ankle-deep in mud. We were next obliged to remain in the open air, awaiting the arrival of the train from Stockerau, which unloaded its freight, and received us in exchange.

At Stockerau I once more took leave of my companions, and was soon securely packed in the post-carriage for transmission.

In travelling this short distance, I had thus entered four carriages; a thing sufficiently disagreeable to an unencumbered person, but infinitely more so to one who has luggage to watch over. The only advantage I could discover in all this was, that we had saved half an hour in coming these seventeen miles. For this, instead of 9 fl. 26 kr. from Vienna to Prague, we paid 10 fl. 10 kr. from Stockerau to Prague, without reckoning expense of omnibus and railway. It was certainly a dearly-bought half-hour. {3}

The little town of Znaim, with its neighbouring convent, is situated on a large plain, extending from Vienna to Budwitz, seventeen miles beyond Znaim; the monotony of the view is only broken here and there by low hills.

Near Schelletau the scenery begins to improve. On the left the view is bounded by a range of high hills, with a ruined castle, suggestive of tragical tales of centuries gone by. Fir and pine forests skirt the road, and lie scattered in picturesque groups over hill and dale.

April 11th.

Yesterday the weather had already begun to be ungracious to us. At Znaim we found the valleys still partly covered with snow, and the fog was at times so thick, that we could not see a hundred paces in advance; but to-day it was incomparably worse. The mist resolved itself into a mild rain, which, however, lost so much of its mildness as we passed from station to station, that every thing around us was soon under water. But not only did we ride through water, we were obliged to sit in it also. The roof of our carriage threatened to become a perfect sieve, and the rain poured steadily in. Had there been room for such a proceeding, we should all have unfurled our umbrellas.

On occasions like these, I always silently admire the patience of my worthy countrymen, who take every thing so good-humouredly. Were I a man, I should pursue a different plan, and should certainly not fail to complain of such careless-ness. But as a woman, I must hold my peace; people would only rail at my sex, and call it ill-humoured. Besides, I thanked my guardian-angel for these discomforts, looking upon them as a preparation for what was to befall me in the far North.

Passing several small towns and villages, we at length entered the Bohemian territory, close behind Iglau. The first town which we saw was Czaslau, with its large open square, and a few neat houses; the latter provided with so-called arbours (or **verandahs**), which enable one to pass round the square dry-footed, even in the most rainy weather.

Journeying onwards, we noticed the fine cathedral and town of Kuttenberg, once famous for its gold and silver mines. {4} Next comes the great tobacco-man-ufactory of Sedlitz, near which we first see the Elbe, but only for a short time, as it soon takes another direction. Passing the small town of Collin, we are whirled close by the battle-field where, in the year 1757, the great King Frederick paid his score to the Austrians. An obelisk, erected a few years since to the memory of General Daun, occupies a small eminence on the right. On the left is the plain of Klephorcz, where the Austrian army was drawn up. {5}

At eleven o'clock on the same night we reached
PRAGUE.

As it was my intention to pursue my journey after two days, my first walk on the following morning was to the police-office, to procure a passport and the all-important pass-warrant; my next to the custom-house, to take possession of a small chest, which I had delivered up five days before my departure, and which, as the expeditor affirmed, I should find ready for me on my arrival at Prague. {6} Ah, Mr.

Expeditor! my chest was not there. After Saturday comes Sunday; but on Sunday the custom-house is closed. So here was a day lost, a day in which I might have gone to Dresden, and even visited the opera.

On Monday morning I once more hastened to the office in anxious expectation; the box was not yet there. An array of loaded wagons had, however, arrived, and in one of these it might be. Ah, how I longed to see my darling little box, in order that I might--**not** press it to my heart, but unpack it in presence of the excise officer!

I took merely a cursory glance at Prague, as I had thoroughly examined every thing there some years before. The beautiful "Graben" and Horse-market once more excited my admiration. It was with a peculiar feeling that I trod the old bridge, from which St. John of Nepomuk was cast into the Moldau for refusing to publish the confession of King Wenceslaus' consort. {7} On the opposite bank I mounted the Hradschin, and paid a visit to the cathedral, in which a large sarcophagus, surrounded and borne by angels, and surmounted by a canopy of crimson damask, is dedicated to the memory of the saint. The monument is of silver, and the worth of the metal alone is estimated at 80,000 florins. The church itself is not spacious, but is built in the noble Gothic style; the lesser altars, however, with their innumerable gilded wooden figures, look by contrast extremely puny. In the chapel are many sarcophagi, on which repose bishops and knights hewn in stone, but so much damaged, that many are without hands and feet, while some lack heads. To the right, at the entrance of the church, is the celebrated chapel of St. Wenceslaus, with its walls ornamented with frescoes, of which the colours and designs are now almost obliterated. It is further enriched with costly stones.

Not far from the cathedral is situated the palace of Count Czernin, a building particularly favoured with windows, of which it has one for every day in the year. I was there in an ordinary year, and saw 365; how they manage in leap-year I do not know. The view from the belvedere of this palace well repays the observer. It takes in the old and new town, the noble river with its two bridges (the ancient venerable-looking stone structure, and the graceful suspension-bridge, six hundred paces long), and the hills round about, clothed with gardens, among which appear neat country-houses.

The streets of the "Kleinseite" are not particularly attractive, being mostly tortuous, steep, and narrow. They contain, however, several remarkable palaces, among which that of Wallenstein Duke of Friedland stands pre-eminent. {8}

After visiting St. Nicholas' Church, remarkable for the height of its spire and its beautifully arched cupola, I betook myself to Wimmer's gardens, and thence to the "Bastei," a place of public resort with the citizens of Prague.

I could now observe the devastation caused by the rising of the water shortly before my arrival. The Moldau had overstepped its banks in so turbulent a manner, as to carry along with it several small houses, and even a little village not far from Prague, besides damaging all the dwellings upon its banks. The water had indeed already fallen, but the walls of the houses were soaked through and through; the doors had been carried away, and from the broken windows no faces looked out upon the passers-by. The water had risen two feet more than in 1784, in which year the Moldau had also attained an unusual height.

From the same tower of observation, I looked down upon the great open space bought a few years ago, and intended to be occupied by the termini of the Vienna and Dresden railroads. Although several houses were only just being pulled down, and the foundations of but few buildings were laid, I was assured that within six months every thing would be completed.

I have still to mention a circumstance which struck me during my morning peregrinations, namely, the curious method in which milk, vegetables, and other provisions are here brought to town. I could have fancied myself transported to Lapland or Greenland, on meeting every where carts to which two, three, or four dogs were harnessed. One pair of dogs will drag three hundredweight on level ground; but when they encounter a hill, the driver must lend a helping hand. These dogs are, besides, careful guardians; and I would not advise any one to approach a car of this kind, as it stands before the inn-door, while the proprietor is quenching his thirst within, on the money he has just earned.

At five o'clock on the morning of the 15th of April I left Prague, and rode for fourteen miles in the mail-carriage, as far as Obristwy on the Elbe, at which place I embarked for Dresden, on board the steamer Bohemia, of fifty-horse power, a miserable old craft, apparently a stranger to beauty and comfort from her youth up. The price charged for this short passage of eight or nine hours is enormously dear. The travellers will, however, soon have their revenge on the extortionate proprietors; a railroad is constructing, by means of which this distance will be traversed in a much shorter time, and at a great saving of expense.

But at any rate the journey by water is the more agreeable; the way lies through very picturesque scenery, and at length through "Saxon Switzerland" itself. The commencement of the journey is, however, far from pleasing. On the right are naked hills, and on the left large plains, over which, last spring, the swollen stream rolled, partly covering the trees and the roofs of the cottages. Here I could for the first time see the whole extent of the calamity. Many houses had been completely torn down, and the crops, and even the loose alluvial earth swept away; as we glided by each dreary scene of devastation, another yet more dismal would appear in its place.

This continued till we reached Melnick, where the trees become higher, and groups of houses peer forth from among the innumerable vineyards. Opposite this little town the Moldau falls into the Elbe. On the left, in the far distance, the traveller can descry St. George's Mount, from which, as the story goes, Czech took possession of all Bohemia.

Below the little town of Raudnitz the hills gave place to mountains, and as many enthusiasts can only find those regions romantic where the mountains are crowned with half-ruined castles and strongholds, good old Time has taken care to plant there two fine ruins, Hafenberg and Skalt, for the delectation of such sentimental observers.

Near Leitmeritz, a small town with a handsome castle, and a church and convent, the Eger flows into the Elbe, and a high-arched wooden bridge connects the two banks. Here our poor sailors had difficult work to lower the mast and the funnel.

The rather pretty village of Gross-Czernoseck is remarkable for its gigantic cellars, hewn out of the rock. A post-carriage could easily turn round in one of these. The vats are of course proportioned to the cellars, particularly the barrels called the "twelve apostles," each of which holds between three and four thousand gallons. It would be no more than fair to stop here awhile, to give every hero of the bottle an opportunity to enjoy a sight of these palace-cellars, and to offer a libation to the twelve apostles; but the steamer passed on, and we were obliged to make the most of the descriptions furnished by those who were more at home in these parts, and had no doubt frequently emerged in an inspired state from the depths of the cellars in question.

The view now becomes more and more charming: the mountains appear to draw closer together, and shut in the bed of the stream; romantic groups of rocks, with summits crowned by rains yet more romantic, tower between. The ancient but well-preserved castle of Schreckenstein, built on a rock rising boldly out of the Elbe, is particularly striking; the approaches to it are by serpentine walks hewn out of the rock.

Near the small town of Aussig we find the most considerable coal-mines in Bohemia. In their neighbourhood is situated the little mountain estate Paschkal, which produces a kind of wine said to resemble champagne.

The mountains now become higher and higher, but above them all towers the gigantic Jungfernsprung (Maiden's Leap). The beauty of this region is only surpassed by the situation of the town and castle of Tetschen. The castle stands on a rock, between twenty and thirty feet high, which seems to rise out of the Elbe; it is surrounded by hot-houses and charming gardens, shelving downwards as far as the town, which lies in a blooming valley, near a little harbour. The valley itself, encompassed by a chain of lofty mountains, seems quite shut out from the rest of the world.

The left bank of the river is here so crowded with masses and walls of rock, that there is only room at intervals for an isolated farm or hut. Suddenly the tops of masts appear between the high rocks, a phenomenon which is soon explained; a large gap in one of the rocky walls forms a beautiful basin.

And now we come to Schandau, a place consisting only of a few houses; it is a frontier town of the Saxon dominions. Custom-house officers, a race of beings ever associated with frontier towns, here boarded our vessel, and rummaged every thing. My daguerreotype apparatus, which I had locked up in a small box, was looked upon with an eye of suspicion; but upon my assertion that it was exclusively intended for my own use, I and my apparatus were graciously dismissed.

In our onward journey we frequently observed rocks of peculiar shapes, which have appropriate names, such as the "Zirkelstein," "Lilienstein," &c. The Konigstein is a collection of jagged masses of rock, on which is built the fortress of the same name, used at present as a prison for great criminals. At the foot of the rocks lies the little town of Konigstein. Not far off, on the right bank, a huge rock, resting on others, bears a striking resemblance to a human head. The more distant groups of rocks are called those of "Rathen," but are considered as belonging to Saxon Switzerland. The "Basteien" (Bastions) of this Switzerland, close by which we now pass, are most wonderful superpositions of lofty and fantastically shaped rocks. Unfortunately, the steamer whirled us so rapidly on our way, that whilst we contemplated one bank, the beauteous scenes on the opposite side had already glided from our view. In much too short a time we had passed the town of Pirna, situate at the commencement of this range of mountains. The very ancient gate of this town towers far above all the other buildings.

Lastly we see the great castle Sonnenstein, built on a rock, and now used as an asylum for lunatics.

All the beautiful and picturesque portion of our passage is now past, and the royal villa of Pillnitz, with its many Chinese gables, looks insignificant enough, after the grand scenes of nature. A chain of hills, covered with the country-houses of citizens, adjoins it; and on the right extends a large plain, at the far end of which we can dimly descry the Saxon metropolis. But what is that in the distance? We have hardly time to arrange our luggage, when the anchor is let go near the fine old Dresden Bridge.

This bridge had not escaped unscathed by the furious river. One of the centre arches had given way, and the cross and watchbox which surmounted it were precipitated into the flood. At first, carriages still passed over the bridge; it was not until some time afterwards that the full extent of the damage was ascertained, and the passage of carriages over the bridge discontinued for many months.

As I had seen the town of Dresden several years before, and the only building new to me was the splendid theatre, I took advantage of the few evening hours of my stay to visit this structure.

Standing in the midst of the beautiful Cathedral-square, its noble rotunda-like form at once rivets the attention. The inner theatre is surrounded by a superb broad and lofty corridor, with fine bow-windows and straight broad staircases, leading in different directions towards the galleries. The interior of the theatre is not so spacious as, judging from the exterior, one would imagine it to be, but the architecture and decorations are truly gorgeous and striking. The boxes are all open, being separated from each other merely by a low partition; the walls and chairs are covered with heavy silken draperies, and the seats of the third and fourth galleries with a mixture of silk and cotton. One single circumstance was disagreeable to me in an acoustic point of view--I could hear the slightest whisper of the prompter as distinctly as though some one had been behind me reading the play. The curtain had scarcely fallen before the whole house was empty, and yet there was no crowding to get out. This first drew my attention to the numerous and excellently contrived doors.

April 16th.

The Dresden omnibuses may be cited as models of comfort; one is certain of plenty of room, and there is no occasion to dread either the corpulent persons or the furs and cloaks of fellow-passengers. A bell-pull is fixed in the interior of the carriage, so that each individual can give the coachman a signal when he or she wishes to alight. These omnibuses call at the principal inns, and wait for a moment; but the traveller who is not ready in advance is left behind.

At half-past five in the morning it called at our hotel. I was ready and waiting, and drove off comfortably to the railway. The distance from Dresden to Leipzig is reckoned at fifty-six miles, and the journey occupied three hours.

The first fourteen miles are very agreeable; gardens, fields, and meadows, pine-forests in the plain and on the hills, and between these, villages, farms, country-houses, and solitary chapels, combine to form a very pretty landscape. But the scene soon changes, and the town of Meissen (famous for its porcelain manufactory), on the right hand, seems to shut out from our view all that is picturesque and beautiful.

From here to Leipzig we travel through a wearisome monotonous plain, enlivened at long intervals by villages and scattered farms. There is nothing to see but a great tunnel, and the river Pleisse--the latter, or rather the Elster, is rendered famous by the death of Prince Poniatowski. {9}

The town of Leipzig, celebrated far and wide for its fairs, and more for its immense publishing trade, presents an appearance of noise and bustle proportionate to its commercial importance. I found streets, squares, and inns alike crowded. {10}

Perhaps there does not exist a town with its houses, and consequently its streets, so disfigured with announcements, in all sizes and shapes, covering its walls, and sometimes projecting several feet, as Leipzig.

Among the public buildings, those which pleased me most were the Augusteum and the Burgerschule. The Bucherhalle (book-hall) I should suppose indebted for its celebrity rather to its literary contents than to its architectural beauty or its exterior. The hall itself is indeed large, and occupies the whole length of the building, while the lower story consists of several rooms. The hall, the chambers, and the exterior are all plain, and without particular decoration. The Tuchhalle (cloth-hall) is simply a large house, with spacious chambers, containing supplies of cloth. The Theatre stands on a very large square, and does not present a very splendid appearance, whether viewed from within or from without. The plan of having stalls in front of the boxes in the second and third galleries was a novelty to me. The orchestra I could only hear, but could not discover its whereabouts; most probably it was posted behind the scenes. On inquiry, I was told that this was only done on extraordinary occasions, when the seats in the orchestra were converted into stalls, as was the case on the night of my visit. The play given was "the original Tartuffe," a popular piece by Gutzkow. It was capitally performed.

In the Leipzig theatre I had a second opportunity of observing, that as regards the love of eating our good Saxons are not a whit behind the much-censured Viennese. In the Dresden theatre I had admired a couple of ladies who sat next me. They came provided with a neat bag, containing a very sufficient supply of confectionery, to which they perseveringly applied themselves between the acts. But at Leipzig I found a delicate-looking mother and her son, a lad of fifteen or sixteen years, regaling themselves with more solid provisions--white bread and small sausages. I could not believe my eyes, and had made up my mind that the sausages were artificially formed out of some kind of confectionery--but alas! my nose came forward but too soon, as a potent witness, to corroborate what I was so unwilling to believe!

Neither did these two episodes take place in the loftiest regions of Thalia's temple, but in the stalls of the second tier.

Beautiful alleys are planted round Leipzig. I took a walk into the Rosenthal (Valley of Roses), which also consists of splendid avenues and lawns. A pretty coffee-house, with a very handsome alcove, built in a semicircular form, invites the weary traveller to rest and refreshment, while a band of agreeable music diffuses mirth and good humour around.

The rest of the scenery around Leipzig presents the appearance of a vast and monotonous plain.

April 17th.

I had intended to continue my journey to Hamburgh via Berlin, but the weather was so cold and stormy, and the rain poured down so heavily, that I preferred the shorter way, and proceeded by rail to Magdeburg. Flying through the dismal plain past Halle, Kothen, and other towns, of which I could only discern groups of houses, we hurriedly recognised the Saale and the Elbe; and towards 10 o'clock in the morning arrived at Magdeburg, having travelled seventy miles in three hours and a quarter.

As the steamer for Hamburgh was not to start until 3 o'clock, I had ample time to look at the town.

Magdeburg is a mixed pattern of houses of ancient, mediaeval, and modern dates. Particularly remarkable in this respect is the principal street, the "Broadway," which runs through the whole of the town. Here we can see houses dating their origin from the most ancient times; houses that have stood proof against sieges and sackings; houses of all colours and forms; some sporting peaked gables, on which stone figures may still be seen; others covered from roof to basement with arabesques; and in one instance I could even detect the remains of frescoes. In the very midst of these relics of antiquity would appear a house built in the newest style. I do not remember ever having seen a street which produced so remarkable an impression on me. The finest building is unquestionably the venerable cathedral. In Italy I had already seen numbers of the most beautiful churches; yet I remained standing in mute admiration before this masterpiece of Gothic architecture.

The monument with the twelve Apostles in this church is a worthy memorial of the celebrated sculptor Vischer. In order to view it, it is necessary to obtain the special permission of the commandant.

The cathedral square is large, symmetrical, and decorated with two alleys of trees; it is also used as a drilling-ground for the soldiers' minor manoeuvres. I was particularly struck with the number of military men to be seen here. Go where I would, I was sure to meet soldiers and officers, frequently in large companies; in time of war it could scarcely have been worse. This was an unmistakeable token that I was on Prussian territory.

The open canals, which come from all the houses, and meander through the streets, are a great disfigurement to the town.

Half-past three o'clock came only too quickly, and I betook myself on board the steamer *Magdeburg*, of sixty-horse power, to proceed to Hamburgh. Of the passage itself I can say nothing, except that a journey on a river through execrable scenery is one of the most miserable things that can well be imagined. When, in addition to this, the weather is bad, the ship dirty, and one is obliged to pass a night on board, the discomfort is increased. It was my lot to endure all this: the weather was bad, the ship was dirty, the distance more than 100 miles, so that we had the pleasant prospect of a delightful night on board the ship. There were, moreover, so many passengers, that we were forced to sit crowded together; so there we sat with exemplary patience, stared at each other, and sighed bitterly. Order was entirely out of the question; no one had time to think of such a thing. Smoking and card-playing were perseveringly carried on all day and all night; it can easily be imagined that things did not go so quietly as at an English whist-party. The incessant rain rendered it impossible to leave the cabin even for a short time. The only consolation I had was, that I made the acquaintance of the amiable composer Lorzing, a circumstance which delighted me the more, as I had always been an admirer of his beautiful original music.

CHAPTER II

Morning dawned at length, and in a short time afterwards we reached the great commercial city, which, half destroyed by the dreadful conflagration of 1842, had risen grander and more majestic from its ashes. {11} I took up my quarters with a cousin, who is married to the Wurtemburg consul, the merchant Schmidt, in whose house I spent a most agreeable and happy week. My cousin-in-law was polite enough to escort me every where himself, and to shew me the lions of Hamburgh.

First of all we visited the Exchange between the hours of one and two, when it is at the fullest, and therefore best calculated to impress a stranger with an idea of the extent and importance of the business transacted there. The building contains a hall of great size, with arcades and galleries, besides many large rooms, which are partly used for consultations, partly for the sale of refreshments. The most interesting thing of all is, however, to sit in the gallery, and looking downwards, to observe the continually increasing crowd passing and repassing each other in the immense hall and through the galleries and chambers, and to listen to the hubbub and noise of the thousands of eager voices talking at once. At half-past one o'clock the hall is at its fullest, and the noise becomes absolutely deafening; for now they are marking up the rates of exchange, by which the merchants regulate their monetary transactions.

Leaving the Exchange, we bent our steps towards the great harbour, and entering a small boat, cruised in and about it in all directions. I had resolved to count only the three-masted ships; but soon gave it up, for their number seemed overwhelming, even without reckoning the splendid steamers, brigs, sloops, and craft. In short, I could only gaze and wonder, for at least 900 ships lay before me.

Let any one fancy an excursion amidst 900 ships, great and small, which lined both shores of the Elbe in tiers of three deep or more; the passing to and fro of countless boats busily employed in loading or unloading these vessels; these things, together with the shouting and singing of the sailors, the rattling of anchors which are being weighed, and the rush and swell of passing steamers, combine to constitute a picture not to be surpassed in any city except in that metropolis of the world, London. {12}

The reason of this unusual activity in the harbour lay in the severity of the past winter. Such a winter had not been experienced for seventy years: the Elbe and the Baltic lay for months in icy chains, and not a ship could traverse the frozen river, not an anchor could be weighed or lowered. It was only a short time before my arrival that the passage had once more become free.

In the neighbourhood of the harbour are situated the greater number of the so-called "yards." I had read concerning them that, viewed from the exterior, they look like common houses; but that they constitute separate communities, and contain alleys and streets, serving as the domicile of innumerable families. I visited several of these places, and can assure the reader that I saw nothing extraordinary in them. Houses with two large wings, forming an alley of from eighty to a hundred paces in length, are to be met with in every large town; and that a number of families should inhabit such a house is not remarkable, considering that they are all poor, and that each only possesses a single small apartment.

The favourite walk in the town is the "Jungfernstieg" (Maiden's Walk), a broad alley, extending round a spacious and beautiful basin of the Alster. On one side are splendid hotels, with which Hamburgh is richly provided; on the other, a number of private residences of equal pretensions. Other walks are, the "Wall," surrounding the town, and the "Botanical Garden," which resembles a fine park. The noblest building, distinguished alike as regards luxury, skill, tastefulness of design, and stability, is the Bazaar. It is truly a gigantic undertaking, and the more to be admired from the fact that it is not built upon shares, but at the expense of a single individual, Herr Carl Sillem; the architect's name is Overdick. The building itself is constructed entirely of stone, and the walls of the great room and of the hall are inlaid with marble. A lofty cupola and an immense glazed dome cover both the great room and the hall; the upper staircases are ornamented with beautiful statues. When in the evening it is brilliantly lighted with gas, and further ornamented by a tasteful display of the richest wares, the spectator can almost fancy himself transported to a fairy palace.

Altogether the shops in Hamburgh are very luxurious. The wares lie displayed in the most tasteful manner behind huge windows of plate-glass, which are often from five to six feet broad, and eight or ten feet high; a single sheet frequently costs 600 florins. This plate-glass luxury is not confined to shops, but extends to windows generally, not only in Hamburgh, but also in Altona, and is also seen in the handsomest country-houses of the Hamburghers. Many a pane costs eight or ten florins; and the glass is insured in case of breakage, like houses in case of fire.

This display of glass is equalled by the costliness of the furniture, which is almost universally of mahogany; a wood which is here in such common use, that in some of the most elegant houses the very stair-banisters are constructed of it. Even the pilots have often mahogany furniture.

The handsomest and most frequented street is the "Neue Wall" (New Wall). I was particularly struck with the number of shops and dwellings underground, to which one descends by a flight of six or eight stairs; an iron railing is generally placed before the entrance, to prevent the passers-by from falling down.

A very practical institution is the great slaughterhouse, in which all cattle are killed on certain days of the week.

Concerning the town of Altona, I have only to observe that it appeared to me a continuation of Hamburgh; from which town, indeed, it is only separated by a wooden door. A very broad, handsome street, or, more properly speaking, an elongated square, planted with a double row of large trees, is the most remarkable thing about Altona, which belongs to the Danish Government, and is considered, after Copenhagen, the most important place in the kingdom.

It is a delicious ride to the village of Blankenese, distant nine miles from Hamburgh; the road lies among beautiful country-houses and large park-like gardens. Blankenese itself consists of cottages, grouped in a picturesque manner round the Sulberg, a hill from which the traveller enjoys a very extended view over the great plain, in which it is the only elevated point. The course of the Elbe, as it winds at moderate speed towards the sea, is here to be traced almost to its embouchure at Cuxhaven.

The breadth of the Elbe at Blankenese exceeds two miles.

Another interesting excursion is to the "New Mills," a little village on the Elbe, not more than half a mile from Altona, and inhabited only by fishermen and pilots. Whoever wishes to form an idea of Dutch prettiness and cleanliness should come here.

The houses are mostly one story high, neatly and tastefully built; the brightest of brass handles adorn the street-doors; the windows are kept scrupulously clean, and furnished with white curtains.

In Saxony I had found many dwellings of the peasantry tidy and neat enough, displaying at any rate more opulence than we are accustomed to find with this class of people; but I had seen none to compete with this pretty village.

Among the peasants' costumes, I only liked that worn by the women from the "Vierlanden." They wear short full skirts of black stuff, fine white chemisettes with long sleeves, and coloured bodices, lightly fastened in front with silk cords or silver buckles. Their straw hats have a most comical appearance; the brim of the hat is turned up in such a manner that the crown appears to have completely sunk in. Many pretty young girls dressed in this manner come to Hamburgh to sell flowers, and take up their position in front of the Exchange.

The 26th of April, the day appointed for my departure, arrived only too speedily. To part is the unavoidable fate of the traveller; but sometimes we part gladly, sometimes with regret. I need not write many pages to describe my feelings at the parting in Hamburgh. I was leaving behind me my last relations, my last friends. Now I was going into the wide world, and among strangers.

At eight o'clock in the morning I left Altona, and proceeded by railway to Kiel.

I noticed with pleasure that on this railway even the third-class carriages were securely covered in, and furnished with glass windows. In fact, they only differed from those of the first and second class in being painted a different colour, and having the seats uncushioned.

The whole distance of seventy miles was passed in three hours; a rapid journey, but agreeable merely by its rapidity, for the whole neighbourhood presents only widely-extended plains, turf-bogs and moorlands, sandy places and heaths, interspersed with a little meadow or arable land. From the nature of the soil, the water in the ditches and fields looked black as ink.

Near Binneburg we notice a few stunted plantations of trees. From Eisholm a branch-line leads to Gluckstadt, and another from Neumunster, a large place with important cloth-factories, to Rendsburg.

From here there is nothing to be seen but a convent, in which many Dukes of Holstein lie buried, and several unimportant lakes; for instance, those of Bernsholm, Einfeld, and Schulhof. The little river Eider would have passed unnoticed by me, had not some of my fellow-passengers made a great feature of it. In the finest countries I have found the natives far less enthusiastic about what was really grand and beautiful, than they were here in praise of what was neither the one nor the other. My neighbour, a very agreeable lady, was untiring in laudation of her beautiful native land. In her eyes the crippled wood was a splendid park, the waste moorland an inexhaustible field for contemplation, and every trifle a matter of real importance. In my heart I wished her joy of her fervid imagination; but unfortunately my colder nature would not catch the infection.

Towards Kiel the plain becomes a region of low hills. Kiel itself is prettily situated on the Baltic, which, viewed from thence, has the appearance of a lake of middling size. The harbour is said to be good; but there were not many ships there. {13} Among these was the steamer destined to carry me to Copenhagen. Little did

I anticipate the good reason I should have to remember this vessel.

Thanks to the affectionate forethought of my cousin Schmidt, I found one of his relations, Herr Brauer, waiting for me at the railway. I was immediately introduced to his family, and passed the few hours of my stay very agreeably in their company.

Evening approached, and with it the hour of embarkation. My kind friends the Brauers accompanied me to the steamer, and I took a grateful leave of them.

I soon discovered the steamer *Christian VIII.*, of 180-horse power, to be a vessel dirtier and more uncomfortable than any with which I had become acquainted in my maritime excursions. Scrubbing and sweeping seemed things unknown here. The approach to the cabin was by a flight of stairs so steep, that great care was requisite to avoid descending in an expeditious but disagreeable manner, by a fall from top to bottom. In the fore-cabin there was no attempt at separate quarters for ladies and gentlemen. In short, the arrangements seemed all to have been made with a view of impressing the ship vividly on the recollection of every traveller.

At nine o'clock we left Kiel. The day and the twilight are here already longer than in the lands lying to the south and the west. There was light enough to enable me to see, looming out of the surrounding darkness, the fortress "Friedrichsort," which we passed at about ten o'clock.

April 27th.

To-day I still rose with the sun; but that will soon be a difficult matter to accomplish; for in the north the goddess of light makes amends in spring and summer for her shortcomings during the winter. I went on deck, and looked on the broad expanse of ocean. No land was to be seen; but soon a coast appeared, then disappeared, and then a new and more distant one rose out of the sea. Towards noon we reached the island of Moen, which lies about forty {14} miles distant from Copenhagen. It forms a beautiful group of rocks, rising boldly from the sea. They are white as chalk, and have a smooth and shining appearance. The highest of these walls of rock towers 400 feet above the level of the surrounding ocean. Soon we saw the coast of Sweden, then the island of Malmo; and at last Copenhagen itself, where we landed at four o'clock in the afternoon. The distance from Kiel to Copenhagen is 136 sea-miles.

I remained seven days at Copenhagen, and should have had ample time to see every thing, had the weather been more favourable. But it blew and rained so violently, that I was obliged to give up all thoughts of visiting the surrounding parks, and was fain to content myself with seeing a few of the nearest walks, which I accomplished with some difficulty.

The first street in Copenhagen which I traversed on coming from the harbour generally produces a great impression. It is called the "Broad Street," and leads from the harbour through the greater part of the town. In addition to its breadth it is very long and regular, and the splendid palaces and houses on either side give it a remarkably grand appearance.

It is a peculiar sight, when, in the midst of this fine quarter, we come suddenly upon a ruin, a giant building resting on huge pillars, but half completed, and partly covered with moss and lichens. It was intended for a splendid church, and is built entirely of marble; but the soft ground would not bear the immense weight. The half-finished building began to sink, and the completion of the undertaking became for ever impossible.

Many other streets rival the "Broad Street" in size and magnificence. Foremost among them comes the Amalienstrasse. The most bustling, but by far not the finest, are the Oster and Gotherstrasse. To walk in these is at first quite a difficult undertaking for a stranger. On one side of the pavement, which is raised about a foot above the carriage-way, he comes continually in contact with stairs, leading sometimes to warehouses above, at others to subterranean warehouses below the level of the street. The approaches to the latter are not guarded by railings as in Hamburgh. The other side of the pavement is bounded by a little unostentatious rivulet, called by unpoetical people "canal," into which tributaries equally sweet pour from all the neighbouring houses. It is therefore necessary to take great care, lest you should fall into the traitorous depths on the one side, or stumble over the projecting steps on the other. The pavement itself is covered with a row of stone slabs, a foot and a half wide, on which one walks comfortably enough. But then every body contends for the possession of these, to avoid the uneven and pointed stones at the side. This, added to the dreadful crowding, renders the street one which would scarcely be chosen for a walk, the less so as the shops do not contain any thing handsome, the houses are neither palace-like nor even tastefully built, and the street itself is neither of the broadest nor of the cleanest.

The squares are all large and regularly built. The finest is the Kongensnytorf (King's New Market). Some fine mansions, the chief guard-house, the theatre, the chief coffee-houses and inns, the academy of the fine arts, and the building belonging to the botanical garden, the two last commonly known by the name of "Charlottenburg," are among the ornaments of this magnificent square, in the midst of which stands a beautiful monument, representing Christian V. on horseback, and surrounded by several figures.

Smaller, but more beautiful in its perfect symmetry, is the "Amalienplatz," containing four royal palaces, built exactly alike, and intersected by four broad streets in the form of a cross. This square also is decorated by a monument standing in the midst, and representing Frederick V. In another fine square, the "Nytorf" (New Market), there is a fountain. Its little statue sends forth very meagre jets of water, and the fountain is merely noticeable as being the only one I could find at Copenhagen.

The traveller can hardly fail of being surprised by the number and magnificence of the palaces, at sight of which he could fancy himself in the metropolis of one of the largest kingdoms. The "Christianensburg" is truly imperial; it was completely destroyed by fire in the year 1794, but has since been rebuilt with increased splendour. The chapel of this palace is very remarkable. The interior has the appearance rather of a concert-room than of a building devoted to purposes of worship. Tastefully decorated boxes, among which we notice that of the king, together with galleries, occupy the upper part of the chapel; the lower is filled with benches covered with red velvet and silk. The pulpit and altar are so entirely without decoration, that, on first entering, they wholly escape notice.

In the "Christianensburg" is also the "Northern Museum," peculiarly rich in specimens of the ornaments, weapons, musical instruments, and other mementoes of northern nations.

The Winter Riding-school, in which concerts are frequently given, is large and symmetrical. I admired the stalls, and yet more the grey horses which occupied them--descendants of the pure Arabian and wild Norwegian breeds--creatures with long manes and tails of fine silky hair. Every one who sees these horses, whether he be a connoisseur or one of the uninitiated, must admire them.

Adjoining the "Christianensburg" is Thorwaldsen's Museum, a square building with fine saloons, lighted from above. When I saw it, it was not completed; the walls were being painted in fresco by some of the first native artists. The sculptured treasures were there, but unfortunately yet unpacked.

In the midst of the courtyard Thorwaldsen's mausoleum is being erected. There his ashes will rest, with his exquisitely finished lion as a gravestone above them. {15}

The largest among the churches is the "Woman's Church." The building has no architectural beauty; the pillars, galleries, and cupola are all of wood, covered with a mixture of sand and plaster. But whatever may be wanting in outward splendour is compensated by its contents, for this church contains the masterpieces of Thorwaldsen. At the high altar stands his glorious figure of our Saviour, in the niches of the wall his colossal twelve apostles.

In the contemplation of these works we forget the plainness of the building which contains them. May the fates be prosperous, and no conflagration reach this church, built as it is half of wood!

The Catholic Church is small, but tasteful beyond expression. The late emperor of Austria presented to it a good full-toned organ, and two oil-paintings, one by Kuppelweiser, the other by a pupil of this master.

In the "Museum of Arts" I was most interested in the ancient chair, used in days of yore by Tycho de Brahe. {16}

The Exchange is a curious ancient building. It is very long and narrow, and surmounted by nine peaks, from the centre of which protrudes a remarkable pointed tower, formed of four crocodiles' tails intertwined.

The hall itself is small, low, and dark; it contains a full-length portrait in oil of Tycho de Brahe. Nearly all the upper part of the building is converted into a kind of bazaar, and the lower portion contains a number of small and dingy booths.

Several canals, having an outlet into the sea, give a peculiar charm to the town. They are, in fact, so many markets; for the craft lying in them are laden with provisions of all kinds, which are here offered for sale.

The Sailors' Town, adjoining Copenhagen, and situated near the harbour, is singularly neat and pretty. It consists of three long, broad, straight streets, built of houses looking so exactly alike, that on a foggy night an accurate knowledge of the locality is requisite to know one from the other. It looks as though, on each side of the way, there were only one long house of a single floor, with a building one story high in the middle. In the latter dwell the commandant and overseers.

The lighting of the streets is managed in Copenhagen in the same way as in our smaller German towns. When "moonlight" is announced in the calendar, not a lamp is lighted. If the lady moon chooses to hide behind dark clouds, that is her fault. It would be insolent to attempt to supply the place of her radiance with miserable lamps--a wise arrangement! (?)

Of the near walks, the garden of the "Rosenburg," within the town, pleased me much; as did also the "Long Line," an alley of beautiful trees extending parallel with the sea, and in which one can either walk or ride. A coffee-house, in front of which there is music in fine weather, attracts many of the loungers. The most beautiful place of all is the "Kastell," above the "Long Line," from whence one can enjoy a beautiful view. The town lies displayed below in all its magnificence: the harbour, with its many ships; the sparkling blue Sound, which spreads its broad expanse between the coasts of Denmark and Sweden, and washes many a beautiful group of islands belonging to one or the other of these countries. The background of the picture alone is uninteresting, as there is no chain of mountains to form a horizon, and the eye wanders over the boundless flats of Denmark.

Among the vessels lying at anchor in the harbour I saw but few three-masters, and still fewer steamers. The ships of the fleet presented a curious appearance; at the first view they look like great houses with flag-staves, for every ship is provided with a roof, out of which the masts rise into the air; they are besides very high out of the water, so that all the port-holes and the windows of the cabins appear in two or three stories, one above the other.

A somewhat more distant excursion, which can be very conveniently made in a capital omnibus, takes you to the royal chateau "Friedrichsberg," lying before the water-gate, two miles distant from the town. Splendid avenues lead to this place, where are to be found all the delights that can combine to draw a citizen into the country. There are a tivoli, a railway, cabinets, and booths with wax-figures, and countless other sights, besides coffee-houses, beer-rooms, and music. The gardens are planted at the sides with a number of small arbours, each containing a table and chairs, and all open in front, so as to shew at one view all the visitors of these pretty natural huts. On Sundays, when the gardens are crowded, this is a very animated sight.

On the way to this "Prater" of Copenhagen, we pass many handsome villas, each standing in a fine garden.

[Picture: Copenhagen: From Frederiesbourg]

The royal palace is situated on the summit of a hill, at the end of the avenue, and is surrounded by a beautiful park; it commands a view of a great portion of the town, with the surrounding country and the sea; still I far prefer the prospect from the "Kastell." The Park contains a considerable island, which, during some part of the year, stands in the midst of an extensive lake. This island is appropriated to the Court, but the rest of the park is open to the public.

Immediately outside the water-gate stands an obelisk, remarkable neither for its beauty nor for the skill displayed in its erection, for it consists of various stones, and is not high, but interesting from the circumstance to which it owes its origin. It was erected by his grateful subjects in memory of the late king Christian VII., to commemorate the abolition of feudal service. Surely no feeling person can contemplate without joyful emotion a monument like this.

I have here given a faithful account of what I saw during my short stay at Copenhagen. It only remains for me to describe a few peculiar customs of the people, and so I will begin as it were at the end, with the burial of the dead. In Denmark, as in fact in the whole of Scandinavia, not excepting Iceland, it is customary not to bury the dead until eight or ten days have elapsed. In winter-time this is not of so much consequence, but in summer it is far from healthy for those under the same roof with the corpse. I was present at Copenhagen at the funeral of Dr. Brandis, physician to the king. Two of the king's carriages and a number of private equipages attended. Nearly all these were empty, and the servants walked beside them. Among the mourners I did not notice a single woman; I supposed that this was only the case at the funerals of gentlemen, but on inquiry I found that the same rule is observed at the burial of women. This consideration for the weaker sex is carried so far, that on the day of the funeral no woman may be seen in the house of mourning. The mourners assemble in the house of the deceased, and partake of cold refreshments. At the conclusion of the ceremony they are again regaled. What particularly pleased me in Copenhagen was, that I never on any occasion saw beggars, or even such miserably clad people as are found only too frequently in our great cities. Here there are no doubt poor people, as there are such every where else in the world, but one does not see them beg. I cannot help mentioning an arrangement which certainly deserves to be universally carried out;--I mean, the setting apart of many large houses, partly belonging to the royal family, partly to rich private people or to companies, for the reception of poor people, who are here lodged at a much cheaper rate than is possible in ordinary dwellings.

The costumes of the peasants did not particularly please me. The women wear dresses of green or black woollen stuff, reaching to the ankle, and trimmed at the skirt with broad coloured woollen borders. The seams of the spenser, and the arm-holes, are also trimmed with smaller coloured borders. On their heads they wear a handkerchief, and over this a kind of shade, like a bonnet. On Sundays I saw many of them in small, pretty caps, worked with silk, with a border of lace of more than a hand's breadth, plaited very stiffly; at the back they have large bows of fine riband, the ends of which reach half down to their feet. I found nothing very remarkable in the dress of the peasants. As far as strength and beauty were concerned, I thought these peasants were neither more nor less gifted than those of Austria. As regards the beauty of the fair sex, I should certainly give the preference to the Austrians. Fair hair and blue eyes predominate.

I saw but few soldiers; their uniforms, particularly those worn by the king's life-guards, are very handsome.

I especially noticed the drummers; they were all little lads of ten or twelve years old. One could almost have exclaimed, "Drum, whither art thou carrying that boy?" To march, and to join in fatiguing manoeuvres, carrying such a drum, and beating it bravely at the same time, is rather cruel work for such young lads. Many a ruined constitution may be ascribed to this custom.

During my stay in Copenhagen I spent many very delightful hours with Professor Mariboe and his amiable family, and with the kind clergyman of the embassy, Herr Zimmermann. They received me with true politeness and hospitality, and drew me into their circle, where I soon felt myself quite at ease. I shall never forget their friendship, and shall make use of every opportunity to shew them my appreciation of it. Herr Edouard Gottschalk and Herr Knudson have also my best thanks. I applied to the first of these gentlemen to procure me a passage to Iceland, and he was kind enough to use his interest with Herr Knudson on my behalf.

Herr Knudson is one of the first general dealers in Copenhagen, and carries on a larger and more extended commerce with Iceland than any other house trading thither. He is already beginning to retire, as the continual journeys are becoming irksome to him; but he still owns a number of great and small vessels, which are partly employed in the fisheries, and partly in bringing all kinds of articles of consumption and luxury to the different harbours of Iceland.

He himself goes in one of his ships every year, and stays a few months in Iceland to settle his affairs there. On the recommendation of Herr Gottschalk, Herr Knudson was kind enough to give me a passage in the ship in which he made the journey himself; a favour which I knew how to value. It is certainly no small kindness to take a lady passenger on such a journey. Herr Knudson knew neither my fortitude nor my perseverance; he did not know whether I should be able to endure the hardships of a journey to the north, whether I would bear sea-sickness philosophically, or even if I had courage enough, in case of storms or bad weather, to abstain from annoying the captain by my fears or complaints at a time when he would only have too much to harass him. The kind man allowed no such considerations to influence him. He believed me when I promised to behave courageously come what might, and took me with him. Indeed his kindness went so far that it is to him I owe every comfort I enjoyed in Iceland, and every assistance in furthering the attainment of my journey's object. I could certainly not have commenced a voyage under better auspices.

All ships visiting Iceland leave Copenhagen at the end of April, or at the latest in the middle of May. After this time only one ship is despatched, to carry the mails of the Danish government. This vessel leaves Copenhagen in October, remains in Iceland during the winter months, and returns in March. The gain or loss of this expedition is distributed in shares among the merchants of Copenhagen.

Besides this, a French frigate comes to Iceland every spring, and cruises among the different harbours until the middle of August. She superintends the fishing vessels, which, attracted by the large profits of the fisheries, visit these seas in great numbers during the summer. {17}

Opportunities of returning from Iceland occur during the summer until the end of September, by means of the merchant-ships, which carry freights from the island to Denmark, England, and Spain.

At length, on Sunday the 4th of May, a favourable wind sprung up. Herr Knudson sent me word to be ready to embark at noon on board the fine brig *John*.

I immediately proceeded on board. The anchor was weighed, and the sails, unfolding themselves like giant wings, wafted us gently out of the harbour of Copenhagen. No parting from children, relations, or old-cherished friends embittered this hour. With a glad heart I bade adieu to the city, in the joyful hope soon to see the fulfilment of my long-expected journey.

The bright sky smiled above us, and a most favourable wind filled our sails. I sat on deck and revelled in the contemplation of scenes so new to me. Behind us lay spread the majestic town; before us the Sound, an immense natural basin, which I could almost compare to a great Swiss lake; on the right and left were the coasts of Sweden and Denmark, which here approach each other so closely that they seem to oppose a barrier to the further progress of the adventurous voyager.

Soon we passed the little Swedish town of Carlscrona, and the desolate island Hveen, on which Tycho de Brahe passed the greater portion of his life, occupied with stellar observations and calculations. Now came a somewhat dangerous part, and one which called into action all the careful seamanship of the captain to bring us safely through the confined sea and the strong current,--the entrance of the Sound into the Cattegat.

The two coasts here approach to within a mile of each other. On the Swedish side lies the pretty little town of Helsingborg, on the Danish side that of Helsingor, and at the extremity of a projecting neck of land the fortress Kronburg, which demands a toll of every passing ship, and shews a large row of threatening cannon in case of non-compliance. Our toll had already been paid before leaving Copenhagen; we had been accurately signalled, and sailed fearlessly by. {18}

The entrance once passed, we entered the Cattegat, which already looked more like the great ocean: the coasts retired on each side, and most of the shifts and barques, which till now had hovered around us on all sides, bade us "farewell." Some bent their course towards the east, others towards the west; and we alone, on the broad desert ocean, set sail for the icy north. Twilight did not set in until 9 o'clock at night; and on the coasts the flaming beacons flashed up, to warn the benighted mariner of the proximity of dangerous rocks.

I now offered up my thanksgiving to Heaven for the protection hitherto vouchsafed me, with a humble prayer for its continuance. Then I descended to the cabin, where I found a convenient bunk (a kind of crib fixed to the side of the ship); I laid myself down, and was soon in a deep and refreshing sleep.

I awoke full of health and spirits, which, however, I enjoyed but for a short time. During the night we had left behind us the "Cattegat" and the "Skagerrack," and were driving through the stormy German Ocean. A high wind, which increased almost to a gale, tumbled our poor ship about in such a manner, that none but a good dancer could hope to maintain an upright position. I had unfortunately been from my youth no votary of Terpsichore, and what was I to do? The naiads of this stormy region seized me, and bandied me to and fro, until they threw me into the arms of what was, according to my experience, if not exactly after Schiller's interpretation, "the horrible of horrors,"--sea-sickness. At first I took little heed of this, thinking that sea-sickness would soon be overcome by a traveller like myself, who should be inured to every thing. But in vain did I bear up; I became worse and worse, till I was at length obliged to remain in my berth with but one consoling thought, namely, that we were to-day on the open sea, where there was nothing worthy of notice. But the following day the Norwegian coast was in sight, and at all hazards I must see it; so I crawled on deck more dead than alive, looked at a row of mountains of moderate elevation, their tops at this early season still sparkling with their snowy covering, and then hurried back, benumbed by the piercing icy wind, to my good warm feather-bed. Those who have never experienced it can have no conception of the biting, penetrating coldness of a gale of wind in the northern seas. The sun shone high in the heavens; the thermometer (I always calculate according to Reaumur) stood 3 degrees above zero; I was dressed much more warmly than I should have thought necessary when, in my fatherland, the thermometer was 8 or 10 degrees *below* zero, and yet I felt chilled to the heart, and could have fancied that I had no clothes on at all.

On the fourth night we sailed safely past the Shetland Islands; and on the evening of the fifth day we passed so near the majestic rocky group of the Feroe Islands, that we were at one time apprehensive of being cast upon the rocks by the unceasing gale. {19}

Already on the seventh day we descried the coast of Iceland. Our passage had been unprecedentedly quick; the sailors declared that a favourable gale was to be preferred even to steam, and that on our present voyage we should certainly have left every steamer in our wake. But I, wretched being that I was, would gladly have dispensed with the services both of gale and steam for the sake of a few hours' rest. My illness increased so much, that on the seventh day I thought I must succumb. My limbs were bathed in a cold perspiration; I was as weak as an infant, and my mouth felt parched and dry. I saw that I must now either make a great effort or give up entirely; so I roused myself, and with the assistance of the cabin-boy gained a seat, and promised to take any and every remedy which should be recommended. They gave me hot-water gruel with wine and sugar; but it was not enough to be obliged to force this down, I was further compelled to swallow small pieces of raw bacon highly peppered, and even a mouthful of rum. I need not say what strong determination was required to make me submit to such a regimen. I had, how-ever, but one choice, either to conquer my repugnance or give myself up a victim to sea-sickness; so with all patience and resignation I received the proffered gifts, and found, after a trial of many hours, that I could manage to retain a small dose. This physicking was continued for two long, long days, and then I began slowly to recover.

I have here circumstantially described both my illness and its cure, because so many people are unfortunately victims to the complaint, and when under its influ-ence cannot summon resolution to take sustenance. I should advise all my friends not to hold out so long as I did, but to take food at once, and continue to do so until the system will receive it.

As I was now convalescent, I tried to recruit my wearied mind by a diligent study of the mode of life and customs of the mariners of the northern seas.

Our ship's company consisted of Herr Knudson, Herr Bruge (a merchant whom we were to land at the Westmann Islands), the captain, the mate, and six or seven sailors. Our mode of life in the cabin was as follows: in the morning, at seven o'clock, we took coffee, but whence this coffee came, heaven knows! I drank it for eleven days, and could never discover any thing which might serve as a clue in my attempt to discover the country of its growth. At ten o'clock we had a meal consisting of bread and butter and cheese, with cold beef or pork, all excellent dishes for those in health; the second course of this morning meal was "tea-water." In Scandina-via, by the way, they never say, "I drink *tea*," the word "water" is always added: "I drink *tea-water*." Our "tea-water" was, if possible, worse than its predecessor, the incomparable coffee. Thus I was beaten at all points; the eatables were too strong for me, the drinkables too--too--I can find no appropriate epithet--probably too artificial. I consoled myself with the prospect of dinner; but, alas, too soon this sweet vision faded into thin air! On the sixth day I made my first appearance at the covered table, and could not help at once remarking the cloth which had been spread over it. At the commencement of our journey it might perhaps have been white; now it was most certainly no longer of that snowy hue. The continual pitching and rolling of the ship had caused each dish to set its peculiar stamp upon the cloth. A sort of wooden network was now laid upon it, in the interstices of which the plates and glasses were set, and thus secured from falling. But before placing it on the table, our worthy cabin-boy took each plate and glass separately, and polished it on a towel which hung near, and in colour certainly rather resembling the dingy floor of the cabin than the bight-hued rainbow. This could still have been endured, but the article in question really did duty *as a towel* in the morning, before extending its salutary influence over plates and glasses for the remainder of the day.

On making discoveries such as these, I would merely turn away my eyes, and try to think that perhaps *my glass* and *my plate* would be more delicately manipulated, or probably escape altogether; and then I would turn my whole attention to the expected dishes.

First came soup; but instead of gravy-soup, it was water-soup, with rice and dried plums. This, when mingled with red wine and sugar, formed a most exquisite dish for Danish appetites, but it certainly did not suit mine. The second and concluding course consisted of a large piece of beef, with which I had no fault to find, except that it was too heavy for one in my weak state of health. At supper we had the same dishes as at dinner, and each meal was followed by "tea-water." At first I could not fancy this bill of fare at all; but within a few days after my convalesence, I had accustomed myself to it, and could bear the sea-diet very well. {20}

As the rich owner of the vessel was on board, there was no lack of the best wines, and few evenings passed on which a bowl of punch was not emptied. There was, however, a reason found why every bottle of wine or bowl of punch should be drunk: for instance, at our embarkation, to drink the health of the friends we were leaving, and to hope for a quick and prosperous voyage; then, when the wind was favourable, its health was drunk, with the request that it would remain so; when it was contrary, with the request that it would change; when we saw land, we saluted it with a glass of wine, or perhaps with several, but I was too ill to count; when we lost sight of it, we drank a farewell glass to its health: so that every day brought with it three or four distinct and separate occasions for drinking wine. {21}

The sailors drank tea-water without sugar every morning and evening, with the addition of a glass of brandy; for dinner they had pease, beans, barley, or potatoes, with salted cod, bacon, "or junk;" good sea-biscuit they could get whenever they chose.

The diet is not the worst part of these poor people's hardships. Their life may be called a continual fight against the elements; for it is precisely during the most dreadful storms, with rain and piercing cold, that they have to be continually upon deck. I could not sufficiently admire the coolness, or rather the cheerfulness and alacrity with which they fulfilled their onerous duties. And what reward have they? Scanty pay, for food the diet I have just described, and for their sleeping-place the smallest and most inconvenient part of the ship, a dark place frequently infested with vermin, and smelling offensively from being likewise used as a receptacle for oil-colours, varnish, tar, salt-fish, &c. &c.

To be cheerful in the midst of all this requires a very quiet and contented mind. That the Danish sailors are contented, I had many opportunities of observing during the voyage of which I am speaking, and on several other occasions.

But after all this long description, it is high time that I should return to the journey itself.

The favourable gale which had thus wafted us to the coast of Iceland within seven days, now unfortunately changed its direction, and drove us back. We drifted about in the storm-tost ocean, and many a Spanish wave {22} broke completely over our ship. Twice we attempted to approach the Westmann Islands {23} (a group belonging to Iceland) to watch an opportunity of casting anchor, and setting ashore our fellow-traveller Herr Bruge; but it was in vain, we were driven back each time. At length, at the close of the eleventh day, we reached Havenfiord, a very good harbour, distant nine miles from Reikjavik, the capital of Iceland.

In spite of the very inopportune change in the direction of the wind, we had had an unprecedentedly quick passage. The distance from Copenhagen to Iceland, in a straight line, is reckoned at 1200 geographical miles; for a sailing vessel, which must tack now and then, and must go as much with the wind as possible, 1500 to 1600 miles. Had the strong wind, which was at first so favourable, instead of changing on the seventh day, held on for thirty or forty hours longer, we should have landed in Iceland on the eighth or ninth day--even the steamer could not have accomplished the passage so quickly.

The shores of Iceland appeared to me quite different from what I had supposed them to be from the descriptions I had read. I had fancied them naked, without tree or shrub, dreary and desert; but now I saw green hills, shrubs, and even what appeared to be groups of stunted trees. As we came nearer, however, I was enabled to distinguish objects more clearly, and the green hills became human dwellings with small doors and windows, while the supposed groups of trees proved in reality to be heaps of lava, some ten or twelve feet high, thickly covered with moss and grass. Every thing was new and striking to me; I waited in great impatience till we could land.

At length the anchor descended; but it was not till next morning that the hour of disembarkation and deliverance came.

But one more night, and then, every difficulty overcome, I should tread the shores of Iceland, the longed-for, and bask as it were in the wonders of this island, so poor in the creations of art, so rich in the phenomena of Nature.

* * * * *

Before I land in Iceland, I must trouble the reader with a few preliminary observations regarding this island. They are drawn from Mackenzie's **Description of Iceland**, a book the sterling value of which is appreciated every where. {24}

The discovery of Iceland, about the year of our Lord 860, is attributed to the spirit of enterprise of some Swedish and Norwegian pirates, who were drifted thither on a voyage to the Feroe Isles. It was not till the year 874 that the island was peopled by a number of voluntary emigrants, who, feeling unhappy under the dominion of Harold Harfraga (fine hair), arrived at the island under the direction of Ingold. {25} As the newcomers are said to have found no traces of dwellings, they are presumed to be the first who took possession of the island.

At this time Iceland was still so completely covered with underwood, that at some points it was necessary to cut a passage. Bringing with them their language, religion, customs, and historical monuments, the Norwegians introduced a kind of feudal system, which, about the year 928, gave place to a somewhat aristocratic government, retaining, however, the name of a republic. The island was divided into four provinces, over each of which was placed an hereditary governor or judge.

The General Assembly of Iceland (called Allthing) was held annually on the shores of the Lake Thingvalla. The people possessed an excellent code of laws, in which provision had been made for every case which could occur.

This state of things lasted for more than 300 years, a period which may be called the golden age of Iceland. Education, literature, and even refined poetry flourished among the inhabitants, who took part in commerce and in the sea-voyages which the Norwegians undertook for purposes of discovery.

The "Sagas," or histories of this country, contain many tales of personal bravery. Its bards and historians visited other climes, became the favourites of monarchs, and returned to their island covered with honour and loaded with presents. The *Edda*, by Samund, is one of the most valued poems of the ancient days of Iceland. The second portion of the *Edda*, called *Skalda*, dates from a later period, and is ascribed by many to the celebrated Snorri Sturluson. Isleif, first Bishop of Skalholt, was the earliest Icelandic historian; after him came the noted Snorri Sturluson, born in 1178, who became the richest and mightiest man in Iceland.

Snorri Sturluson was frequently followed to the General Assembly of Iceland by a splendid retinue of 800 armed men. He was a great historian and poet, and possessed an accurate knowledge of the Greek and Latin tongues, besides being a powerful orator. He was also the author of the *Heims-kringla*.

The first school was founded at Skalholt, about the middle of the eleventh century, under Isleif, first Bishop of Iceland; four other schools and several convents soon followed. Poetry and music seem to have formed a staple branch of education.

The climate of Iceland appears to have been less inclement than is now the case; corn is said to have grown, and trees and shrubs were larger and thicker than we find them at present. The population of Iceland was also much more numerous than it is now, although there were neither towns nor villages. The people lived scattered throughout the island; and the General Assembly was held at Thingvalla, in the open air.

Fishing constituted the chief employment of the Icelanders. Their clothing was woven from the wool of their sheep. Commerce with neighbouring countries opened to them another field of occupation.

The doctrines of Christianity were first introduced into Iceland, in the year 981, by Friederich, a Saxon bishop. Many churches were built, and tithes established for the maintenance of the clergy. Isleif, first Bishop of Skalholt, was ordained in the year 1057. After the introduction of Christianity, all the Icelanders enjoyed an unostentatious but undisturbed practice of their religion.

Greenland and the most northern part of America are said to have been discovered by Icelanders.

In the middle of the thirteenth century Iceland came into the power of the Norwegian kings. In the year 1380 Norway was united to the crown of Denmark; and Iceland incorporated, without resistance, in the Danish monarchy. Since the cession of the island to Norway, and then to Denmark, peace and security took the place of the internal commotions with which, before this time, Iceland had been frequently disturbed; but this state of quiet brought forth indolence and apathy. The voyages of discovery were interfered with by the new government, and the commerce gradually passed into the hands of other nations. The climate appears also to have changed; and the lessened industry and want of perseverance in the inhabitants have brought agriculture completely into decline.

In the year 1402 the plague broke out upon the island, and carried off two-thirds of the population.

The first printing-press was established at Hoolum, about the year 1530, under the superintendence of the Bishop, John Areson.

The reformation in the Icelandic Church was not brought about without disturbance. It was legally established in the year 1551.

During the fifteenth century the Icelanders suffered more from the piratical incursions of foreigners. As late as the year 1616 the French and English nations took part in these enormities. The most melancholy occurrence of this kind took place in 1627, in which year a great number of Algerine pirates made a descent upon the Icelandic coast, murdered about fifty of the inhabitants, and carried off nearly 400 others into captivity. {26}

The eighteenth century commenced with a dreadful mortality from the small-pox; of which disease more than 16,000 of the inhabitants died. In 1757 a famine swept away about 10,000 souls.

The year 1783 was distinguished by most dreadful volcanic outbreaks in the interior of the island. Tremendous streams of lava carried all before them; great rivers were checked in their course, and formed lakes. For more than a year a thick cloud of smoke and volcanic ashes covered the whole of Iceland, and nearly darkened the sunlight. Horned cattle, sheep, and horses were destroyed; famine came, with its accompanying illnesses; and once more appeared the malignant small-pox. In a few years more than 11,000 persons had died; more than one-fourth of the whole present population of the island.

Iceland lies in the Atlantic ocean; its greatest breadth is 240 geographical miles, and its extreme length from north to south 140 miles. The number of inhabitants is estimated at 48,000, and the superficial extent of the island at 29,800 square miles.

CHAPTER III

On the morning of the 16th of May I landed in the harbour of Havenfiord, and for the first time trod the shores of Iceland. Although I was quite bewildered by sea-sickness, and still more by the continual rocking of the ship, so that every object round me seemed to dance, and I could scarcely make a firm step, still I could not rest in the house of Herr Knudson, which he had obligingly placed at my disposal. I must go out at once, to see and investigate every thing. I found that Havenfiord consisted merely of three wooden houses, a few magazines built of the same material, and some peasants' cottages.

The wooden houses are inhabited by merchants or by their factors, and consist only of a ground-floor, with a front of four or six windows. Two or three steps lead up to the entrance, which is in the centre of the building, and opens upon a hall from which doors lead into the rooms to the right and left. At the back of the house is situated the kitchen, which opens into several back rooms and into the yard. A house of this description consists only of five or six rooms on the ground-floor and a few small attic bedrooms.

The internal arrangements are quite European. The furniture--which is often of mahogany,--the mirrors, the cast-iron stoves, every thing, in short, come from Copenhagen. Beautiful carpets lie spread before the sofas; neat curtains shade the windows; English prints ornament the whitewashed walls; porcelain, plate, cut-glass, &c., are displayed on chests and on tables; and flower-pots with roses, mignonnette, and pinks spread a delicious fragrance around. I even found a grand pianoforte here. If any person could suddenly, and without having made the journey, be transported into one of these houses, he would certainly fancy himself in some continental town, rather than in the distant and barren island of Iceland. And as in Havenfiord, so I found the houses of the more opulent classes in Reikjavik, and in all the places I visited.

From these handsome houses I betook myself to the cottages of the peasants, which have a more indigenous, Icelandic appearance. Small and low, built of lava, with the interstices filled with earth, and the whole covered with large pieces of turf, they would present rather the appearance of natural mounds of earth than of human dwellings, were it not that the projecting wooden chimneys, the low-browed entrances, and the almost imperceptible windows, cause the spectator to conclude that they are inhabited. A dark narrow passage, about four feet high, leads on one side into the common room, and on the other to a few compartments, some of which are used as storehouses for provisions, and the rest as winter stables for the cows and sheep. At the end of this passage, which is purposely built so low, as an additional defence against the cold, the fireplace is generally situated. The rooms of the poorer class have neither wooden walls nor floors, and are just large enough to admit of the inhabitants sleeping, and perhaps turning round in them. The whole interior accommodation is comprised in bedsteads with very little covering, a small table, and a few drawers. Beds and chests of drawers answer the purpose of benches and chairs. Above the beds are fixed rods, from which depend clothes, shoes, stockings, &c. A small board, on which are arranged a few books, is generally to be observed. Stoves are considered unnecessary; for as the space is very confined, and the house densely populated, the atmosphere is naturally warm.

Rods are also placed round the fireplace, and on these the wet clothes and fishes are hung up in company to dry. The smoke completely fills the room, and slowly finds its way through a few breathing-holes into the open air.

Fire-wood there is none throughout the whole island. The rich inhabitants have it brought from Norway or Denmark; the poor burn turf, to which they frequently add bones and other offal of fish, which naturally engender a most disagreeable smoke.

On entering one of these cottages, the visitor is at a loss to determine which of the two is the more obnoxious--the suffocating smoke in the passage or the poisoned air of the dwelling-room, rendered almost insufferable by the crowding together of so many persons. I could almost venture to assert, that the dreadful eruption called Lepra, which is universal throughout Iceland, owes its existence rather to the total want of cleanliness than to the climate of the country or to the food.

Throughout my subsequent journeys into the interior, I found the cottages of the peasants every where alike squalid and filthy. Of course I speak of the majority, and not of the exceptions; for here I found a few rich peasants, whose dwellings looked cleaner and more habitable, in proportion to the superior wealth or sense of decency of the owners. My idea is, that the traveller's estimate of a country should be formed according to the habits and customs of the generality of its inhabitants, and not according to the doings of a few individuals, as is often the case. Alas, how seldom did I meet with these creditable exceptions!

The neighbourhood of Havenfiord is formed by a most beautiful and picturesque field of lava, at first rising in hills, then sinking into hollows, and at length terminating in a great plain which extends to the base of the neighbouring mountains. Masses of the most varied forms, often black and naked, rise to the height of ten or fifteen feet, forming walls, ruined pillars, small grottoes, and hollow spaces. Over these latter large slabs often extend, and form bridges. Every thing around consists of suddenly cooled heaped-up masses of lava, in some instances covered to their summits with grass and moss; this circumstance gives them, as already stated, the appearance of groups of stunted trees. Horses, sheep, and cows were clambering about, diligently seeking out every green place. I also clambered about diligently; I could not tire of gazing and wondering at this terribly beautiful picture of destruction.

After a few hours I had so completely forgotten the hardships of my passage, and felt myself so much strengthened, that I began my journey to Reikjavik at five o'clock on the evening of the same day. Herr Knudson seemed much concerned for me; he warned me that the roads were bad, and particularly emphasised the dangerous abysses I should be compelled to pass. I comforted him with the assurance that I was a good horsewoman, and could hardly have to encounter worse roads than those with which I had had the honour to become acquainted in Syria. I therefore took leave of the kind gentleman, who intended to stay a week or ten days in Havenfiord, and mounting a small horse, set out in company of a female guide.

In my guide I made the acquaintance of a remarkable antiquity of Iceland, who is well worthy that I should devote a few words to her description. She is above seventy years of age, but looks scarcely fifty; her head is surrounded by tresses of rich fair hair. She is dressed like a man; undertakes, in the capacity of messenger, the longest and most fatiguing journeys; rows a boat as skilfully as the most practised fisherman; and fulfils all her missions quicker and more exactly than a man, for she does not keep up so good an understanding with the brandy-bottle. She marched on so sturdily before me, that I was obliged to incite my little horse to greater speed with my riding-whip.

At first the road lay between masses of lava, where it certainly was not easy to ride; then over flats and small acclivities, from whence we could descry the immense plain in which are situated Havenfiord, Bassastadt, Reikjavik, and other places. Bassastadt, a town built on a promontory jutting out into the sea, contains one of the principal schools, a church built of masonry, and a few cottages. The town of Reikjavik cannot be seen, as it is hidden behind a hill. The other places consist chiefly of a few cottages, and only meet the eye of the traveller when he approaches them nearly. Several chains of mountains, towering one above the other, and sundry "Jokuls," or glaciers, which lay still sparkling in their wintry garb, surround this interminable plain, which is only open at one end, towards the sea. Some of the plains and hills shone with tender green, and I fancied I beheld beautiful meadows. On a nearer inspection, however, they proved to be swampy places, and hundreds upon hundreds of little acclivities, sometimes resembling mole-hills, at others small graves, and covered with grass and moss.

I could see over an area of at least thirty or forty miles, and yet could not descry a tree or a shrub, a bit of meadow-land or a friendly village. Every thing seemed dead. A few cottages lay scattered here and there; at long intervals a bird would hover in the air, and still more seldom I heard the kindly greeting of a passing inhabitant. Heaps of lava, swamps, and turf-bogs surrounded me on all sides; in all the vast expanse not a spot was to be seen through which a plough could be driven.

After riding more than four miles, I reached a hill, from which I could see Reikjavik, the chief harbour, and, in fact, the only town on the island. But I was deceived in my expectations; the place before me was a mere village.

The distance from Havenfiord to Reikjavik is scarcely nine miles; but as I was unwilling to tire my good old guide, I took three hours to accomplish it. The road was, generally speaking, very good, excepting in some places, where it lay over heaps of lava. Of the much-dreaded dizzy abysses I saw nothing; the startling term must have been used to designate some unimportant declivities, along the brow of which I rode, in sight of the sea; or perhaps the "abysses" were on the lava-fields, where I sometimes noticed small chasms of fifteen or sixteen feet in depth at the most.

Shortly after eight o'clock in the evening I was fortunate enough to reach Reikjavik safe and well. Through the kind forethought of Herr Knudson, a neat little room had been prepared for me in one of his houses occupied by the family of the worthy baker Bernhoft, and truly I could not have been better received any where.

During my protracted stay the whole family of the Bernhofts shewed me more kindness and cordiality than it has been my lot frequently to find. Many an hour has Herr Bernhoft sacrificed to me, in order to accompany me in my little excursions. He assisted me most diligently in my search for flowers, insects, and shells, and was much rejoiced when he could find me a new specimen. His kind wife and dear children rivalled him in willingness to oblige. I can only say, may Heaven requite them a thousand-fold for their kindness and friendship!

I had even an opportunity of hearing my native language spoken by Herr Bernhoft, who was a Holsteiner by birth, and had not quite forgotten our dear German tongue, though he had lived for many years partly in Denmark, partly in Iceland.

So behold me now in the only town in Iceland, {27} the seat of the so-called cultivated classes, whose customs and mode of life I will now lay before my honoured readers.

Nothing was more disagreeable to me than a certain air of dignity assumed by the ladies here; an air which, except when it is natural, or has become so from long habit, is apt to degenerate into stiffness and incivility. On meeting an acquaintance, the ladies of Reikjavik would bend their heads with so stately and yet so careless an air as we should scarcely assume towards the humblest stranger. At the conclusion of a visit, the lady of the house only accompanies the guest as far as the chamber-door. If the husband be present, this civility is carried a little further; but when this does not happen to be the case, a stranger who does not know exactly through which door he can make his exit, may chance to feel not a little embarrassed. Excepting in the house of the "Stiftsamtmann" (the principal official on the island), one does not find a footman who can shew the way. In Hamburgh I had already noticed the beginnings of this dignified coldness; it increased as I journeyed further north, and at length reached its climax in Iceland.

Good letters of recommendation often fail to render the northern grandees polite towards strangers. As an instance of this fact, I relate the following trait:

Among other kind letters of recommendation, I had received one addressed to Herr von H---, the "Stiftsamtmann" of Iceland. On my arrival at Copenhagen, I heard that Herr von H--- happened to be there. I therefore betook myself to his residence, and was shewn into a room where I found two young ladies and three children. I delivered my letter, and remained quietly standing for some time. Finding at length that no one invited me to be seated, I sat down unasked on the nearest chair, never supposing for an instant that the lady of the house could be present, and neglect the commonest forms of politeness which should be observed towards every stranger. After I had waited for some time, Herr von H--- graciously made his appearance, and expressed his regret that he should have very little time to spare for me, as he intended setting sail for Iceland with his family in a short time, and in the interim had a number of weighty affairs to settle at Copenhagen; in conclusion, he gave me the friendly advice to abandon my intention of visiting Iceland, as the fatigues of travelling in that country were very great; finding, however, that I persevered in my intention, he promised, in case I set sail for Reikjavik earlier than himself, to give me a letter of recommendation. All this was concluded in great haste, and we stood during the interview. I took my leave, and at first determined not to call again for the letter. On reflection, however, I changed my mind, ascribed my unfriendly reception to important and perhaps disagreeable business, and called again two days afterwards. Then the letter was handed to me by a servant; the high people, whom I could hear conversing in the adjoining apartment, probably considered it too much trouble to deliver it to me personally.

On paying my respects to this amiable family in Reikjavik, I was not a little surprised to recognise in Frau von H--- one of those ladies who in Copenhagen had not had the civility to ask me to be seated. Five or six days afterwards, Herr von H--- returned my call, and invited me to an excursion to Vatne. I accepted the invitation with much pleasure, and mentally asked pardon of him for having formed too hasty an opinion. Frau von H---, however, did not find her way to me until the fourth week of my stay in Reikjavik; she did not even invite me to visit her again, so of course I did not go, and our acquaintance terminated there. As in duty bound, the remaining dignitaries of this little town took their tone from their chief. My visits were unreturned, and I received no invitations, though I heard much during my stay of parties of pleasure, dinners, and evening parties. Had I not fortunately been able to employ myself, I should have been very badly off. Not one of the ladies had kindness and delicacy enough to consider that I was alone here, and that the society of educated people might be necessary for my comfort. I was less annoyed at the want of politeness in the gentlemen; for I am no longer young, and that accounts for every thing. When the women were wanting in kindliness, I had no right to expect consideration from the gentlemen.

I tried to discover the reason of this treatment, and soon found that it lay in a national characteristic of these people--their selfishness.

It appears I had scarcely arrived at Reikjavik before diligent inquiries were set on foot as to whether I was *rich*, and should see much company at my house, and, in fact, whether much could be got out of me.

To be well received here it is necessary either to be rich, or else to travel as a naturalist. Persons of the latter class are generally sent by the European courts to investigate the remarkable productions of the country. They make large collections of minerals, birds, &c.; they bring with them numerous presents, sometimes of considerable value, which they distribute among the dignitaries; they are, moreover, the projectors of many an entertainment, and even of many a little ball, &c.; they buy up every thing they can procure for their cabinets, and they always travel in company; they have much baggage with them, and consequently require many horses, which cannot be hired in Iceland, but must be bought. On such occasions every one here is a dealer: offers of horses and cabinets pour in on all sides.

The most welcome arrival of all is that of the French frigate, which visits Iceland every year; for sometimes there are ***dejeuners a la fourchette*** on board, sometimes little evening parties and balls. There is at least something to be got besides the rich presents; the "Stiftsamtmann" even receives 600 florins per annum from the French government to defray the expense of a few return balls which he gives to the naval officers.

With me this was not the case: I gave no parties--I brought no presents--they had nothing to expect from me; and therefore they left me to myself. {28}

For this reason I affirm that he only can judge of the character of a people who comes among them without claim to their attention, and from whom they have nothing to expect. To such a person only do they appear in their true colours, because they do not find it worth while to dissemble and wear a mask in his presence. In these cases the traveller is certainly apt to make painful discoveries; but when, on the other hand, he meets with good people, he may be certain of their sincerity; and so I must beg my honoured readers to bear with me, when I mention the names of all those who heartily welcomed the undistinguished foreigner; it is the only way in which I can express my gratitude towards them.

As I said before, I had intercourse with very few people, so that ample time remained for solitary walks, during which I minutely noticed every thing around me.

The little town of Reikjavik consists of a single broad street, with houses and cottages scattered around. The number of inhabitants does not amount to 500.

The houses of the wealthier inhabitants are of wood-work, and contain merely a ground-floor, with the exception of a single building of one story, to which the high school, now held at Bassastadt, will be transferred next year. The house of the "Stiftsamtmann" is built of stone. It was originally intended for a prison; but as criminals are rarely to be met with in Iceland, the building was many years ago transformed into the residence of the royal officer. A second stone building, discernible from Reikjavik, is situated at Langarnes, half a mile from the town. It lies near the sea, in the midst of meadows, and is the residence of the bishop.

The church is capable of holding only at the most from 100 to 150 persons; it is built of stone, with a wooden roof. In the chambers of this roof the library, consisting of several thousand volumes, is deposited. The church contains a treasure which many a larger and costlier edifice might envy,--a baptismal font by Thor-waldsen, whose parents were of Icelandic extraction. The great sculptor himself was born in Denmark, and probably wished, by this present, to do honour to the birth-place of his ancestors.

To some of the houses in Reikjavik pieces of garden are attached. These gardens are small plots of ground where, with great trouble and expense, salad, spinach, parsley, potatoes, and a few varieties of edible roots, are cultivated. The beds are separated from each other by strips of turf a foot broad, seldom boasting even a few field-flowers.

The inhabitants of Iceland are generally of middle stature, and strongly built, with light hair, frequently inclining to red, and blue eyes. The men are for the most part ugly; the women are better favoured, and among the girls I noticed some very sweet faces. To attain the age of seventy or eighty years is here considered an extraordinary circumstance. {29} The peasants have many children, and yet few; many are born, but few survive the first year. The mothers do not nurse them, and rear them on very bad food. Those who get over the first year look healthy enough; but they have strangely red cheeks, almost as though they had an eruption. Whether this appearance is to be ascribed to the sharp air, to which the delicate skin is not yet accustomed, or to the food, I know not.

In some places on the coast, when the violent storms prevent the poor fishermen for whole weeks from launching their boats, they live almost entirely on dried fishes' heads. {30} The fishes themselves have been salted down and sold, partly to pay the fishermen's taxes, and partly to liquidate debts for the necessaries of the past season, among which brandy and snuff unfortunately play far too prominent a part.

Another reason why the population does not increase is to be found in the numerous catastrophes attending the fisheries during the stormy season of the year. The fishermen leave the shore with songs and mirth, for a bright sky and a calm sea promise them good fortune. But, alas, tempests and snow-storms too often overtake the unfortunate boatmen! The sea is lashed into foam, and mighty waves overwhelm boats and fishermen together, and they perish inevitably. It is seldom that the father of a family embarks in the same boat with his sons. They divide themselves among different parties, in order that, if one boat founder, the whole family may not be destroyed.

I found the cottages of the peasants at Reikjavik smaller, and in every respect worse provided, than those at Havenfiord. This seems, however, to be entirely owing to the indolence of the peasants themselves; for stones are to be had in abundance, and every man is his own builder. The cows and sheep live through the winter in a wretched den, built either in the cottage itself or in its immediate neighbourhood. The horses pass the whole year under the canopy of heaven, and must find their own provender. Occasionally only the peasant will shovel away the snow from a little spot, to assist the poor animals in searching for the grass or moss concealed beneath. It is then left to the horses to finish clearing away the snow with their feet. It may easily be imagined that this mode of treatment tends to render them very hardy; but the wonder is, how the poor creatures manage to exist through the winter on such spare diet, and to be strong and fit for work late in the spring and in summer. These horses are so entirely unused to being fed with oats, that they will refuse them when offered; they are not even fond of hay.

As I arrived in Iceland during the early spring, I had an opportunity of seeing the horses and sheep in their winter garments. The horses seemed to be covered, not with hair, but with a thick woolly coat; their manes and tails are very long, and of surprising thickness. At the end of May or the beginning of June the tail and mane are docked and thinned, their woolly coat falls of itself, and they then look smooth enough. The sheep have also a very thick coat during the winter. It is not the custom to shear them, but at the beginning of June the wool is picked off piece by piece with the hand. A sheep treated in this way sometimes presents a very comical appearance, being perfectly naked on one side, while on the other it is still covered with wool.

The horses and cows are considerably smaller than those of our country. No one need journey so far north, however, to see stunted cattle. Already, in Galicia, the cows and horses of the peasants are not a whit larger or stronger than those in Iceland. The Icelandic cows are further remarkable only for their peculiarly small horns; the sheep are also smaller than ours.

Every peasant keeps horses. The mode of feeding them is, as already shewn, very simple; the distances are long, the roads bad, and large rivers, moorlands, and swamps must frequently be passed; so every one rides, both men, women, and children. The use of carriages is as totally unknown throughout the island as in Syria.

The immediate vicinity of Reikjavik is pretty enough. Some of the townspeople go to much trouble and expense in sometimes collecting and sometimes breaking the stones around their dwellings. With the little ground thus obtained they mix turf, ashes, and manure, until at length a soil is formed on which something will grow. But this is such a gigantic undertaking, that the little culture bestowed on the spots wholly neglected by nature cannot be wondered at. Herr Bernhoft shewed me a small meadow which he had leased for thirty years, at an annual rent of thirty kreutzers. In order, however, to transform the land he bought into a meadow, which yields winter fodder for only one cow, it was necessary to expend more than 150 florins, besides much personal labour and pains. The rate of wages for peasants is very high when compared with the limited wants of these people: they receive thirty or forty kreutzers per diem, and during the hay-harvest as much as a florin.

For a long distance round the town the ground consists of stones, turf, and swamps. The latter are mostly covered with hundreds upon hundreds of great and small mounds of firm ground. By jumping from one of these mounds to the next, the entire swamp may be crossed, not only without danger, but dry-footed.

In spite of all this, one of these swamps put me in a position of much difficulty and embarrassment during one of my solitary excursions. I was sauntering quietly along, when suddenly a little butterfly fluttered past me. It was the first I had seen in this country, and my eagerness to catch it was proportionately great. I hastened after it; thought neither of swamp nor of danger, and in the heat of the chase did not observe that the mounds became every moment fewer and farther between. Soon I found myself in the middle of the swamp, and could neither advance nor retreat. Not a human being could I descry; the very animals were far from me; and this circumstance confirmed me as to the dangerous nature of the ground. Nothing remained for me but to fix my eyes upon one point of the landscape, and to step out boldly towards it. I was often obliged to hazard two or three steps into the swamp itself, in order to gain the next acclivity, upon which I would then stand triumphantly, to determine my farther progress. So long as I could distinguish traces of horses' hoofs, I had no fear; but even these soon disappeared, and I stood there alone in the morass. I could not remain for ever on my tower of observation, and had no resource but to take to the swamp once more. I must confess that I experienced a very uncomfortable feeling of apprehension when my foot sank suddenly into the soft mud; but when I found that it did not rise higher than the ankles, my courage returned; I stepped out boldly, and was fortunate enough to escape with the fright and a thorough wetting.

The most arduous posts in the country are those of the medical men and clergymen. Their sphere of action is very enlarged, particularly that of the medical man, whose practice sometimes extends over a distance of eighty to a hundred miles. When we add to this the severity of the winter, which lasts for seven or eight months, it seems marvellous that any one can be found to fill such a situation.

In winter the peasants often come with shovels, pickaxes, and horses to fetch the doctor. They then go before him, and hastily repair the worst part of the road; while the doctor rides sometimes on one horse, sometimes on another, that they may not sink under the fatigue. And thus the procession travels for many, many miles, through night and fog, through storm and snow, for on the doctor's promptitude life and death often hang. When he then returns, quite benumbed, and half dead with cold, to the bosom of his family, in the expectation of rest and refreshment, and to rejoice with his friends over the dangers and hardships he has escaped, the poor doctor is frequently compelled to set off at once on a new and important journey, before he has even had time to greet the dear ones at home.

Sometimes he is sent for by sea, where the danger is still greater on the storm-tost element.

Though the salary of the medical men is not at all proportionate to the hardships they are called upon to undergo, it is still far better than that of the priests.

The smallest livings bring in six to eight florins annually, the richest 200 florins. Besides this, the government supplies for each priest a house, often not much better than a peasant's cottage, a few meadows, and some cattle. The peasants are also required to give certain small contributions in the way of hay, wool, fish, &c. The greater number of priests are so poor, that they and their families dress exactly like the peasants, from whom they can scarcely be distinguished. The clergyman's wife looks after the cattle, and milks cows and ewes like a maid-servant; while her husband proceeds to the meadow, and mows the grass with the labourer. The intercourse of the pastor is wholly confined to the society of peasants; and this constitutes the chief element of that "patriarchal life" which so many travellers describe as charming. I should like to know which of them would wish to lead such a life!

The poor priest has, besides, frequently to officiate in two, three, or even four districts, distant from four to twelve miles from his residence. Every Sunday he must do duty at one or other of these districts, taking them in turn, so that divine service is only performed at each place once in every three or four weeks. The journeys of the priest, however, are not considered quite so necessary as those of the doctor; for if the weather is very bad on Sundays, particularly during the winter, he can omit visiting the most distant places. This is done the more readily, as but few of the peasants would be at church; all who lived at a distance remaining at home.

The Sysselmann (an officer similar to that of the sheriff of a county) is the best off. He has a good salary with little to do, and in some places enjoys in addition the "strand-right," which is at times no inconsiderable privilege, from the quantity of drift timber washed ashore from the American continent.

Fishing and the chase are open to all, with the exception of the salmon-fisheries in the rivers; these are farmed by the government. Eider-ducks may not be shot, under penalty of a fine. There is no military service, for throughout the whole island no soldiers are required. Even Reikjavik itself boasts only two police-officers.

Commerce is also free; but the islanders possess so little commercial spirit, that even if they had the necessary capital, they would never embark in speculation.

The whole commerce of Iceland thus lies in the hands of Danish merchants, who send their ships to the island every year, and have established factories in the different ports where the retail trade is carried on.

These ships bring every thing to Iceland, corn, wood, wines, manufactured goods, and colonial produce, &c. The imports are free, for it would not pay the government to establish offices, and give servants salaries to collect duties upon the small amount of produce required for the island. Wine, and in fact all colonial produce, are therefore much cheaper than in other countries.

The exports consist of fish, particularly salted cod, fish-roe, tallow, train-oil, eider-down, and feathers of other birds, almost equal to eider-down in softness, sheep's wool, and pickled or salted lamb. With the exception of the articles just enumerated, the Icelanders possess nothing; thirteen years ago, when Herr Knudson established a bakehouse, {31} he was compelled to bring from Copenhagen, not only the builder, but even the materials for building, stones, lime, &c.; for although the island abounds with masses of stone, there are none which can be used for building an oven, or which can be burnt into lime: every thing is of lava.

Two or three cottages situated near each other are here dignified by the name of a "place." These places, as well as the separate cottages, are mostly built on little acclivities, surrounded by meadows. The meadows are often fenced in with walls of stone or earth, two or three feet in height, to prevent the cows, sheep, and horses from trespassing upon them to graze. The grass of these meadows is made into hay, and laid up as a winter provision for the cows.

I did not hear many complaints of the severity of the cold in winter; the temperature seldom sinks to twenty degrees below zero; the sea is sometimes frozen, but only a few feet from the shore. The snowstorms and tempests, however, are often so violent, that it is almost impossible to leave the house. Daylight lasts only for five or six hours, and to supply its place the poor Icelanders have only the northern light, which is said to illumine the long nights with a brilliancy truly marvellous.

The summer I passed in Iceland was one of the finest the inhabitants had known for years. During the month of June the thermometer often rose at noon to twenty degrees. The inhabitants found this heat so insupportable, that they complained of being unable to work or to go on messages during the day-time. On such warm days they would only begin their hay-making in the evening, and continued their work half the night.

The changes in the weather are very remarkable. Twenty degrees of heat on one day would be followed by rain on the next, with a temperature of only five degrees; and on the 5th of June, at eight o'clock in the morning, the thermometer stood at one degree below zero. It is also curious that thunderstorms happen in Iceland in winter, and are said never to occur during the summer.

From the 16th or 18th of June to the end of the month there is no night. The sun appears only to retire for a short time behind a mountain, and forms sunset and morning-dawn at the same time. As on one side the last beam fades away, the orb of day re-appears at the opposite one with redoubled splendour.

During my stay in Iceland, from the 15th of May to the 29th of July, I never retired to rest before eleven o'clock at night, and never required a candle. In May, and also in the latter portion of the month of July, there was twilight for an hour or two, but it never became quite dark. Even during the last days of my stay, I could read until half-past ten o'clock. At first it appeared strange to me to go to bed in broad daylight; but I soon accustomed myself to it, and when eleven o'clock came, no sunlight was powerful enough to cheat me of my sleep. I found much pleasure in walking at night, at past ten o'clock, not in the pale moonshine, but in the broad blaze of the sun.

It was a much more difficult task to accustom myself to the diet. The baker's wife was fully competent to superintend the cooking according to the Danish and Icelandic schools of the art; but unfortunately these modes of cookery differ widely from ours. One thing only was good, the morning cup of coffee with cream, with which the most accomplished gourmand could have found no fault: since my departure from Iceland I have not found such coffee. I could have wished for some of my dear Viennese friends to breakfast with me. The cream was so thick, that I at first thought my hostess had misunderstood me, and brought me curds. The butter made from the milk of Icelandic cows and ewes did not look very inviting, and was as white as lard, but the taste was good. The Icelanders, however, find the taste not sufficiently "piquant," and generally qualify it with train-oil. Altogether, train-oil plays a very prominent part in the Icelandic kitchen; the peasant considers it a most delicious article, and thinks nothing of devouring a quantity of it without bread, or indeed any thing else. {32}

I did not at all relish the diet at dinner; this meal consisted of two dishes, namely, boiled fish, with vinegar and melted butter instead of oil, and boiled potatoes. Unfortunately I am no admirer of fish, and now this was my daily food. Ah, how I longed for beef-soup, a piece of meat, and vegetables, in vain! As long as I remained in Iceland, I was compelled quite to give up my German system of diet.

After a time I got on well enough with the boiled fish and potatoes, but I could not manage the delicacies of the island. Worthy Madame Bernhoft, it was so kindly meant on her part; and it was surely not her fault that the system of cookery in Iceland is different from ours; but I could not bring myself to like the Icelandic delicacies. They were of different kinds, consisting sometimes of fishes, hard-boiled eggs, and potatoes chopped up together, covered with a thick brown sauce, and seasoned with pepper, sugar, and vinegar; at others, of potatoes baked in butter and sugar. Another delicacy was cabbage chopped very small, rendered very thin by the addition of water, and sweetened with sugar; the accompanying dish was a piece of cured lamb, which had a very unpleasant "pickled" flavour.

On Sundays we sometimes had "Prothe Grutze," properly a Scandinavian dish, composed of fine sago boiled to a jelly, with currant-juice or red wine, and eaten with cream or sugar. Tapfen, a kind of soft cheese, is also sometimes eaten with cream and sugar.

In the months of June and July the diet improved materially. We could often procure splendid salmon, sometimes roast lamb, and now and then birds, among which latter dainties the snipes were particularly good. In the evening came butter, cheese, cold fish, smoked lamb, and eggs of eider-ducks, which are coarser than hen's eggs. In time I became so accustomed to this kind of food, that I no longer missed either soup or beef, and felt uncommonly well.

My drink was always clear fresh water; the gentlemen began their dinner with a small glass of brandy, and during the meal all drank beer of Herr Bernhoft's own brewing, which was very good. On Sundays, a bottle of port or Bordeaux sometimes made its appearance at our table; and as we fared at Herr Bernhoft's, so it was the custom in the houses of all the merchants and officials.

At Reikjavik I had an opportunity of witnessing a great religious ceremony. Three candidates of theology were raised to the ministerial office. Though the whole community here is Lutheran, the ceremonies differ in many respects from those of the continent of Europe, and I will therefore give a short sketch of what I saw. The solemnity began at noon, and lasted till four o'clock. I noticed at once that all the people covered their faces for a moment on entering the church, the men with their hats, and the women with their handkerchiefs. Most of the congregation sat with their faces turned towards the altar; but this rule had its exceptions. The vestments of the priests were the same as those worn by our clergymen, and the commencement of the service also closely resembled the ritual of our own Church; but soon this resemblance ceased. The bishop stepped up to the altar with the candidates, and performed certain ceremonies; then one would mount the pulpit and read part of a sermon, or sing a psalm, while the other clergymen sat round on chairs, and appeared to listen; then a second and a third ascended the pulpit, and afterwards another sermon was preached from the altar, and another psalm sung; then a sermon was again read from the pulpit. While ceremonies were performed at the altar, the sacerdotal garments were often put on and taken off again.

I frequently thought the service was coming to a close, but it always began afresh, and lasted, as I said before, until four o'clock. The number of forms surprised me greatly, as the ritual of the Lutheran Church is in general exceedingly simple.

On this occasion a considerable number of the country people were assembled, and I had thus a good opportunity of noticing their costumes. The dresses worn by the women and girls are all made of coarse black woollen stuffs. The dress consists of a long skirt, a spencer, and a coloured apron. On their heads they wear a man's nightcap of black cloth, the point turned downwards, and terminating in a large tassel of wool or silk, which hangs down to the shoulder. Their hair is unbound, and reaches only to the shoulder: some of the women wear it slightly curled. I involuntarily thought of the poetical descriptions of the northern romancers, who grow enthusiastic in praise of ideal "angels' heads with golden tresses." The hair is certainly worn in this manner here, and our poets may have borrowed their descriptions from the Scandinavians. But the beautiful faces which are said to beam forth from among those golden locks exist only in the poet's vivid imagination.

Ornamental additions to the costume are very rare. In the whole assembly I only noticed four women who were dressed differently from the others. The cords which fastened their spencers, and also their girdles, were ornamented with a garland worked in silver thread. Their skirts were of fine black cloth, and decorated with a border of coloured silk a few inches broad. Round their necks they wore a kind of stiff collar of black velvet with a border of silver thread, and on their heads a black silk handkerchief with a very strange addition. This appendage consisted of a half-moon fastened to the back of the head, and extending five or six inches above the forehead. It was covered with white lawn arranged in folds; its breadth at the back of the head did not exceed an inch and a half, but in front it widened to five or six inches.

The men, I found, were clothed almost like our peasants. They wore small-clothes of dark cloth, jackets and waistcoats, felt hats, or fur caps; and instead of boots a kind of shoe of ox-hide, sheep, or seal-skin, bound to the feet by a leather strap. The women, and even the children of the officials, all wear shoes of this description.

It was very seldom that I met people so wretchedly and poorly clad as we find them but too often in the large continental towns. I never saw any one without good warm shoes and stockings.

The better classes, such as merchants, officials, &c. are dressed in the French style, and rather fashionably. There is no lack of silk and other costly stuffs. Some of these are brought from England, but the greater part come from Denmark.

On the king's birthday, which is kept every year at the house of the Stiftsamt-mann, the festivities are said to be very grand; on this occasion the matrons appear arrayed in silk, and the maidens in white jaconet; the rooms are lighted with wax tapers.

Some speculative genius or other has also established a sort of club in Reik-javik. He has, namely, hired a couple of rooms, where the townspeople meet of an evening to discuss "tea-water," bread and butter, and sometimes even a bottle of wine or a bowl of punch. In winter the proprietor gives balls in these apart-ments, charging 20 kr. for each ticket of admission. Here the town grandees and the handicraftsmen, in fact all who choose to come, assemble; and the ball is said to be conducted in a very republican spirit. The shoemaker leads forth the wife of the Stiftsamtmann to the dance, while that official himself has perhaps chosen the wife or daughter of the shoemaker or baker for his partner. The refreshments consist of "tea-water" and bread and butter, and the room is lighted with tallow candles. The music, consisting of a kind of three-stringed violin and a pipe, is said to be exqui-sitely horrible.

In summer the dignitaries make frequent excursions on horse-back; and on these occasions great care is taken that there be no lack of provisions. Commonly each person contributes a share: some bring wine, others cake; others, again, cof-fee, and so on. The ladies use fine English side-saddles, and wear elegant riding-habits, and pretty felt hats with green veils. These jaunts, however, are confined to Reikjavik; for, as I have already observed, there is, with the exception of this town, no place in Iceland containing more than two or three stores and some half-dozen cottages.

To my great surprise, I found no less than six square piano-fortes belonging to different families in Reikjavik, and heard waltzes by our favourite composers, besides variations of Herz, and some pieces of Liszt, Wilmers, and Thalberg. But such playing! I do not think that these talented composers would have recognised their own works.

In conclusion, I must offer a few remarks relative to the travelling in this country.

The best time to choose for this purpose is from the middle of June to the end of August at latest. Until June the rivers are so swollen and turbulent, by reason of the melting snows, as to render it very dangerous to ride through them. The traveller must also pass over many a field of snow not yet melted by the sun, and frequently concealing chasms and masses of lava; and this is attended with danger almost as great. At every footstep the traveller sinks into the snow; and he may thank his lucky stars if the whole rotten surface does not give way. In September the violent storms of wind and rain commence, and heavy falls of snow may be expected from day to day.

A tent, provisions, cooking utensils, pillows, bed-clothes, and warm garments, are highly necessary for the wayfarer's comfort. This paraphernalia would have been too expensive for me to buy, and I was unprovided with any thing of the kind; consequently I was forced to endure the most dreadful hardships and toil, and was frequently obliged to ride an immense distance to reach a little church or a cottage, which would afford me shelter for the night. My sole food for eight or ten days together was often bread and cheese; and I generally passed the night upon a chest or a bench, where the cold would often prevent my closing my eyes all night.

It is advisable to be provided with a waterproof cloak and a sailor's tarpaulin hat, as a defence against the rain, which frequently falls. An umbrella would be totally useless, as the rain is generally accompanied by a storm, or, at any rate, by a strong wind; when we add to this, that it is necessary in some places to ride quickly, it will easily be seen that holding an umbrella open is a thing not to be thought of.

Altogether I found the travelling in this country attended with far more hardship than in the East. For my part, I found the dreadful storms of wind, the piercing air, the frequent rain, and the cold, much less endurable than the Oriental heat, which never gave me either cracked lips or caused scales to appear on my face. In Iceland my lips began to bleed on the fifth day; and afterwards the skin came off my face in scales, as if I had had the scrofula. Another source of great discomfort is to be found in the long riding-habit. It is requisite to be very warmly clad; and the heavy skirts, often dripping with rain, coil themselves round the feet of the wearer in such a manner, as to render her exceedingly awkward either in mounting or dismounting. The worst hardship of all, however, is the being obliged to halt to rest the horses in a meadow during the rain. The long skirts suck up the water from the damp grass, and the wearer has often literally not a dry stitch in all her garments.

Heat and cold appear in this country to affect strangers in a remarkable degree. The cold seemed to me more piercing, and the heat more oppressive in Iceland, than when the thermometer stood at the same points in my native land.

In summer the roads are marvellously good, so that one can generally ride at a pretty quick pace. They are, however, impracticable for vehicles, partly because they are too narrow, and partly also on account of some very bad places which must occasionally be encountered. On the whole island not a single carriage is to be found.

The road is only dangerous when it leads through swamps and moors, or over fields of lava. Among these fields, such as are covered with white moss are peculiarly to be feared, for the moss frequently conceals very dangerous holes, into which the horse can easily stumble. In ascending and descending the hills very formidable spots sometimes oppose the traveller's progress. The road is at times so hidden among swamps and bogs, that not a trace of it is to be distinguished, and I could only wonder how my guide always succeeded in regaining the right path. One could almost suppose that on these dangerous paths both horse and man are guided by a kind of instinct.

Travelling is more expensive in Iceland than any where else, particularly when one person travels alone, and must bear all the expense of the baggage, the guide, ferries, &c. Horses are not let out on hire, they must be bought. They are, however, very cheap; a pack-horse costs from eighteen to twenty-four florins, and a riding-horse from forty to fifty florins. To travel with any idea of comfort it is necessary to have several pack-horses, for they must not be heavily laden; and an additional servant must likewise be hired, as the guide only looks after the saddle-horses, and, at most, one or two of the pack-horses. If the traveller, at the conclusion of the journey, wishes to sell the horses, such a wretchedly low price is offered, that it is just as well to give them away at once. This is a proof of the fact that men are every where alike ready to follow up their advantage. These people are well aware that the horses must be left behind at any rate, and therefore they will not bid for them. I must confess that I found the character of the Icelanders in every respect below the estimate I had previously formed of it, and still further below the standard given in books.

In spite of their scanty food, the Icelandic horses have a marvellous power of endurance; they can often travel from thirty-five to forty miles per diem for several consecutive days. But the only difficulty is to keep the horse moving. The Iceland-ers have a habit of continually kicking their heels against the poor beast's sides; and the horse at last gets so accustomed to this mode of treatment, that it will hardly go if the stimulus be discontinued. In passing the bad pieces of road it is necessary to keep the bridle tight in hand, or the horse will stumble frequently. This and the continual urging forward of the horse render riding very fatiguing. {33}

Not a little consideration is certainly required before undertaking a journey into the far north; but nothing frightened me,--and even in the midst of the greatest dangers and hardships I did not for one moment regret my undertaking, and would not have relinquished it under any consideration.

I made excursions to every part of Iceland, and am thus enabled to place before my readers, in regular order, the chief curiosities of this remarkable country. I will commence with the immediate neighbourhood of Reikjavik.

CHAPTER IV

May 25th.

Stiftsamtmann von H--- was to-day kind enough to pay me a visit, and to in-vite me to join his party for a ride to the great lake Vatne. I gladly accepted the invitation, for, according to the description given by the Stiftsamtmann, I hoped to behold a very Eden, and rejoiced at the prospect of observing the recreations of the higher classes, and at the same time gaining many acquisitions in specimens of plants, butterflies, and beetles. I resolved also to test the capabilities of the Icelandic horses more thoroughly than I had been able to do during my first ride from Ha-venfiord to Reikjavik, as I had been obliged on that occasion to ride at a foot-pace, on account of my old guide.

The hour of starting was fixed for two o'clock. Accustomed as I am to strict punctuality, I was ready long before the appointed time, and at two o'clock was about to hasten to the place of rendezvous, when my hostess informed me I had plenty of time, for Herr von H--- was still at dinner. Instead of meeting at two o'clock, we did not assemble until three, and even then another quarter of an hour elapsed before the cavalcade started. Oh, Syrian notions of punctuality and dispatch! Here, almost at the very antipodes, did I once more greet ye.

The party consisted of the nobility and the town dignitaries. Among the former class may be reckoned Stiftsamtmann von H--- and his lady; a privy councillor, Herr von B---, who had been sent from Copenhagen to attend the "Allthing" (political assembly); and a Danish baron, who had accompanied the councillor. I noticed among the town dignitaries the daughter and wife of the apothecary, and the daughters of some merchants resident here.

Our road lay through fields of lava, swamps, and very poor grassy patches, in a great valley, swelling here and there into gentle acclivities, and shut in on three sides by several rows of mountains, towering upwards in the most diversified shapes. In the far distance rose several jokuls or glaciers, seeming to look proudly down upon the mountains, as though they asked, "Why would ye draw men's eyes upon you, where we glisten in our silver sheen?" In the season of the year at which I beheld them, the glaciers were still very beautiful; not only their summits, but their entire surface, as far as visible, being covered with snow. The fourth side of the valley through which we travelled was washed by the ocean, which melted as it were into the horizon in immeasurable distance. The coast was dotted with small bays, having the appearance of so many lakes.

As the road was good, we could generally ride forward at a brisk pace. Occasionally, however, we met with small tracts on which the Icelandic horse could exercise its sagacity and address. My horse was careful and free from vice; it carried me securely over masses of stone and chasms in the rocks, but I cannot describe the suffering its trot caused me. It is said that riding is most beneficial to those who suffer from liver-complaints. This may be the case; but I should suppose that any one who rode upon an Icelandic horse, with an Icelandic side-saddle, every day for the space of four weeks, would find, at the expiration of that time, her liver shaken to a pulp, and no part of it remaining.

All the rest of the party had good English saddles, mine alone was of Icelandic origin. It consisted of a chair, with a board for the back. The rider was obliged to sit crooked upon the horse, and it was impossible to keep a firm seat. With much difficulty I trotted after the others, for my horse would not be induced to break into a gallop.

At length, after a ride of an hour and a half, we reached a valley. In the midst of a tolerably green meadow I descried what was, for Iceland, a farm of considerable dimensions, and not far from this farm was a very small lake. I did not dare to ask if this was the *great* lake Vatne, or if this was the delicious prospect I had been promised, for my question would have been taken for irony. I could not refrain from wonder when Herr von H--- began praising the landscape as exquisite, and farther declaring the effect of the lake to be bewitching. I was obliged, for politeness' sake, to acquiesce, and leave them in the supposition that I had never seen a larger lake nor a finer prospect.

We now made a halt, and the whole party encamped in the meadow. While the preparations for a social meal were going on, I proceeded to satisfy my curiosity.

The peasant's house first attracted my attention. I found it to consist of one large chamber, and two of smaller size, besides a storeroom and extensive stables, from which I judged that the proprietor was rich in cattle. I afterwards learnt that he owned fifty sheep, eight cows, and five horses, and was looked upon as one of the richest farmers in the neighbourhood. The kitchen was situated at the extreme end of the building, and was furnished with a chimney that seemed intended only as a protection against rain and snow, for the smoke dispersed itself throughout the whole kitchen, drying the fish which hung from the ceiling, and slowly making its exit through an air-hole.

The large apartment boasted a wooden bookshelf, containing about forty volumes. Some of these I turned over, and in spite of my limited knowledge of the Danish language, could make out enough to discover that they were chiefly on religious subjects. But the farmer seemed also to love poetry; among the works of this class in his library, I noticed Kleist, Muller, and even Homer's *Odyssey*. I could make nothing of the Icelandic books; but on inquiring their contents, I was told that they all treated of religious matters.

After inspecting these, I walked out into the meadow to search for flowers and herbs. Flowers I found but few, as it was not the right time of the year for them;

my search for herbs was more successful, and I even found some wild clover. I saw neither beetles nor butterflies; but, to my no small surprise, heard the humming of two wild bees, one of which I was fortunate enough to catch, and took home to preserve in spirits of wine.

On rejoining my party, I found them encamped in the meadow around a table, which had in the meantime been spread with butter, cheese, bread, cake, roast lamb, raisins and almonds, a few oranges, and wine. Neither chairs nor benches were to be had, for even wealthy peasants only possess planks nailed to the walls of their rooms; so we all sat down upon the grass, and did ample justice to the capital coffee which made the commencement of the meal. Laughter and jokes predominated to such an extent, that I could have fancied myself among impulsive Italians instead of cold Northmen.

There was no lack of wit; but to-day I was unfortunately its butt. And what was my fault?--only my stupid modesty. The conversation was carried on in the Danish language; some members of our party spoke French and others German, but I purposely abstained from availing myself of their acquirements, in order not to disturb the hilarity of the conversation. I sat silently among them, and was perfectly contented in listening to their merriment. But my behaviour was set down as proceeding from stupidity, and I soon gathered from their discourse that they were comparing me to the "stone guest" in Mozart's **Don Giovanni**. If these kind people had only surmised the true reason of my keeping silence, they would perhaps have thanked me for doing so.

As we sat at our meal, I heard a voice in the farmhouse singing an Icelandic song. At a distance it resembled the humming of bees; on a nearer approach it sounded monotonous, drawling, and melancholy.

While we were preparing for our departure, the farmer, his wife, and the servants approached, and shook each of us by the hand. This is the usual mode of saluting such **high** people as we numbered among our party. The true national salutation is a hearty kiss.

On my arrival at home the effect of the strong coffee soon began to manifest itself. I could not sleep at all, and had thus ample leisure to make accurate observations as to the length of the day and of the twilight. Until eleven o'clock at night I could read ordinary print in my room. From eleven till one o'clock it was dusk, but never so dark as to prevent my reading in the open air. In my room, too, I could distinguish the smallest objects, and even tell the time by my watch. At one o'clock I could again read in my room.

EXCURSION TO VIDOE.

The little island of Vidoe, four miles distant from Reikjavik, is described by most travellers as the chief resort of the eider-duck. I visited the island on the 8th of June, but was disappointed in my expectations. I certainly saw many of these birds on the declivities and in the chasms of the rocks, sitting quietly on their nests, but nothing approaching the thousands I had been led to expect. On the whole, I may perhaps have seen from one hundred to a hundred and fifty nests.

The most remarkable circumstance connected with the eider-ducks is their tameness during the period of incubation. I had always regarded as myths the stories told about them in this respect, and should do so still had I not convinced myself of the truth of these assertions by laying hands upon the ducks myself. I could go quite up to them and caress them, and even then they would not often leave their nests. Some few birds, indeed, did so when I wished to touch them; but they did not fly up, but contented themselves with coolly walking a few paces away from the nest, and there sitting quietly down until I had departed. But those which already had live young, beat out boldly with their wings when I approached, struck at me with their bills, and allowed themselves to be taken up bodily rather than leave the nest. They are about the size of our ducks; their eggs are of a greenish grey, rather larger than hen's eggs, and taste very well. Altogether they lay about eleven eggs. The finest down is that with which they line their nests at first; it is of a dark grey colour. The Icelanders take away this down, and the first nest of eggs. The poor bird now robs herself once more of a quantity of down (which is, however, not of so fine a quality as the first), and again lays eggs. For the second time every thing is taken from her; and not until she has a third time lined the nest with her down is the eider-duck left in peace. The down of the second, and that of the third quality especially, are much lighter than that of the first. I also was sufficiently cruel to take a few eggs and some down out of several of the nests. {34}

I did not witness the dangerous operation of collecting this down from between the clefts of rocks and from unapproachable precipices, where people are let down, or to which they are drawn up, by ropes, at peril of their lives. There are, however, none of these break-neck places in the neighbourhood of Reikjavik.

SALMON FISHERY.

I made another excursion to a very short distance (two miles) from Reikjavik, in the company of Herr Bernhoft and his daughter, to the Laxselv (salmon river) to witness the salmon-fishing, which takes place every week from the middle of June to the middle of August. It is conducted in a very simple manner. The fish come up the river in the spawning season; the stream is then dammed up with several walls of stone loosely piled to the height of some three feet; and the retreat of the fish to the sea is thus cut off. When the day arrives on which the salmon are to be caught, a net is spread behind each of these walls. Three or four such dams are erected at intervals, of from eighty to a hundred paces, so that even if the fishes escape one barrier, they are generally caught at the next. The water is now made to run off as much as possible; the poor salmon dart to and fro, becoming every moment more and more aware of the sinking of the water, and crowd to the weirs, cutting themselves by contact with the sharp stones of which they are built. This is the deepest part of the water; and it is soon so thronged with fish, that men, stationed in readiness, can seize them in their hands and fling them ashore.

The salmon possess remarkable swiftness and strength. The fisherman is obliged to take them quickly by the head and tail, and to throw them ashore, when they are immediately caught by other men, who fling them still farther from the water. If this is not done with great quickness and care, many of the fishes escape. It is wonderful how these creatures can struggle themselves free, and leap into the air. The fishermen are obliged to wear woollen mittens, or they would be quite unable to hold the smooth salmon. At every day's fishing, from five hundred to a thousand fish are taken, each weighing from five to fifteen pounds. On the day when I was present eight hundred were killed. This salmon-stream is farmed by a merchant of Reikjavik.

The fishermen receive very liberal pay,--in fact, one-half of the fish taken. And yet they are dissatisfied, and show so little gratitude, as seldom to finish their work properly. So, for instance, they only brought the share of the merchant to the harbour of Reikjavik, and were far too lazy to carry the salmon from the boat to the warehouse, a distance certainly not more than sixty or seventy paces from the shore. They sent a message to their employer, bidding him "send some fresh hands, for they were much too tired." Of course, in a case like this, all remonstrance is unavailing.

As in the rest of the world, so also in Iceland, every occasion that offers is seized upon for a feast or a merry-making. The day on which I witnessed the salmon-fishing happened to be one of the few fine days that occur during a summer in Iceland. It was therefore unanimously concluded by several merchants, that the day and the salmon-fishing should be celebrated by a *dejeuner a la fourchette*. Every one contributed something, and a plentiful and elegant breakfast was soon arranged, which quite resembled an entertainment of the kind in our country; this one circumstance excepted, that we were obliged to seat ourselves on the ground, by reason of a scarcity of tables and benches. Spanish and French wines, as well as cold punch, were there in plenty, and the greatest hilarity prevailed.

I made a fourth excursion, but to a very inconsiderable distance,--in fact, only a mile and a half from Reikjavik. It was to see a hot and slightly sulphurous spring, which falls into a river of cold water. By this lucky meeting of extremes, water can be obtained at any temperature, from the boiling almost to the freezing point. The townspeople take advantage of this good opportunity in two ways, for bathing and for washing clothes. The latter is undoubtedly the more important purpose of application, and a hut has been erected, in order to shield the poor people from wind and rain while they are at work. Formerly this hut was furnished with a good door and with glazed windows, and the key was kept at an appointed place in the town, whence any one might fetch it. But the servants and peasant girls were soon too lazy to go for the key; they burst open the lock, and smashed the windows, so that now the hut has a very ruinous appearance, and affords but little protection against the weather. How much alike mankind are every where, and how seldom they do right, except when it gives them no trouble, and then, unfortunately, there is not much merit to be ascribed to them, as their doing right is merely the result of a lucky chance! Many people also bring fish and potatoes, which they have only to lay in the hot water, and in a short time both are completely cooked.

This spring is but little used for the purpose of bathing; at most perhaps by a few children and peasants. Its medicinal virtues, if it possesses any, are completely unknown.

THE SULPHUR-SPRINGS AND SULPHUR-MOUNTAINS OF KRISUVIK.

The 4th of June was fixed for my departure. I had only to pack up some bread and cheese, sugar and coffee, then the horses were saddled, and at seven o'clock the journey was happily commenced. I was alone with my guide, who, like the rest of his class, could not be considered as a very favourable specimen of humanity. He was very lazy, exceedingly self-interested, and singularly loath to devote any part of his attention either to me or to the horses, preferring to concentrate it upon brandy, an article which can unfortunately be procured throughout the whole country.

I had already seen the district between Reikjavik and Havenfiord at my first arrival in Iceland. At the present advanced season of the year it wore a less gloomy aspect: strawberry-plants and violets,--the former, however, without blossoms, and the latter inodorous,--were springing up between the blocks of lava, together with beautiful ferns eight or ten inches high. In spite of the trifling distance, I noticed, as a rule, that vegetation was here more luxuriant than at Reikjavik; for at the latter place I had found no strawberry-plants, and the violets were not yet in blossom. This difference in the vegetation is, I think, to be ascribed to the high walls of lava existing in great abundance round Havenfiord; they protect the tender plants and ferns from the piercing winds. I noticed that both the grass and the plants before mentioned throve capitally in the little hollows formed by masses of lava.

A couple of miles beyond Havenfiord I saw the first birch-trees, which, however, did not exceed two or three feet in height, also some bilberry-plants. A number of little butterflies, all of one colour, and, as it seemed to me, of the same species, fluttered among the shrubs and plants.

The manifold forms and varied outline of the lava-fields present a remarkable and really a marvellous appearance. Short as this journey is--for ten hours are amply sufficient for the trip to Krisuvik,--it presents innumerable features for contemplation. I could only gaze and wonder. I forgot every thing around me, felt neither cold nor storm, and let my horse pick his way as slowly as he chose, so that I had once almost become separated from my guide.

One of the most considerable of the streams of lava lay in a spacious broad valley. The lava-stream itself, about two miles long, and of a considerable breadth, traversing the whole of the plain, seemed to have been called into existence by magic, as there was no mountain to be seen in the neighbourhood from which it could have emerged. It appeared to be the covering of an immense crater, formed, not of separate stones and blocks, but of a single and slightly porous mass of rock ten or twelve feet thick, broken here and there by clefts about a foot in breadth.

Another, and a still larger valley, many miles in circumference, was filled with masses of lava shaped like waves, reminding the beholder of a petrified sea. From the midst rose a high black mountain, contrasting beautifully with the surrounding masses of light-grey lava. At first I supposed the lava must have streamed forth from this mountain, but soon found that the latter was perfectly smooth on all sides, and terminated in a sharp peak. The remaining mountains which shut in the valley were also perfectly closed, and I looked in vain for any trace of a crater.

We now reached a small lake, and soon afterwards arrived at a larger one, called Kleinfarvatne. Both were hemmed in by mountains, which frequently rose abruptly from the waters, leaving no room for the passage of the horses. We were obliged sometimes to climb the mountains by fearfully dizzy paths; at others to scramble downwards, almost clinging to the face of the rock. At some points we were even compelled to dismount from our horses, and scramble forward on our hands and knees. In a word, these dangerous points, which extended over a space of about seven miles, were certainly quite as bad as any I had encountered in Syria; if any thing, they were even more formidable.

I was, however, assured that I should have no more such places to encounter during all my further journeys in Iceland, and this information quite reconciled me to the roads in this country. For the rest, the path was generally tolerably safe even during this tour, which continually led me across fields of lava.

A journey of some eight-and-twenty miles brought us at length into a friendly valley; clouds of smoke, both small and great, were soon discovered rising from the surrounding heights, and also from the valley itself; these were the sulphur-springs and sulphur-mountains.

I could hardly restrain my impatience while we traversed the couple of miles which separated us from Krisuvik. A few small lakes were still to be crossed; and at length, at six o'clock in the evening, we reached our destination.

With the exception of a morsel of bread and cheese, I had eaten nothing since the morning; still I could not spare time to make coffee, but at once dismounted, summoned my guide, and commenced my pilgrimage to the smoking mountains. At the outset our way lay across swampy places and meadow lands; but soon we had to climb the mountains themselves, a task rendered extremely difficult by the elastic, yielding soil, in which every footstep imprinted itself deeply, suggesting to the traveller the unpleasant possibility of his sinking through,--a contingency rendered any thing but agreeable by the neighbourhood of the boiling springs. At length I gained the summit, and saw around me numerous basins filled with boiling water, while on all sides, from hill and valley, columns of vapour rose out of numberless clefts in the rocks. From a cleft in one rock in particular a mighty column of vapour whirled into the air. On the windward side I could approach this place very closely. The ground was only lukewarm in some places, and I could hold my hand for several moments to the gaps from which steam issued. No trace of a crater was to be seen. The bubbling and hissing of the steam, added to the noise of the wind, occasioned such a deafening clamour, that I was very glad to feel firmer ground beneath my feet, and to leave the place in haste. It really seemed as if the interior of the mountain had been a boiling caldron. The prospect from these mountains is very fine. Numerous valleys and mountains innumerable offered themselves to my view, and I could even discern the isolated black rock past which I had ridden five or six hours previously.

I now commenced my descent into the valley; at a few hundred paces the bubbling and hissing were already inaudible. I supposed that I had seen every thing worthy of notice; but much that was remarkable still remained. I particularly noticed a basin some five or six feet in diameter, filled with boiling mud. This mud has quite the appearance of fine clay dissolved in water; its colour was a light grey.

From another basin, hardly two feet in diameter, a mighty column of steam shot continually into the air with so much force and noise that I started back half stunned, and could have fancied the vault of heaven would burst. This basin is situated in a corner of the valley, closely shut in on three sides by hills. In the neighbourhood many hot springs gushed forth; but I saw no columns of water, and my guide assured me that such a phenomenon was never witnessed here.

There is more danger in passing these spots than even in traversing the mountains. In spite of the greatest precautions, I frequently sank in above the ankles, and would then draw back with a start, and find my foot covered with hot mud. From the place where I had broken through, steam and hot mud, or boiling water, rose into the air.

Though my guide, who walked before me, carefully probed the ground with his stick, he several times sank through half-way to the knee. These men are, however, so much accustomed to contingencies of this kind that they take little account of them. My guide would quietly repair to the next spring and cleanse his clothes from mud. As I was covered with it to above the ankles, I thought it best to follow his example.

For excursions like these it is best to come provided with a few boards, five or six feet in length, with which to cover the most dangerous places.

At nine o'clock in the evening, but yet in the full glare of the sun, we arrived at Krisuvik. I now took time to look at this place, which I found to consist of a small church and a few miserable huts.

I crept into one of these dens; it was so dark that a considerable time elapsed before I could distinguish objects, the light was only admitted through a very small aperture. I found in this hut a few persons who were suffering from the eruption called "lepra," a disease but too commonly met with in Iceland. Their hands and faces were completely covered with this eruption; if it spreads over the whole body the patient languishes slowly away, and is lost without remedy.

Churches are in this country not only used for purposes of public worship, but also serve as magazines for provisions, clothes, &c., and as inns for travellers. I do not suppose that a parallel instance of desecration could be met with even among the most uncivilised nations. I was assured, indeed, that these abuses were about to be remedied. A reform of this kind ought to have been carried out long ago; and even now the matter seems to remain an open point; for wherever I came the church was placed at my disposal for the night, and every where I found a store of fish, tallow, and other equally odoriferous substances.

The little chapel at Krisuvik is only twenty-two feet long by ten broad; on my arrival it was hastily prepared for my reception. Saddles, ropes, clothes, hats, and other articles which lay scattered about, were hastily flung into a corner; mattresses and some nice soft pillows soon appeared, and a very tolerable bed was prepared for me on a large chest in which the vestments of the priest, the coverings of the altar, &c., were deposited. I would willingly have locked myself in, eaten my frugal supper, and afterwards written a few pages of my diary before retiring to rest; but this was out of the question. The entire population of the village turned out to see me, old and young hastened to the church, and stood round in a circle and gazed at me.

Irksome as this curiosity was, I was obliged to endure it patiently, for I could not have sent these good people away without seriously offending them; so I began quietly to unpack my little portmanteau, and proceeded to boil my coffee over a spirit-lamp. A whispering consultation immediately began; they seemed particularly struck by my mode of preparing coffee, and followed every one of my movements with eager eyes. My frugal meal dispatched, I resolved to try the patience of my audience, and, taking out my journal, began to write. For a few minutes they remained quiet, then they began to whisper one to another, "She writes, she writes," and this was repeated numberless times. There was no sign of any disposition to depart; I believe I could have sat there till doomsday, and failed to tire my audience out. At length, after this scene had lasted a full hour, I could stand it no longer, and was fain to request my amiable visitors to retire, as I wished to go to bed.

My sleep that night was none of the sweetest. A certain feeling of discomfort always attaches to the fact of sleeping in a church alone, in the midst of a graveyard. Besides this, on the night in question such a dreadful storm arose that the wooden walls creaked and groaned as though their foundations were giving way. The cold was also rather severe, my thermometer inside the church shewing only two degrees above zero. I was truly thankful when approaching day brought with it the welcome hour of departure.

June 5th.

The heavy sleepiness and extreme indolence of an Icelandic guide render departure before seven o'clock in the morning a thing not to be thought of. This is, however, of little consequence, as there is no night in Iceland at this time of year.

Although the distance was materially increased by returning to Reikjavik by way of Grundivik and Keblevik, I chose this route in order to pass through the wildest of the inhabited tracts in Iceland.

The first stage, from Krisuvik to Grundivik, a distance of twelve to fourteen miles, lay through fields of lava, consisting mostly of small blocks of stone and fragments, filling the valley so completely that not a single green spot remained. I here met with masses of lava which presented an appearance of singular beauty. They were black mounds, ten or twelve feet in height, piled upon each other in the most varied forms, their bases covered with a broad band of whitish-coloured moss, while the tops were broken into peaks and cones of the most fantastic shapes. These lava-streams seem to date from a recent period, as the masses are somewhat scaly and glazed.

Grundivik, a little village of a few wretched cottages, lies like an oasis in this desert of lava.

My guide wished to remain here, asserting that there was no place between this and Keblevik where I could pass the night, and that it would be impossible for our horses, exhausted as they were with yesterday's march, to carry us to Keblevik that night. The true reason of this suggestion was that he wished to prolong the journey for another day.

Luckily I had a good map with me, and by dint of consulting it could calculate distances with tolerable accuracy; it was also my custom before starting on a journey to make particular inquiries as to how I should arrange the daily stages.

So I insisted upon proceeding at once; and soon we were wending our way through fields of lava towards Stad, a small village six or seven miles distant from Grundivik.

On the way I noticed a mountain of most singular appearance. In colour it closely resembled iron; its sides were perfectly smooth and shining, and streaks of the colour of yellow ochre traversed it here and there.

Stad is the residence of a priest. Contrary to the assertions of my guide, I found this place far more cheerful and habitable than Grundivik. Whilst our horses were resting, the priest paid me a visit, and conducted me, not, as I anticipated, into his house, but into the church. Chairs and stools were quickly brought there, and my host introduced his wife and children to me, after which we partook of coffee, bread and cheese, &c. On the rail surrounding the altar hung the clothes of the priest and his family, differing little in texture and make from those of the peasants.

The priest appeared to be a very intelligent, well-read man. I could speak the Danish language pretty fluently, and was therefore able to converse with him on various subjects. On hearing that I had already been in Palestine, he put a number of questions to me, from which I could plainly see that he was alike well acquainted with geography, history, natural science, &c. He accompanied me several miles on my road, and we chatted away the time very pleasantly.

The distance between Krisuvik and Keblevik is about forty-two miles. The road lies through a most dreary landscape, among vast desert plains, frequently twenty-five to thirty miles in circumference, entirely divested of all traces of vegetation, and covered throughout their extreme area by masses of lava--gloomy monuments of volcanic agency. And yet here, at the very heart of the subterranean fire, I saw only a single mountain, the summit of which had fallen in, and presented the appearance of a crater. The rest were all completely closed, terminating sometimes in a beautiful round top, and sometimes in sharp peaks; in other instances they formed long narrow chains.

Who can tell whence these all-destroying masses of lava have poured forth, or how many hundred years they have lain in these petrified valleys?

Keblevik lies on the sea-coast; but the harbour is insecure, so that ships remain here at anchor only so long as is absolutely necessary; there are frequently only two or three ships in the harbour.

A few wooden houses, two of which belong to Herr Knudson, and some peasants' cottages, are the only buildings in this little village. I was hospitably received, and rested from the toils of the day at the house of Herr Siverson, Herr Knudson's manager.

On the following day (June 6th) I had a long ride to Reikjavik, thirty-six good miles, mostly through fields of lava.

The whole tract of country from Grundivik almost to Havenfiord is called "The lava-fields of Reikianes."

Tired and almost benumbed with cold, I arrived in the evening at Reikjavik, with no other wish than to retire to rest as fast as possible.

In these three days I had ridden 114 miles, besides enduring much from cold, storms, and rain. To my great surprise, the roads had generally been good; there were, however, many places highly dangerous and difficult.

But what mattered these fatigues, forgotten, as they were, after a single night's rest? what were they in comparison to the unutterably beautiful and marvellous phenomena of the north, which will remain ever present to my imagination so long as memory shall be spared me?

The distances of this excursion were: From Reikjavik to Krisuvik, 37 miles; from Krisuvik to Keblevik, 39 miles; from Keblevik to Reikjavik, 38 miles: total,

114 miles.

CHAPTER V

As the weather continued fine, I wished to lose no time in continuing my wanderings. I had next to make a tour of some 560 miles; it was therefore necessary that I should take an extra horse, partly that it might carry my few packages, consisting of a pillow, some rye-bread, cheese, coffee, and sugar, but chiefly that I might be enabled to change horses every day, as one horse would not have been equal to the fatigue of so long a journey.

My former guide could not accompany me on my present journey, as he was unacquainted with most of the roads. My kind protectors, Herr Knudson and Herr Bernhoft, were obliging enough to provide another guide for me; a difficult task, as it is a rare occurrence to find an Icelander who understands the Danish language, and who happens to be sober when his services are required. At length a peasant was found who suited our purpose; but he considered two florins per diem too little pay, so I was obliged to give an additional zwanziger. On the other hand, it was arranged that the guide should also take two horses, in order that he might change every day.

The 16th of June was fixed for the commencement of our journey. From the very first day my guide did not shew himself in an amiable point of view. On the morning of our departure his saddle had to be patched together, and instead of coming with two horses, he appeared with only one. He certainly promised to buy a second when we should have proceeded some miles, adding that it would be cheaper to buy one at a little distance from the "capital." I at once suspected this was merely an excuse of the guide's, and that he wished thereby to avoid having the care of four horses. The event proved I was right; not a single horse could be found that suited, and so my poor little animal had to carry the guide's baggage in addition to my own.

Loading the pack-horses is a business of some difficulty, and is conducted in the following manner: sundry large pieces of dried turf are laid upon the horse's back, but not fastened; over these is buckled a round piece of wood, furnished with two or three pegs. To these pegs the chests and packages are suspended. If the weight is not quite equally balanced, it is necessary to stop and repack frequently, for the whole load at once gets askew.

The trunks used in this country are massively constructed of wood, covered with a rough hide, and strengthened on all sides with nails, as though they were intended to last an eternity. The poor horses have a considerable weight to bear in empty boxes alone, so that very little real luggage can be taken. The weight which a horse has to carry during a long journey should never exceed 150lbs.

It is impossible to remember how many times our baggage had to be repacked during a day's journey. The great pieces of turf would never stay in their places, and every moment something was wrong. Nothing less than a miracle, however, can prevail on an Icelander to depart from his regular routine. His ancestors packed in such and such a manner, and so he must pack also. {35}

We had a journey of above forty miles before us the first day, and yet, on account of the damaged saddle, we could not start before eight o'clock in the morning.

The first twelve or fourteen miles of our journey lay through the great valley in which Reikjavik is situated; the valley contains many low hills, some of which we had to climb. Several rivers, chief among which was the Laxselv, opposed our progress, but at this season of the year they could be crossed on horseback without danger. Nearly all the valleys through which we passed to-day were covered with lava, but nevertheless offered many beautiful spots.

Many of the hills we passed seemed to me to be extinct volcanoes; the whole upper portion was covered with colossal slabs of lava, as though the crater had been choked up with them. Lava of the same description and colour, but in smaller pieces, lay strewed around.

For the first twelve or fourteen miles the sea is visible from the brow of every successive hill. The country is also pretty generally inhabited; but afterwards a distance of nearly thirty miles is passed, on which there is not a human habitation. The traveller journeys from one valley into another, and in the midst of these hill-girt deserts sees a single small hut, erected for the convenience of those who, in the winter, cannot accomplish the long distance in one day, and must take up their quarters for the night in the valley. No one must, however, rashly hope to find here a human being in the shape of a host. The little house is quite uninhabited, and consists only of a single apartment with four naked walls. The visitor must depend on the accommodation he carries with him.

The plains through which we travelled to-day were covered throughout with one and the same kind of lava. It occurs in masses, and also in smaller stones, is not very porous, of a light grey colour, and mixed, in many instances, with sand or earth.

Some miles from Thingvalla we entered a valley, the soil of which is fine, but nevertheless only sparingly covered with grass, and full of little acclivities, mostly clothed with delicate moss. I have no doubt that the indolence of the inhabitants alone prevents them from materially improving many a piece of ground. The worst soil is that in the neighbourhood of Reikjavik; yet there we see many a garden, and many a piece of meadow-land, wrung, as it were, from the barren earth by labour and pains. Why should not the same thing be done here--the more so as nature has already accomplished the preliminary work?

Thingvalla, our resting-place for to-night, is situate on a lake of the same name, and only becomes visible when the traveller is close upon it. The lake is rather considerable, being almost three miles in length, and at some parts certainly more than two miles in breadth; it contains two small islands,--Sandey and Nesey.

My whole attention was still riveted by the lake and its naked and gloomy circle of mountains, when suddenly, as if by magic, I found myself standing on the brink of a chasm, into which I could scarcely look without a shudder; involuntarily I thought of Weber's *Freyschutz* and the "Wolf's Hollow." {36}

The scene is the more startling from the circumstance that the traveller approaching Thingvalla in a certain direction sees only the plains beyond this chasm, and has no idea of its existence. It was a fissure some five or six fathoms broad, but several hundred feet in depth; and we were forced to descend by a small, steep, dangerous path, across large fragments of lava. Colossal blocks of stone, threatening the unhappy wanderer with death and destruction, hang loosely, in the form of pyramids and of broken columns, from the lofty walls of lava, which encircle the whole long ravine in the form of a gallery. Speechless, and in anxious suspense, we descend a part of this chasm, hardly daring to look up, much less to give utterance to a single sound, lest the vibration should bring down one of these avalanches of stone, to the terrific force of which the rocky fragments scattered around bear ample testimony. The distinctness with which echo repeats the softest sound and the lightest footfall is truly wonderful.

The appearance presented by the horses, which are allowed to come down the ravine after their masters have descended, is most peculiar. One could fancy they were clinging to the walls of rock.

This ravine is known by the name of Almanagiau. Its entire length is about a mile, but a small portion only can be traversed; the rest is blocked up by masses of lava heaped one upon the other. On the right hand, the rocky wall opens, and forms an outlet, over formidable masses of lava, into the beautiful valley of Thingvalla. I could have fancied I wandered through the depths of a crater, which had piled around itself these stupendous barriers during a mighty eruption in times long gone by.

The valley of Thingvalla is considered one of the most beautiful in Iceland. It contains many meadows, forming, as it were, a place of refuge for the inhabitants, and enabling them to keep many head of cattle. The Icelanders consider this little green valley the finest spot in the world. Not far from the opening of the ravine, on the farther bank of the river Oxer, lies the little village of Thingvalla, consisting of three or four cottages and a small chapel. A few scattered farms and cottages are situated in the neighbourhood.

Thingvalla was once one of the most important places in Iceland; the stranger is still shewn the meadow, not far from the village, on which the Allthing (general assembly) was held annually in the open air. Here the people and their leaders met, pitching their tents after the manner of nomads. Here it was also that many an opinion and many a decree were enforced by the weight of steel.

The chiefs appeared, ostensibly for peace, at the head of their tribe; yet many of them returned not again, but beneath the sword-stroke of their enemies obtained that peace which no man seeketh, but which all men find.

On one side the valley is skirted by the lake, on the other it is bounded by lofty mountains, some of them still partly covered with snow. Not far from the entrance of the ravine, the river Oxer rushes over a wall of rock of considerable height, forming a beautiful waterfall.

It was still fine clear daylight when I reached Thingvalla, and the sky rose pure and cloudless over the far distance. It seemed therefore the more singular to me to see a few clouds skimming over the surface of the mountains, now shrouding a part of them in vapour, now wreathing themselves round their summits, now vanishing entirely, to reappear again at a different point.

This is a phenomenon frequently observed in Iceland during the finest days, and one I had often noticed in the neighbourhood of Reikjavik. Under a clear and cloudless sky, a light mist would appear on the brow of a mountain,--in a moment it would increase to a large cloud, and after remaining stationary for a time, it frequently vanished suddenly, or soared slowly away. However often it may be repeated, this appearance cannot fail to interest the observer.

Herr Beck, the clergyman at Thingvalla, offered me the shelter of his hut for the night; as the building, however, did not look much more promising than the peasants' cottages by which it was surrounded, I preferred quartering myself in the church, permission to do so being but too easily obtained on all occasions. This chapel is not much larger than that at Krisuvik, and stands at some distance from the few surrounding cottages. This was perhaps the reason why I was not incommoded by visitors. I had already conquered any superstitious fears derived from the proximity of my silent neighbours in the churchyard, and passed the night quietly on one of the wooden chests of which I found several scattered about. Habit is certainly every thing; after a few nights of gloomy solitude one thinks no more about the matter.

June 17th.

Our journey of to-day was more formidable than that of yesterday. I was assured that Reikholt (also called Reikiadal) was almost fifty miles distant. Distances cannot always be accurately measured by the map; impassable barriers, only to be avoided by circuitous routes, often oppose the traveller's progress. This was the case with us to-day. To judge from the map, the distance from Thingvalla to Reikholt seemed less by a great deal than that from Reikjavik to Thingvalla, and yet we were full fourteen hours accomplishing it--two hours longer than on our yesterday's journey.

So long as our way lay through the valley of Thingvalla there was no lack of variety. At one time there was an arm of the river Oxer to cross, at another we traversed a cheerful meadow; sometimes we even passed through little shrubberies,-

-that is to say, according to the Icelandic acceptation of the term. In my country these lovely shrubberies would have been cleared away as useless underwood. The trees trail along the ground, seldom attaining a height of more than two feet. When one of these puny stems reaches four feet in height, it is considered a gigantic tree. The greater portion of these miniature forests grow on the lava with which the valley is covered.

The formation of the lava here assumes a new character. Up to this point it has mostly appeared either in large masses or in streams lying in strata one above the other; but here the lava covered the greater portion of the ground in the form of immense flat slabs or blocks of rock, often split in a vertical direction. I saw long fissures of eight or ten feet in breadth, and from ten to fifteen feet in depth. In these clefts the flowers blossom earlier, and the fern grows taller and more luxuriantly, than in the boisterous upper world.

After the valley of Thingvalla has been passed the journey becomes very monotonous. The district beyond is wholly uninhabited, and we travelled many miles without seeing a single cottage. From one desert valley we passed into another; all were alike covered with light-grey or yellowish lava, and at intervals also with fine sand, in which the horses sunk deeply at every step. The mountains surrounding these valleys were none of the highest, and it was seldom that a jokul or glacier shone forth from among them. The mountains had a certain polished appearance, their sides being perfectly smooth and shining. In some instances, however, masses of lava formed beautiful groups, bearing a great resemblance to ruins of ancient buildings, and standing out in peculiarly fine relief from the smooth walls.

These mountains are of different colours; they are black or brown, grey or yellow, &c.; and the different shades of these colours are displayed with marvellous effect in the brilliant sunshine.

Nine hours of uninterrupted riding brought us into a large tract of moorland, very scantily covered with moss. Yet this was the first and only grazing-place to be met with in all the long distance from Thingvalla. We therefore made a halt of two hours, to let our poor horses pick a scanty meal. Large swarms of minute gnats, which seemed to fly into our eyes, nose, and mouth, annoyed us dreadfully during our stay in this place.

On this moor there was also a small lake; and here I saw for the first time a small flock of swans. Unfortunately these creatures are so very timid, that the most cautious approach of a human being causes them to rise with the speed of lightning into the air. I was therefore obliged perforce to be content with a distant view of these proud birds. They always keep in pairs, and the largest flock I saw did not consist of more than four such pairs.

Since my first arrival in Iceland I had considered the inhabitants an indolent race of people; to-day I was strengthened in my opinion by the following slight circumstance. The moorland on which we halted to rest was separated from the adjoining fields of lava by a narrow ditch filled with water. Across this ditch a few stones and slabs had been laid, to form a kind of bridge. Now this bridge was so full of holes that the horses could not tell where to plant their feet, and refused obstinately to cross it, so that in the end we were obliged to dismount and lead them across. We had scarcely passed this place, and sat down to rest, when a caravan of fifteen horses, laden with planks, dried fish, &c. arrived at the bridge. Of course the poor creatures observed the dangerous ground, and could only be driven by hard blows to advance. Hardly twenty paces off there were stones in abundance; but rather than devote a few minutes to filling up the holes, these lazy people beat their horses cruelly, and exposed them to the risk of breaking their legs. I pitied the poor animals, which would be compelled to recross the bridge, so heartily, that, after they are gone, I devoted a part of my resting-time to collecting stones and filling up the holes,--a business which scarcely occupied me a quarter of an hour.

It is interesting to notice how the horses know by instinct the dangerous spots in the stony wastes, and in the moors and swamps. On approaching these places they bend their heads towards the earth, and look sharply round on all sides. If they cannot discover a firm resting-place for the feet, they stop at once, and cannot be urged forward without many blows.

After a halt of two hours we continued our journey, which again led us across fields of lava. At past nine o'clock in the evening we reached an elevated plain, after traversing which for half an hour we saw stretched at our feet the valley of Reikholt or Reikiadal; it is fourteen to seventeen miles long, of a good breadth, and girt round by a row of mountains, among which several jokuls sparkle in their icy garments.

A sunset seen in the sublime wildness of Icelandic scenery has a peculiarly beautiful effect. Over these vast plains, divested of trees or shrubs, covered with dark lava, and shut in by mountains almost of a sable hue, the parting sun sheds an almost magical radiance. The peaks of the mountains shine in the bright parting rays, the jokuls are shrouded in the most delicate roseate hue, while the lower parts of the mountains lie in deep shadow, and frown darkly on the valleys, which resemble a sheet of dark blue water, with an atmosphere of a bluish-red colour floating above it. The most impressive feature of all is the profound silence and solitude; not a sound can be heard, not a living creature is to be seen; every thing appears dead. Throughout the broad valleys not a town nor a village, no, not even a solitary house or a tree or shrub, varies the prospect. The eye wanders over the vast desert, and finds not one familiar object on which it can rest.

To-night, as at past eleven o'clock we reached the elevated plain, I saw a sunset which I shall never forget. The sun disappeared behind the mountains, and in its stead a gorgeous ruddy gleam lighted up hill and valley and glacier. It was long ere I could turn away my eyes from the glittering heights, and yet the valley also offered much that was striking and beautiful.

Throughout almost its entire length this valley formed a meadow, from the extremities of which columns of smoke and boiling springs burst forth. The mists had almost evaporated, and the atmosphere was bright and clear, more transparent even than I had seen it in any other country. I now for the first time noticed, that in the valley itself the radiance was almost as clear as the light of day, so that the most minute objects could be plainly distinguished. This was, however, extremely necessary, for steep and dangerous paths lead over masses of lava into the valley. On one side ran a little river, forming many picturesque waterfalls, some of them above thirty feet in height.

I strained my eyes in vain to discover any where, in this great valley, a little church, which, if it only offered me a hard bench for a couch, would at any rate afford me a shelter from the sharp night-wind; for it is really no joke to ride for fifteen hours, with nothing to eat but bread and cheese, and then not even to have the pleasant prospect of a hotel *a la villa de Londres* or *de Paris*. Alas, my wishes were far more modest. I expected no porter at the gate to give the signal of my arrival, no waiter, and no chambermaid; I only desired a little spot in the neighbourhood of the dear departed Icelanders. I was suddenly recalled from these happy delusions by the voice of the guide, who cried out: "Here we are at our destination for to-night." I looked joyfully round; alas! I could only see a few of those cottages which are never observed until you almost hit your nose against one of them, as the grass-covered walls can hardly be distinguished from the surrounding meadow.

It was already midnight. We stopped, and turned our horses loose, to seek supper and rest in the nearest meadow. Our lot was a less fortunate one. The inhabitants were already buried in deep slumbers, from which even the barking set up by the dogs at our approach failed to arouse them. A cup of coffee would certainly have been very acceptable to me; yet I was loath to rouse any one merely for this. A piece of bread satisfied my hunger, and a draught of water from the nearest spring tasted most deliciously with it. After concluding my frugal meal, I sought out a corner beside a cottage, where I was partially sheltered from the too-familiar wind; and wrapping my cloak around me, lay down on the ground, having wished myself, with all my heart, a good night's rest and pleasant dreams, in the broad daylight, {37} under the canopy of heaven. Just dropping off to sleep, I was surprised by a mild rain, which, of course, at once put to flight every idea of repose. Thus, after all, I was obliged to wake some one up, to obtain the shelter of a roof.

The best room, *i.e.* the store-room, was thrown open for my accommodation, and a small wooden bedstead placed at my disposal. Chambers of this kind are luckily found wherever two or three cottages lie contiguous to each other; they are certainly far from inviting, as dried fish, train-oil, tallow, and many other articles of the same description combine to produce a most unsavoury atmosphere. Yet they are infinitely preferable to the dwellings of the peasants, which, by the by, are the most filthy dens that can be imagined. Besides being redolent of every description of bad odour, these cottages are infested with vermin to a degree which can certainly not be surpassed, except in the dwellings of the Greenlanders and Laplanders.

June 18th.

Yesterday we had been forced to put upon our poor horses a wearisome distance of more than fifty miles, as the last forty miles led us through desert and uninhabited places, boasting not even a single cottage. To-day, however, our steeds had a light duty to perform, for we only proceeded seven miles to the little village of Reikiadal, where I halted to-day, in order to visit the celebrated springs.

The inconsiderable village called Reikiadal, consisting only of a church and a few cottages, is situated amidst pleasant meadows. Altogether this valley is rich in beautiful meadow-lands; consequently one sees many scattered homesteads and cottages, with fine herds of sheep, and a tolerable number of horses; cows are less plentiful.

The church at Reikiadal is among the neatest and most roomy of those which came under my observation. The dwelling of the priest too, though only a turf-covered cottage, is large enough for the comfort of the occupants. This parish extends over a considerable area, and is not thinly inhabited.

My first care on my arrival was to beg the clergyman, Herr Jonas Jonason, to procure for me, as expeditiously as possible, fresh horses and a guide, in order that I might visit the springs. He promised to provide me with both within half an hour; and yet it was not until three hours had been wasted, that, with infinite pains, I saw my wish fulfilled. Throughout my stay in Iceland, nothing annoyed me more than the slowness and unconcern displayed by the inhabitants in all their undertakings. Every wish and every request occupies a long time in its fulfilment. Had I not been continually at the good pastor's side, I believe I should scarcely have attained my object. At length every thing was ready, and the pastor himself was kind enough to be my guide.

We rode about four miles through this beautiful vale, and in this short distance were compelled at least six times to cross the river Sidumule, which rolls its most tortuous course through the entire valley. At length the first spring was reached; it emerges from a rock about six feet in height, standing in the midst of a moor. The upper cavity of the natural reservoir, in which the water continually boils and seethes, is between two and three feet in diameter. This spring never stops; the jet of water rises two, and sometimes even four feet high, and is about eighteen inches thick. It is possible to increase the volume of the jet for a few seconds, by throwing large stones or lumps of earth into the opening, and thus stirring up the spring. The stones are cast forcibly forth, and the lumps of earth, dissolved by the action of the water, impart to the latter a dingy colour.

Whoever has seen the jet of water at Carlsbad, in Bohemia, can well imagine the appearance of this spring, which closely resembles that of Carlsbad. {38}

In the immediate neighbourhood of the spring is an abyss, in which water is continually seething, but never rises into the air. At a little distance, on a high rock, rising out of the river Sidumule, not far from the shore, are other springs. They are three in number, each at a short distance from the next, and occupy nearly the entire upper surface of the rock. Lower down we find a reservoir of boiling water; and at the foot of the rock, and on the nearest shore, are many more hot springs; but most of these are inconsiderable. Many of these hot springs emerge almost from the cold river itself.

The chief group, however, lies still farther off, on a rock which may be about twenty feet in height, and fifty in length. It is called Tunga Huer, and rises from the midst of a moor. On this rock there are no less than sixteen springs, some emerging from its base, others rather above the middle, but none from the top of the rock.

The construction of the basins and the height and diameter of the jets were precisely similar to those I have already described. All these sixteen springs are so near each other that they do not even occupy two sides of the rock. It is impossible to form an idea of the magnificence of this singular spectacle, which becomes really fairy-like, if the beholder have the courage to climb the rock itself, a proceeding of some danger, though of little difficulty. The upper stratum of the rock is soft and warm, presenting almost the appearance of mud thickened with sand and small stones. Every footstep leaves a trace behind it, and the visitor has continually before his eyes the fear of breaking through, and falling into a hot spring hidden from view by a thin covering. The good pastor walked in advance of me, with a stick, and probed the dangerous surface as much as possible. I was loath to stay behind, and suddenly we found ourselves at the summit of the rock. Here we could take in, at one view, the sixteen springs gushing from both its sides. If the view from below had been most interesting and singular, how shall I describe its appearance as seen from above? Sixteen jets of water seen at one glance, sixteen reservoirs, in all their diversity of form and construction, opening at once beneath the feet of the beholder, seemed almost too wonderful a sight. Forgetting all pusillanimous feelings, I stood and honoured the Creator in these his marvellous works. For a long time I stood, and could not tire of gazing into the abysses from whose darkness the masses of white and foaming water sprung hissing into the air, to fall again, and hasten in quiet union towards the neighbouring river. The good pastor found it necessary to remind me several times that our position here was neither of the safest nor of the most comfortable, and that it was therefore high time to abandon it. I had ceased to think of the insecurity of the ground we trod, and scarcely noticed the mighty clouds of hot vapour which frequently surrounded and threatened to suffocate us, obliging us to step suddenly back with wetted faces. It was fortunate that these waters contain but a very small quantity of brimstone, otherwise we could scarcely have long maintained our elevated position.

The rock from which these springs rise is formed of a reddish mass, and the bed of the river into which the water flows is also completely covered with little stones of the same colour.

On our way back we noticed, near a cottage, another remarkable phenomenon. It was a basin, in whose depths the water boils and bubbles violently; and near this basin are two unsightly holes, from which columns of smoke periodically rise with a great noise. Whilst this is going on, the basin fills itself more and more with water, but never so much as to overflow, or to force a jet of water into the air; then the steam and the noise cease in both cavities, and the water in the reservoir sinks several feet.

This strange phenomenon generally lasts about a minute, and is repeated so regularly, that a bet could almost be made, that the rising and falling of the water, and the increased and lessened noise of the steam, shall be seen and heard sixty or sixty-five times within an hour.

In communication with this basin is another, situate at a distance of about a hundred paces in a small hollow, and filled like the former with boiling water. As the water in the upper basin gradually sinks, and ceases to seethe, it begins to rise in the lower one, and is at length forced two or three feet into the air; then it falls again, and thus the phenomenon is continually repeated in the upper and the lower basin alternately.

At the upper spring there is also a vapour-bath. This is formed by a small chamber situate hard by the basin, built of stones and roofed with turf. It is further provided with a small and narrow entrance, which cannot be passed in an upright position. The floor is composed of stone slabs, probably covering a hot spring, for they are very warm. The person wishing to use this bath betakes himself to this room, and carefully closes every cranny; a suffocating heat, which induces violent perspiration over the whole frame, is thus generated. The people, however, seldom avail themselves of this bath.

On my return I had still to visit a basin with a jet of water, in a fine meadow near the church; a low wall of stone has been erected round this spring to prevent the cattle from scalding themselves if they should approach too near in the ardour of grazing. Some eighty paces off is to be seen the wool-bath erected by Snorri Sturluson. It consists of a stone basin three or four feet in depth, and eighteen or twenty in diameter. The approach is by a few steps leading to a low stone bench, which runs round the basin. The water is obtained from the neighbouring spring, but is of so high a temperature that it is impossible to bathe without previously cooling it. The bath stands in the open air, and no traces are left of the building which once covered it. It is now used for clothes and sheep's wool.

I had now seen all the interesting springs on this side of the valley. Some columns of vapour, which may be observed from the opposite end of the valley, proceed from thermal springs, that offer no remarkable feature save their heat.

On our return the priest took me to the churchyard, which lay at some distance from his dwelling, and showed me the principal graves. Though I thought the sight very impressive, it was not calculated to invigorate me, when I considered that I must pass the approaching night alone in the church, amidst these resting-places of the departed.

The mound above each grave is very high, and the greater part of them are surmounted by a kind of wooden coffin, which at first sight conveys the impression that the dead person is above ground. I could not shake off a feeling of discomfort; and such is the power of prejudice, that--I acknowledge my weakness--I was even induced to beg that the priest would remove one of the covers. Though I knew full well that the dead man was slumbering deep in the earth, and not in this coffin, I felt a shudder pass over me as the lid was removed, and I saw--as the priest had assured me I should do--merely a tombstone with the usual inscription, which this coffin-like covering is intended to protect against the rude storms of the winter.

Close beside the entrance to the church is the mound beneath which rest the bones of Snorri Sturluson, the celebrated poet; {39} over this grave stands a small runic stone of the length of the mound itself. This stone is said to have once been completely covered with runic characters; but all trace of these has been swept away by the storms of five hundred winters, against which the tomb had no protecting coffin. The stone, too, is split throughout its entire length into two pieces. The mound above the grave is often renewed, so that the beholder could often fancy he saw a new-made grave. I picked all the buttercups I could find growing on the grave, and preserved them carefully in a book. Perhaps I may be able to give pleasure to several of my countrywomen by offering them a floweret from the grave of the greatest of Icelandic poets.

June 19th.

In order to pursue my journey without interruption, I hired fresh horses, and allowed my own, which were rather fatigued, to accompany us unloaded. My object in this further excursion was to visit the very remarkable cavern of Surthellir, distant a good thirty-three miles from this place. The clergyman was again kind enough to make the necessary arrangements for me, and even to act as my Mentor on the journey.

Though we were only three strong, we departed with a retinue of seven horses, and for nearly ten miles rode back the same way by which I had come from Reikholt on the preceding morning; then we turned off to the left, and crossing hills and acclivities, reached other valleys, which were partly traversed by beautiful streams of lava, and partly interspersed with forests--*forests*, as I have already said, according to Icelandic notions. The separate stems were certainly slightly higher than those in the valley of Thingvalla.

At Kalmannstunga we left the spare horses, and took with us a man to serve as guide in the cavern, from which we were now still some seven miles distant. The great valley in which this cavern lies is reckoned among the most remarkable in Iceland. It is a most perfect picture of volcanic devastation. The most beautiful masses of lava, in the most varied and picturesque forms, occupy the whole immeasurable valley. Lava is to be seen there in a rough glassy state, forming exquisite flames and arabesques; and in immense slabs, lying sometimes scattered, sometimes piled in strata one above the other, as though they had been cast there by a flood. Among these, again, lie mighty isolated streams, which must have been frozen in the midst of their course. From the different colours of the lava, and their transitions from light grey to black, we can judge of the eruptions which have taken place at different periods. The mountains surrounding this valley are mostly of a sombre hue; some are even black, forming a striking contrast to the neighbouring jokuls, which, in their large expanse, present the appearance almost of a sea of ice. I found one of these jokuls of a remarkable size; its shining expanse extended far down into the valley, and its upper surface was almost immeasurable.

The other mountains were all smooth, as though polished by art; in the fore-ground I only noticed one which was covered with wonderful forms of dried lava. A deathlike silence weighed on the whole country round, on hill and on valley alike. Every thing seemed dead, all round was barren and desert, so that the effect was truly Icelandic. The greater portion of Iceland might be with justice designated the "Northern Desert."

The cavern of Surthellir lies on a slightly elevated extended plain, where it would certainly not be sought for, as we are accustomed to see natural phenomena of this description only in the bowels of rocks. It is, therefore, with no little sur-prise that the traveller sees suddenly opening before him a large round basin about fifteen fathoms in diameter, and four in depth. It was with a feeling of awe that I looked downwards on the countless blocks of rock piled one upon the other, ex-tending on one side to the edge of the hollow, across which the road led to the dark ravines farther on.

We were compelled to scramble forward on our hands and knees, until we reached a long broad passage, which led us at first imperceptibly downwards, and then ran underneath the plain, which formed a rocky cavern above our heads. I es-timated the different heights of this roof at not less than from eighteen to sixty feet; but it seldom reached a greater elevation than the latter. Both roof and walls are in some places very pointed and rough: a circumstance to be ascribed to the stalactites which adhere to them, without, however, forming figures or long sharp points.

From this principal path several smaller ones lead far into the interior of this stony region; but they do not communicate with each other, and one is compelled to return from each side-path into the main road. Some of these by-paths are short, narrow, and low; others, on the contrary, are long, broad, and lofty.

In one of the most retired of these by-paths I was shewn a great number of bones, which, I was told, were those of slaughtered sheep and other animals. I could gather, from the account given by the priest of the legend concerning them, that, in days of yore, this cave was the resort of a mighty band of robbers. This must have been a long, long time ago, as this is related as a legend or a fable.

For my part, I could not tell what robbers had to do in Iceland. Pirates had often come to the island; but for these gentry this cavern was too far from the sea.

I cannot even imagine beasts of prey to have been there; for the whole country round about is desert and uninhabited, so that they could have found nothing to prey upon. In fact, I turned over in my mind every probability, and can only say that it appeared to me a most remarkable circumstance to find in this desert place, so far from any living thing, a number of bones, which, moreover, looked as fresh as if the poor animals to whom they once belonged had been eaten but a short time ago. Unfortunately I could obtain no satisfactory information on this point.

It is difficult to imagine any thing more laborious than to wander about in this cavern. As the road had shewed itself at the entrance of the cavern, so it continued throughout its whole extent. The path consisted entirely of loose fragments of lava heaped one upon the other, over which we had to clamber with great labour. None of us could afford to help the others; each one was fully occupied with himself. There was not a single spot to be seen on which we could have stood without holding fast at the same time with our hands. We were sometimes obliged to seat ourselves on a stone, and so to slide down; at others, to take hands and pull one another to the top of high blocks of stone.

We came to several immense basins, or craters, which opened above our heads, but were inaccessible, the sides being too steep for us to climb. The light which entered through these openings was scarcely enough to illumine the principal path, much less the numerous by-paths.

At Kalmannstunga I had endeavoured to procure torches, but was obliged to consider myself fortunate in getting a few tapers. It is necessary to provide oneself with torches at Reikjavik.

The parts of the cavern beneath the open craters were still covered with a considerable quantity of snow, by which our progress was rendered very dangerous. We frequently sunk in, and at other times caught our feet between the stones, so that we could scarcely maintain our balance. In the by-paths situated near these openings an icy rind had formed itself, which was now covered with water. Farther on, the ice had melted; but it was generally very dirty, as a stratum of sand mixed with water lay there in place of the stones. The chief path alone was covered with blocks of lava; in the smaller paths I found only strata of sand and small pieces of lava.

The magical illumination produced by the sun's rays shining through one of these craters into the cavern produced a splendid effect. The sun shone perpendicularly through the opening, spread a dazzling radiance over the snow, and diffused a pale delicate light around us. The effect of this point of dazzling light was the more remarkable from its contrasting strongly with the two dark chasms, from the first of which we had emerged to continue our journey through the obscurity of the second.

This subterranean labyrinth is said to extend in different directions for many miles. We explored a portion of the chief path and several by-paths, and after a march of two hours returned heartily tired to the upper world. We then rested a quarter of an hour, and afterwards returned at a good round pace to Kalmannstunga.

Unfortunately I do not possess sufficient geognostic knowledge to be able to set this cavern down as an extinct volcano. But in travelling in a country where every hill and mountain, every thing around, in fact, consists of lava, even the uninitiated in science seeks to discover the openings whence these immense masses have poured. The stranger curiously regards the top of each mountain, thinking every where to behold a crater, but both hill and dale appear smooth and closed. With what joy then does he hail the thought of having discovered, in this cavern, something to throw light upon the sources of these things! I, at least, fancied myself walking on the hearth of an extinct volcano; for all I saw, from the masses of stone piled beneath my feet and the immense basin above my head, were both of lava. If I am right in my conjecture, I do not know; I only speak according to my notions and my views.

I was obliged to pass this night in a cottage. Kalmannstunga contains three such cottages, but no chapel. Luckily I found one of these houses somewhat larger and more cleanly than its neighbours; it could almost come under the denomination of a farm. The occupants, too, had been employed during my ride to the cavern in cleansing the best chamber, and preparing it, as far as possible, for my reception. The room in question was eleven feet long by seven broad; the window was so small and so covered with dirt that, although the sun was shining in its full glory, I could scarcely see to write. The walls, and even the floor, were boarded--a great piece of luxury in a country where wood is so scarce. The furniture consisted of a broad bedstead, two chests of drawers, and a small table. Chairs and benches are a kind of ***terra incognita*** in the dwellings of the Icelandic peasantry; besides, I do not know where such articles could be stowed in a room of such dimensions as that which I occupied.

My hostess, the widow of a wealthy peasant, introduced to me her four children, who were very handsome, and very neatly dressed. I begged the good mother to tell me the names of the young ones, so that I might at least know a few Icelandic names. She appeared much flattered at my request, and gave me the names as follows: Sigrudur, Gudrun, Ingebor, and Lars.

I should have felt tolerably comfortable in my present quarters, accustomed as I am to bear privations of all kinds with indifference, if they would but have left me in peace. But the reader may fancy my horror when the whole population, not only of the cottage itself, but also of the neighbouring dwellings, made their appearance, and, planting themselves partly in my chamber and partly at the door, held me in a far closer state of siege than even at Krisuvik. I was, it appeared, quite a novel phenomenon in the eyes of these good people, and so they came one and all and stared at me; the women and children were, in particular, most unpleasantly familiar; they felt my dress, and the little ones laid their dirty little countenances in my lap. Added to this, the confined atmosphere from the number of persons present, their lamentable want of cleanliness, and their filthy habit of spitting, &c., all combined to form a most dreadful whole. During these visits I did more penance than by the longest fasts; and fasting, too, was an exercise I seldom escaped, as I could touch few Icelandic dishes. The cookery of the Icelandic peasants is wholly confined to the preparation of dried fish, with which they eat fermented milk that has often been kept for months; on very rare occasions they have a preparation of barley-meal, which is eaten with flat bread baked from Icelandic moss ground fine.

I could not but wonder at the fact that most of these people expected to find me acquainted with a number of things generally studied only by men; they seemed to have a notion that in foreign parts women should be as learned as men. So, for instance, the priests always inquired if I spoke Latin, and seemed much surprised on finding that I was unacquainted with the language. The common people requested my advice as to the mode of treating divers complaints; and once, in the course of one of my solitary wanderings about Reikjavik, on my entering a cottage, they brought before me a being whom I should scarcely have recognised as belonging to the same species as myself, so fearfully was he disfigured by the eruption called "lepra." Not only the face, but the whole body also was covered with it; the patient was quite emaciated, and some parts of his body were covered with sores. For a surgeon this might have been an interesting sight, but I turned away in disgust.

But let us turn from this picture. I would rather tell of the angel's face I saw in Kalmannstunga. It was a girl, ten or twelve years of age, beautiful and lovely beyond description, so that I wished I had been a painter. How gladly would I have taken home with me to my own land, if only on canvass, the delicate face, with its roguish dimples and speaking eyes! But perhaps it is better as it is; the picture might by some unlucky chance have fallen into the hands of some too-susceptible youth, who, like Don Sylvio de Rosalva, in Wieland's **Comical Romance**, would immediately have proceeded to travel through half the world to find the original of this enchanting portrait. His spirit of inquiry would scarcely have carried him to Iceland, as such an apparition would never be suspected to exist in such a country, and thus the unhappy youth would be doomed to endless wandering.

June 20th.

The distance from Kalmannstunga to Thingvalla is fifty-two miles, and the journey is certainly one of the most dreary and fatiguing of all that can be made in Iceland. The traveller passes from one desert valley into another; he is always surrounded by high mountains and still higher glaciers, and wherever he turns his eyes, nature seems torpid and dead. A feeling of anxious discomfort seizes upon the wanderer, he hastens with redoubled speed through the far-stretched deserts, and eagerly ascends the mountains piled up before him, in the hope that better things lie beyond. It is in vain; he only sees the same solitudes, the same deserts, the same mountains.

On the elevated plateaux several places were still covered with snow; these we were obliged to cross, though we could frequently hear the rushing of the water beneath its snowy covering. We were compelled also to pass over coatings of ice spread lightly over rivers, and presenting that blue colour which is a certain sign of danger.

Our poor horses were sometimes very restive; but it was of no use; they were beaten without mercy until they carried us over the dangerous places. The pack-horse was always driven on in front with many blows; it had to serve as pioneer, and try if the road was practicable. Next came my guide, and I brought up the rear. Our poor horses frequently sank up to their knees in the snow, and twice up to the saddle-girths. This was one of the most dangerous rides I have ever had. I could not help continually thinking what I should do if my guide were to sink in so deeply that he could not extricate himself; my strength would not have been sufficient to rescue him, and whither should I turn to seek for help? All around us was nothing but a desert and snow. Perhaps my lot might have been to die of hunger. I should have wandered about seeking dwellings and human beings, and have entangled myself so completely among these wastes that I could never have found my way.

When at a distance I descried a new field of snow (and unfortunately we came upon them but too frequently), I felt very uncomfortable; those alone who have themselves been in a similar situation can estimate the whole extent of my anxiety.

If I had been travelling in company with others, these fears would not have disturbed me; for there reciprocal assistance can be rendered, and the consciousness of this fact seems materially to diminish the danger.

During the season in which the snow ceases to form a secure covering, this road is but little travelled. We saw nowhere a trace of footsteps, either of men or animals; we were the only living beings in this dreadful region. I certainly scolded my guide roundly for bringing me by such a road. But what did I gain by this? It would have been as dangerous to turn back as to go on.

A change in the weather, which till now had been rather favourable, increased the difficulties of this journey. Already when we left Kalmannstunga, the sky began to be overcast, and the sun enlivened us with its rays only for a few minutes at a time. On our reaching the higher mountains the weather became worse; for here we encountered clouds and fog, which wreaked their vengeance upon us, and which only careered by to make room for others. An icy storm from the neighbouring glaciers was their constant companion, and made me shiver so much that I could scarcely keep my saddle. We had now ridden above thirteen hours. The rain poured down incessantly, and we were half dead with cold and wet; so I at length determined to halt for the night at the first cottage: at last we found one between two or three miles from Thingvalla. I had now a roof above my head; but beyond this I had gained nothing. The cottage consisted of a single room, and was almost completely filled by four broad bedsteads. I counted seven adults and three children, who had all to be accommodated in these four beds. In addition to this, the kvef, a kind of croup, prevailed this spring to such an extent that scarcely any one escaped it. Wherever I went, I found the people afflicted with this complaint; and here this was also the case; the noise of groaning and coughing on all sides was quite deplorable. The floor, moreover, was revoltingly dirty.

The good people were so kind as immediately to place one of their beds at my disposal; but I would rather have passed the night on the threshold of the door than in this disgusting hole. I chose for my lodging-place the narrow passage which separated the kitchen from the room; I found there a couple of blocks, across which a few boards had been laid, and this constituted the milk-room: it might have been more properly called the smoke-room; for in the roof were a few air-holes, through which the smoke escaped. In this smoke or milk-room--whichever it may be called--I prepared to pass the night as best I could. My cloak being wet through, I had been compelled to hang it on a stick to dry; and thus found myself under the necessity of borrowing a mattress from these unhealthy people. I laid myself down boldly, and pretended sleepiness, in order to deliver myself from the curiosity of my entertainers. They retired to their room, and so I was alone and undisturbed. But yet I could not sleep; the cold wind, blowing in upon me through the air-holes, chilled and wetted as I already was, kept me awake against my will. I had also another misfortune to endure. As often as I attempted to sit upright on my luxurious couch, my head would receive a severe concussion. I had forgotten the poles which are fixed across each of these antechambers, for the purpose of hanging up fish to dry, &c. Unfortunately I could not bear this arrangement in mind until after I had received half a dozen salutations of this description.

June 21st.

At length the morning so long sighed for came; the rain had indeed ceased; but the clouds still hung about the mountains, and promised a speedy fall; I nevertheless resolved rather to submit myself to the fury of the elements than to remain longer in my present quarters, and so ordered the horses to be saddled.

Before my departure roast lamb and butter were offered me. I thanked my entertainers; but refrained from tasting any thing, excusing myself on the plea of not feeling hungry, which was in reality the case; for if I only looked at the dirty people who surrounded me, my appetite vanished instantly. So long as my stock of bread and cheese lasted, I kept to it, and ate nothing else.

Taking leave of my good hosts, we continued our journey to Reikjavik, by the same road on which I had travelled on my journey hither. This had not been my original plan on starting from Reikjavik; I had intended to proceed from Thingvalla directly to the Geyser, to Hecla, &c.; but the horses were already exhausted, and the weather so dreadfully bad, without prospect of speedy amendment, that I preferred returning to Reikjavik, and waiting for better times in my pleasant little room at the house of the good baker.

We rode on as well as we could amidst ceaseless storms of wind and rain. The most disagreeable circumstance of all was our being obliged to spend the hours devoted to rest in the open air, under a by no means cloudless sky, as during our whole day's journey we saw not a single hut, save the solitary one in the lava desert, which serves as a resting-place for travellers during the winter. So we continued our journey until we reached a scanty meadow. Here I had my choice either to walk about for two hours, or to sit down upon the wet grass. I could find nothing better to do than to turn my back upon the wind and rain, to remain standing on one spot, to have patience, and for amusement to observe the direction in which the clouds scudded by. At the same time I discussed my frugal meal, more for want of something to do than from hunger; if I felt thirsty, I had only to turn round and open my mouth.

If there are natures peculiarly fitted for travelling, I am fortunate in being blessed with such an one. No rain or wind was powerful enough to give me even a cold. During this whole excursion I had tasted no warm or nourishing food; I had slept every night upon a bench or a chest; had ridden nearly 255 miles in six days; and had besides scrambled about bravely in the cavern of Surthellir; and, in spite of all this privation and fatigue, I arrived at Reikjavik in good health and spirits.

Short summary of this journey:

	Miles
First day, from Reikjavik to	46

CHAPTER VI

The weather soon cleared up, and I continued my journey to the Geyser and to Mount Hecla on the 24th June. On the first day, when we rode to Thingvalla, we passed no new scenery, but saw instead an extremely beautiful atmospheric phenomenon.

As we approached the lake, some thin mist-clouds lowered over it and over the earth, so that it seemed as if it would rain. One portion of the firmament glowed with the brightest blue; while the other part was obscured by thick clouds, through which the sun was just breaking. Some of its rays reached the clouds of mist, and illuminated them in a wonderfully beautiful manner. The most delicate shades of colour seemed breathed, as it were, over them like a dissolving rainbow, whose glowing colours were intermingled and yet singly perceptible. This play of colours continued for half an hour, then faded gradually till it vanished entirely, and the ordinary atmosphere took its place. It was one of the most beautiful appearances I had ever witnessed.

June 25th.

The roads separate about a mile behind the little town of Thingvalla; the one to the left goes to Reikholt, the right-hand one leads to the Geyser. We rode for some time along the shores of the lake, and found at the end of the valley an awful chasm in the rock, similar to the one of Almanagiau, which we had passed on such a wretched road.

The contiguous valley bore a great resemblance to that of Thingvalla; but the third one was again fearful. Lava covered it, and was quite overgrown with that whitish moss, which has a beautiful appearance when it only covers a portion of the lava, and when black masses rise above it, but which here presented a most monotonous aspect.

We also passed two grottoes which opened at our feet. At the entrance of one stood a pillar of rock supporting an immense slab of lava, which formed an awe-inspiring portal. I had unfortunately not known of the existence of these caves, and was consequently unprepared to visit them. Torches, at least, would have been requisite. But I subsequently heard that they were not at all deep, and contained nothing of interest.

In the course of the day we passed through valleys such as I had seen nowhere else in Iceland. Beautiful meadow-lawns, perfectly level, covered the country for miles. These rich valleys were, of course, tolerably well populated; we frequently passed three or four contiguous cottages, and saw horses, cows, and sheep grazing on these fields in considerable numbers.

The mountains which bounded these valleys on the left seemed to me very remarkable; they were partly brown, black, or dark blue, like the others; but the bulk of which they were composed I considered to be fine loam-soil layers, if I may trust my imperfect mineralogical knowledge. Some of these mountains were topped by large isolated lava rocks, real giants; and it seemed inexplicable to me how they could stand on the soft soil beneath.

In one of these valleys we passed a considerable lake, on and around which rose circling clouds of steam proceeding from hot springs, but of no great size. But after we had already travelled about twenty-five miles, we came to the most remarkable object I had ever met with; this was a river with a most peculiar bed.

This river-bed is broad and somewhat steep; it consists of lava strata, and is

divided lengthwise in the middle by a cleft eighteen to twenty feet deep, and fifteen to eighteen feet broad, towards which the bubbling and surging waters rush,
so that the sound is heard at some distance. A little wooden bridge, which stands
in the middle of the stream, and over which the high waves constantly play, leads
over the chasm. Any one not aware of the fact can hardly explain this appearance
to himself, nor understand the noise and surging of the stream. The little bridge in
the centre would be taken for the ruins of a fallen bridge, and the chasm is not seen
from the shore, because the foaming waves overtop it. An indescribable fear would
seize upon the traveller when he beheld the venturous guide ride into the stream,
and was obliged to follow without pity or mercy.

The priest of Thingvalla had prepared me for the scene, and had advised me
to *walk* over the bridge; but as the water at this season stood so high that the waves
from both sides dashed two feet above the bridge, I could not descend from my
horse, and was obliged to ride across.

The whole passage through the stream is so peculiar, that it must be seen, and
can scarcely be described. The water gushes and plays on all sides with fearful force;
it rushes into the chasm with impetuous violence, forms waterfalls on both sides,
and breaks itself on the projecting rocks. Not far from the bridge the cleft termi-
nates; and the whole breadth of the waters falls over rocks thirty to forty feet high.
The nearer we approached the centre, the deeper, more violent, and impetuous
grew the stream, and the more deafening was the noise. The horses became restless
and shy; and when we came to the bridge, they began to tremble, they reared, they
turned to all sides but the right one, and refused to obey the bridle. With infinite
trouble we at last succeeded in bringing them across this dangerous place.

The valley which is traversed by this peculiar river is narrow, and quite enclosed by lava mountains and hills; the inanimate, silent nature around is perfectly
adapted to imprint this scene for ever on the traveller's memory.

This remarkable stream had been the last difficulty; and now we proceeded
quietly and safely through the beautiful valleys till we approached the Geyser,
which a projecting hillock enviously concealed from my anxiously curious gaze.
At last this hillock was passed; and I saw the Geyser with its surrounding scenery,
with its immense steam pillars, and the clouds and cloudlets rising from it. The hill
was about two miles distant from the Geyser and the other hot springs. There they

were, boiling and bubbling all around, and through the midst lay the road to the basin. Eighty paces from it we halted.

And now I stood before the chief object of my journey; I saw it, it was so near me, and yet I did not venture to approach it. But a peasant who had followed us from one of the neighbouring cottages, and had probably guessed my anxiety and my fear, took me by the hand and constituted himself my cicerone. He had unfortunately, it being Sunday, paid too great a devotion to the brandy-bottle, so that he staggered rather than walked, and I hesitated to trust myself to the guidance of this man, not knowing whether he had reason enough left to distinguish how far we might with safety venture. My guide, who had accompanied me from Reikjavik, assured me indeed that I might trust him in spite of his intoxication, and that he would himself go with us to translate the peasant's Icelandic jargon into Danish; but nevertheless I followed with great trepidation.

He led me to the margin of the basin of the great Geyser, which lies on the top of a gentle elevation of about ten feet, and contains the outer and the inner basins. The diameter of the outer basin may be about thirty feet; that of the inner one six to seven feet. Both were filled to the brim, the water was pure as crystal, but boiled and bubbled only slightly. We soon left this spot; for when the basins are quite filled with water it is very dangerous to approach them, as they may empty themselves any moment by an eruption. We therefore went to inspect the other springs.

My unsteady guide pointed those out which we might unhesitatingly approach, and warned me from the others. Then we returned to the great Geyser, where he gave me some precautionary rules, in case of an intervening eruption, and then left me to prepare some accommodation for my stay. I will briefly enumerate the rules he gave me.

"The pillar of water always rises perpendicularly, and the overflowing water has its chief outlets on one and the same side. The water does indeed escape on the other side, but only in inconsiderable quantities, and in shapeless little ducts, which one may easily evade. On this side one may therefore approach within forty paces even during the most violent eruptions. The eruption announces itself by a dull roaring; and as soon as this is heard, the traveller must hastily retire to the above-named distance, as the eruption always follows very quickly after the noise. The water, however, does not rise high every time, often only very inconsiderably, so that, to see a very fine explosion, it is often necessary to stay some days here."

The French scholar, M. P. Geimard, has provided for the accommodation of travellers with a truly noble disinterestedness. He traversed the whole of Iceland some years ago and left two large tents behind him; one here, and the other in Thingvalla. The one here is particularly appropriate, as travellers are frequently obliged, as stated above, to wait several days for a fine eruption. Every traveller certainly owes M. Geimard the warmest thanks for this convenience. A peasant, the same who guides travellers to the springs, has the charge of it, and is bound to pitch it for any one for a fee of one or two florins.

When my tent was ready it was nearly eleven o'clock. My companions retired, and I remained alone.

It is usual to watch through the night in order not to miss an eruption. Now, although an alternate watching is no very arduous matter for several travellers, it became a very hard task for me alone, and an Icelandic peasant cannot be trusted; an eruption of Mount Hecla would scarcely arouse him.

I sat sometimes before and sometimes in my tent, and listened with anxious expectation for the coming events; at last, after midnight--the witching hour--I heard some hollow sounds, as if a cannon were being fired at a great distance, and its echoing sounds were borne by the breeze. I rushed from my tent and expected subterranean noises, violent cracking and trembling of the earth, according to the descriptions I had read. I could scarcely repress a slight sensation of fear. To be alone at midnight in such a scene is certainly no joke.

Many of my friends may remember my telling them, before my departure, that I expected I should need the most courage on my Icelandic journey during the nights at the Geyser.

These hollow sounds were repeated, at very short intervals, thirteen times; and each time the basin overflowed and ejected a considerable quantity of water. The sounds did not seem to proceed from subterranean ragings, but from the violent agitation of the waters. In a minute and a half all was over; the water no longer overflowed, the caldron and basin remained filled, and I returned to my tent disappointed in every way. This phenomenon was repeated every two hours and a half, or, at the latest, every three hours and a half. I saw and heard nothing else all night, the next day, or the second night. I waited in vain for an eruption.

When I had accustomed myself to these temporary effusions of my neighbour, I either indulged in a gentle slumber in the intermediate time, or I visited the other springs and explored. I wished to discover the boiling vapour and the coloured springs which many travellers assert they have seen here.

All the hot-springs are united with a circumference of 800 to 900 paces: several of them are very remarkable, but the majority insignificant.

They are situated in the angle of an immense valley at the foot of a hill, behind which extends a chain of mountains. The valley is entirely covered with grass, and the vegetation only decreases a little in the immediate vicinity of the springs. Cottages are built every where in the neighbourhood; the nearest to the springs are only about 700 to 800 paces distant.

I counted twelve large basins with boiling and gushing springs; of smaller ones there were many more.

Among the gushing springs the Strokker is the most remarkable. It boils and bubbles with most extraordinary violence at a depth of about twenty feet, shoots up suddenly, and projects its waters into the air. Its eruptions sometimes last half an hour, and the column occasionally ascends to a height of forty feet. I witnessed several of its eruptions; but unfortunately not one of the largest. The highest I saw could not have been above thirty feet, and did not last more than a quarter of an hour. The Strokker is the only spring, except the Geyser, which has to be approached with great caution. The eruptions sometimes succeed each other quickly, and sometimes cease for a few hours, and are not preceded by any sign. Another spring spouts constantly, but never higher than three to four feet. A third one lies about four or five feet deep, in a rather broad basin, and produces only a few little bubbles. But this calmness is deceptive: it seldom lasts more than half a minute, rarely two or three minutes; then the spring begins to bubble, to boil, and to wave and spout to a height of two or three feet; without, however, reaching the level of the basin. In some springs I heard boiling and foaming like a gentle bellowing; but saw no water, sometimes not even steam, rising.

Two of the most remarkable springs which can perhaps be found in the world are situated immediately above the Geyser, in two openings, which are separated by a wall of rock scarcely a foot wide. This partition does not rise above the surface of the soil, but descends into the earth; the water boils slowly, and has an equable, moderate discharge. The beauty of these springs consists in their remarkable transparency. All the varied forms and caves, the projecting peaks, and edges of rock, are visible far down, until the eye is lost in the depths of darkness. But the greatest beauty of the spring is the splendid colouring proceeding from the rock; it is of the tenderest, most transparent, pale blue and green, and resembles the reflection of a Bengal flame. But what is most strange is, that this play of colour proceeds from the rock, and only extends eight to ten inches from it, while the other water is colourless as common water, only more transparent, and purer.

I could not believe it at first, and thought it must be occasioned by the sun; I therefore visited the springs at different times, sometimes when the sun shone brightly, sometimes when it was obscured by clouds, once even after its setting; but the colouring always remained the same.

One may fearlessly approach the brink of these springs. The platform which projects directly from them, and under which one can see in all directions, is indeed only a thin ledge of rock, but strong enough to prevent any accident. The beauty consists, as I have said, in the magical illumination, and in the transparency, by which all the caves and grottoes to the greatest depths become visible to the eye. Involuntarily I thought of Schiller's **Diver**. {40} I seemed to see the goblet hang on the peaks and jags of the rock; I could fancy I saw the monsters rise from the bottom. It must be a peculiar pleasure to read this splendid poem in such an appropriate spot.

I found scarcely any basins of Brodem or coloured waters. The only one of the kind which I saw was a small basin, in which a brownish-red substance, rather denser than water, was boiling. Another smaller spring, with dirty brown water, I should have quite overlooked, if I had not so industriously searched for these curiosities.

At last, after long waiting, on the second day of my stay, on the 27th June, at half-past eight in the morning, I was destined to see an eruption of the Geyser in its greatest perfection. The peasant, who came daily in the morning and in the evening to inquire whether I had already seen an eruption, was with me when the hollow sounds which precede it were again heard. We hastened out, and I again despaired of seeing any thing; the water only overflowed as usual, and the sound was already ceasing. But all at once, when the last sounds had scarcely died away, the explosion began. Words fail me when I try to describe it: such a magnificent and overpowering sight can only be seen once in a lifetime.

All my expectations and suppositions were far surpassed. The water spouted upwards with indescribable force and bulk; one pillar rose higher than the other; each seemed to emulate the other. When I had in some measure recovered from the surprise, and regained composure, I looked at the tent. How little, how dwarfish it seemed as compared to the height of these pillars of water! And yet it was about twenty feet high. It did, indeed, lie ten feet lower than the basin of the Geyser; but if tent had been raised above tent, these ten feet could only be deducted once, and I calculated, though my calculation may not be correct, that one would need to pile up five or six tents to have the height of one of the pillars. Without exaggeration, I think the largest spout rose above one hundred feet high, and was three to four feet in diameter.

Fortunately I had looked at my watch at the beginning of the hollow sounds, the forerunners of the eruption, for during its continuance I should probably have forgotten to do so. The whole lasted four minutes, of which the greater half must have been taken up by the eruption itself.

When this wonderful scene was over, the peasant accompanied me to the basin. We could now approach it and the boiler without danger, and examine both at leisure. There was now nothing to fear; the water had entirely disappeared from the outer basin. We entered it and approached the inner basin, in which the water had sunk seven or eight feet, where it boiled and bubbled fiercely.

With a hammer I broke some crust out of the outer as well as out of the inner basin; the former was white, the latter brown. I also tasted the water; it had not an unpleasant taste, and can only contain an inconsiderable proportion of sulphur, as the steam does not even smell of it.

I went to the basin of the Geyser every half hour to observe how much time was required to fill it again. After an hour I could still descend into the outer basin; but half an hour later the inner basin was already full, and commenced to overflow. As long as the water only filled the inner basin it boiled violently; but the higher it rose in the outer one, the less it boiled, and nearly ceased when the basin was filled: it only threw little bubbles here and there.

After a lapse of two hours--it was just noon--the basin was filled nearly to the brim; and while I stood beside it the water began again to bubble violently, and to emit the hollow sounds. I had scarcely time to retreat, for the pillars of water rose immediately. This time they spouted during the noise, and were more bulky than those of the first explosion, which might proceed from their not rising so high, and therefore remaining more compact. Their height may have been from forty to fifty feet. The basins this time remained nearly as full after the eruption as before.

I had now seen two eruptions of the Geyser, and felt amply compensated for my persevering patience and watchfulness. But I was destined to be more fortunate, and to experience its explosions in all their variety. The spring spouted again at seven o'clock in the evening, ascended higher than at noon, and brought up some stones, which looked like black spots and points in the white frothy water-column. And during the third night it presented itself under another phase: the water rose in dreadful, quickly-succeeding waves, without throwing rays; the basin overflowed violently, and generated such a mass of steam as is rarely seen. The wind accidentally blew it to the spot where I stood, and it enveloped me so closely that I could scarcely see a few feet off. But I perceived neither smell nor oppression, merely a slight degree of warmth.

June 28th.

As I had now seen the Geyser play so often and so beautifully, I ordered my horses for nine o'clock this morning, to continue my journey. I made the more haste to leave, as a Dutch prince was expected, who had lately arrived at Reikjavik, with a large retinue, in a splendid man-of-war.

I had the luck to see another eruption before my departure at half-past eight o'clock; and this one was nearly as beautiful as the first. This time also the outer basin was entirely emptied, and the inner one to a depth of six or seven feet. I could therefore again descend into the basin, and bid farewell to the Geyser at the very brink of the crater, which, of course, I did.

I had now been three nights and two days in the immediate vicinity of the Geyser, and had witnessed five eruptions, of which two were of the most considerable that had ever been known. But I can assure my readers that I did not find every thing as I had anticipated it according to the descriptions and accounts I had read. I never heard a greater noise than I have mentioned, and never felt any trembling of the earth, although I paid the greatest attention to every little circumstance, and held my head to the ground during an eruption.

It is singular how many people repeat every thing they hear from others--how some, with an over-excited imagination, seem to see, hear, and feel things which do not exist; and how others, again, tell the most unblushing falsehoods. I met an example of this in Reikjavik, in the house of the apothecary Moller, in the person of an officer of a French frigate, who asserted that he had "ridden to the very edge of the crater of Mount Vesuvius." He probably did not anticipate meeting any one in Reikjavik who had also been to the crater of Vesuvius. Nothing irritates me so much as such falsehoods and boastings; and I could not therefore resist asking him how he had managed that feat. I told him that I had been there, and feared danger as little as he could do; but that I had been compelled to descend from my donkey near the top of the mountain, and let my feet carry me the remainder of the journey. He seemed rather embarrassed, and pretended he had meant to say **nearly** to the crater; but I feel convinced he will tell this story so often that he will at last believe it himself.

I hope I do not weary my readers by dwelling so long on the subject of the Geyser. I will now vary the subject by relating a few circumstances that came under my notice, which, though trifling in themselves, were yet very significant. The most unimportant facts of an almost unknown country are often interesting, and are often most conclusive evidences of the general character of the nation.

I have already spoken of my intoxicated guide. It is yet inexplicable to me how he could have conducted me so safely in such a semi-conscious state; and had he not been the only one, I should certainly not have trusted myself to his guidance.

Of the want of cleanliness of the Icelanders, no one who has not witnessed it can have any idea; and if I attempted to describe some of their nauseous habits, I might fill volumes. They seem to have no feeling of propriety, and I must, in this respect, rank them as far inferior to the Bedouins and Arabs--even to the Greenlanders. I can, therefore, not conceive how this nation could once have been distinguished for wealth, bravery, and civilisation.

On this day I proceeded on my journey about twenty-eight miles farther to Skalholt.

For the first five miles we retraced our former road; then we turned to the left and traversed the beautiful long valley in which the Geyser is situated. For many miles we could see its clouds of steam rising to the sky. The roads were tolerable only when they passed along the sides of hills and mountains; in the plains they were generally marshy and full of water. We sometimes lost all traces of a road, and only pushed on towards the quarter in which the place of our destination was situated; and feared withal to sink at every pace into the soft and unresisting soil.

I found the indolence of the Icelandic peasants quite unpardonable. All the valleys through which we passed were large morasses richly overgrown with grass. If the single parishes would unite to dig trenches and drain the soil, they would have the finest meadows. This is proved near the many precipices where the water has an outlet; in these spots the grass grows most luxuriantly, and daisies and herbs flourish there, and even wild clover. A few cottages are generally congregated on these oases.

Before arriving at the village of Thorfastadir, we already perceived Hecla surrounded by the beautiful jokuls.

I arrived at Thorfastadir while a funeral was going on. As I entered the church the mourners were busily seeking courage and consolation in the brandy-bottle. The law commands, indeed, that this be not done in the church; but if every one obeyed the law, what need would there be of judges? The Icelanders must think so, else they would discontinue the unseemly practice.

When the priest came, a psalm or a prayer--I could not tell which it was, being Icelandic--was so earnestly shouted by peasants under the leadership of the priest and elders, that the good people waxed quite warm and out of breath. Then the priest placed himself before the coffin, which, for want of room, had been laid on the backs of the seats, and with a very loud voice read a prayer which lasted more than half an hour. With this the ceremony within the church was concluded, and the coffin was carried round the church to the grave, followed by the priest and the rest of the company. This grave was deeper than any I had ever seen. When the coffin had been lowered, the priest threw three handfuls of earth upon it, but none of the mourners followed his example. Among the earth which had been dug out of the grave I noticed four skulls, several human bones, and a board of a former coffin. These were all thrown in again upon the coffin, and the grave filled in presence of the priest and the people. One man trod the soil firm, then a little mound was made and covered with grass-plots which were lying ready. The whole business was completed with miraculous speed.

The little town of Skalholt, my station this night, was once as celebrated in religious matters as Thingvalla had been politically famous. Here, soon after the introduction of Christianity, the first bishopric was founded in 1098, and the church is said to have been one of the largest and richest. Now Skalholt is a miserable place, and consists of three or four cottages, and a wretched wooden church, which may perhaps contain a hundred persons; it has not even its own priest, but belongs to Thorfastadir.

My first business on arriving was to inspect the yet remaining relics of past ages. First I was shewn an oil-picture which hangs in the church, and is said to represent the first bishop of Skalholt, Thorlakur, who was worshipped almost as a saint for his strict and pious life.

After this, preparations were made to clear away the steps of the altar and several boards of the flooring. I stood expectantly looking on, thinking that I should now have to descend into a vault to inspect the embalmed body of the bishop. I must confess this prospect was not the most agreeable, when I thought of the approaching night which I should have to spend in this church, perhaps immediately over the grave of the old skeleton. I had besides already had too much to do with the dead for one day, and could not rid myself of the unpleasant grave-odour which I had imbibed in Thorfastadir, and which seemed to cling to my dress and my nose. {41} I was therefore not a little pleased when, instead of the dreaded vault and mummy, I was only shewn a marble slab, on which were inscribed the usual notifications of the birth, death, &c. of this great bishop. Besides this, I saw an old embroidered stole and a simple golden chalice, both of which are said to be relics of the age of Thorlakar.

Then we ascended into the so-called store-room, which is only separated from the lower portion of the church by a few boards, and which extends to the altar. Here are kept the bells and the organ, if the church possesses one, the provisions, and a variety of tools. They opened an immense chest for me there, which seemed to contain only large pieces of tallow made in the form of cheeses; but under this tallow I found the library, where I discovered an interesting treasure. This was, besides several very old books in the Icelandic tongue, three thick folio volumes, which I could read very easily; they were German, and contained Luther's doctrines, letters, epistles, &c.

I had now seen all there was to be seen, and began to satisfy my physical wants by calling for some hot water to make coffee, &c. As usual, all the inhabitants of the place ranged themselves in and before the church, probably to increase their knowledge of the human race by studying my peculiarities. I soon, however, closed the door, and prepared a splendid couch for myself. At my first entrance into the church, I had noticed a long box, quite filled with sheep's wool. I threw my rugs over this, and slept as comfortably as in the softest bed. In the morning I carefully teased the wool up again, and no one could then have imagined where I had passed the night.

Nothing amused me more, when I had lodgings of this description, than the curiosity of the people, who would rush in every morning, as soon as I opened the door. The first thing they said to each other was always, "Krar hefur hun sovid" (Where can she have slept?). The good people could not conceive how it was possible to spend a night *alone* in a church surrounded by a churchyard; they perhaps considered me an evil spirit or a witch, and would too gladly have ascertained how such a creature slept. When I saw their disappointed faces, I had to turn away not to laugh at them.

June 29th.

Early the next morning I continued my journey. Not far from Skalholt we came to the river Thiorsa, which is deep and rapid. We crossed in a boat; but the horses had to swim after us. It is often very troublesome to make the horses enter these streams; they see at once that they will have to swim. The guide and boatmen cannot leave the shore till the horses have been forced into the stream; and even then they have to throw stones, to threaten them with the whip, and to frighten them by shouts and cries, to prevent them from returning.

When we had made nearly twelve miles on marshy roads, we came to the beautiful waterfall of the Huitha. This fall is not so remarkable for its height, which is scarcely more than fifteen to twenty feet, as for its breadth, and for its quantity of water. Some beautiful rocks are so placed at the ledge of the fall, that they divide it into three parts; but it unites again immediately beneath them. The bed of the river, as well as its shores, is of lava.

The colour of the water is also a remarkable feature in this river; it inclines so much to milky white, that, when the sun shines on it, it requires no very strong imaginative power to take the whole for milk.

Nearly a mile above the fall we had to cross the Huitha, one of the largest rivers in Iceland. Thence the road lies through meadows, which are less marshy than the former ones, till it comes to a broad stream of lava, which announces the vicinity of the fearful volcano of Hecla.

I had hitherto not passed over such an expanse of country in Iceland as that from the Geyser to this place without coming upon streams of lava. And this lava-stream seemed to have felt some pity for the beautiful meadows, for it frequently separated into two branches, and thus enclosed the verdant plain. But it could not withstand the violence of the succeeding masses; it had been carried on, and had spread death and destruction everywhere. The road to it, through plains covered with dark sand, and over steep hills intervening, was very fatiguing and laborious.

We proceeded to the little village of Struvellir, where we stopped to give our horses a few hours' rest. Here we found a large assembly of men and animals. {42} It happened to be Sunday, and a warm sunny day, and so a very full service was held in the pretty little church. When it was over, I witnessed an amusing rural scene. The people poured out of the church,--I counted ninety-six, which is an extraordinarily numerous assemblage for Iceland,--formed into little groups, chatting and joking, not forgetting, however, to moisten their throats with brandy, of which they had taken care to bring an ample supply. Then they bridled their horses and prepared for departure; now the kisses poured in from all sides, and there was no end of leave-taking, for the poor people do not know whether they shall ever meet again, and when.

In all Iceland welcome and farewell is expressed by a loud kiss,--a practice not very delightful for a non-Icelander, when one considers their ugly, dirty faces, the snuffy noses of the old people, and the filthy little children. But the Icelanders do not mind this. They all kissed the priest, and the priest kissed them; and then they kissed each other, till the kissing seemed to have no end. Rank is not considered in this ceremony; and I was not a little surprised to see how my guide, a common farm-labourer, kissed the six daughters of a judge, or the wife and children of a priest, or a judge and the priest themselves, and how they returned the compliment without reserve. Every country has its peculiar customs!

The religious ceremonies generally begin about noon, and last two or three hours. There being no public inn in which to assemble, and no stable in which the horses can be fastened, all flock to the open space in front of the church, which thus becomes a very animated spot. All have to remain in the open air.

When the service was over, I visited the priest, Herr Horfuson; he was kind enough to conduct me to the Salsun, nine miles distant, principally to engage a guide to Hecla for me.

I was doubly rejoiced to have this good man at my side, as we had to cross a dangerous stream, which was very rapid, and so deep that the water rose to the horses' breasts. Although we raised our feet as high as possible, we were yet thoroughly wet. This wading across rivers is one of the most unpleasant modes of travelling. The horse swims more than it walks, and this creates a most disagreeable sensation; one does not know whither to direct one's eyes; to look into the stream would excite giddiness, and the sight of the shore is not much better, for that seems to move and to recede, because the horse, by the current, is forced a little way down the river. To my great comfort the priest rode by my side to hold me, in case I should not be able to keep my seat. I passed fortunately through this probation; and when we reached the other shore, Herr Horfuson pointed out to me how far the current had carried us down the river.

The valley in which Salsun and the Hecla are situated is one of those which are found only in Iceland. It contains the greatest contrasts. Here are charming fields covered with a rich green carpet of softest grass, and there again hills of black, shining lava; even the fertile plains are traversed by streams of lava and spots of sand. Mount Hecla notoriously has the blackest lava and the blackest sand; and it may be imagined how the country looks in its immediate neighbourhood. One hill only to the left of Hecla is reddish brown, and covered with sand and stones of a similar colour. The centre is much depressed, and seems to form a large crater. Mount Hecla is directly united with the lava-mountains piled round it, and seems from the plain only as a higher point. It is surrounded by several glaciers, whose dazzling fields of snow descend far down, and whose brilliant plains have probably never been trod by human feet; several of its sides were also covered with snow. To the left of the valley near Salsun, and at the foot of a lava-hill, lies a lovely lake, on whose shores a numerous flock of sheep were grazing. Near it rises another beautiful hill, so solitary and isolated, that it looks as if it had been cast out by its neighbours and banished hither. Indeed, the whole landscape here is so peculiarly Icelandic, so strange and remarkable, that it will ever remain impressed on my memory.

Salsun lies at the foot of Mount Hecla, but is not seen before one reaches it.

Arrived at Salsun, our first care was to seek a guide, and to bargain for every thing requisite for the ascension of the mountain. The guide was to procure a horse for me, and to take me and my former guide to the summit of Hecla. He demanded five thaler and two marks (about fifteen shillings), a most exorbitant sum, on which he could live for a month. But what could we do? He knew very well that there was no other guide to be had, and so I was forced to acquiesce. When all was arranged, my kind companion left me, wishing me success on my arduous expedition.

I now looked out for a place in which I could spend the night, and a filthy hole fell to my lot. A bench, rather shorter that my body, was put into it, to serve as my bed; beside it hung a decayed fish, which had infected the whole room with its smell. I could scarcely breathe; and as there was no other outlet, I was obliged to open the door, and thus receive the visits of the numerous and amiable inhabitants. What a strengthening and invigorating preparation for the morrow's expedition!

At the foot of Mount Hecla, and especially in this village, every thing seems to be undermined. Nowhere, not even on Mount Vesuvius, had I heard such hollow, droning sounds as here,--the echoes of the heavy footsteps of the peasants. These sounds made a very awful impression on me as I lay all night alone in that dark hole.

My Hecla guide, as I shall call him to distinguish him from my other guide, advised me to start at two o'clock in the morning, to which I assented, well knowing, however, that we should not have mounted our horses before five o'clock.

As I had anticipated, so it happened. At half-past five we were quite prepared and ready for departure. Besides bread and cheese, a bottle of water for myself, and one of brandy for my guides, we were also provided with long sticks, tipped with iron points to sound the depth of the snow, and to lean upon.

We were favoured by a fine warm sunny morning, and galloped briskly over the fields and the adjoining plains of sand. My guide considered the fine weather a very lucky omen, and told me that M. Geimard, the before-mentioned French scholar, had been compelled to wait three days for fine weather. Nine years had elapsed, and no one had ascended the mountain since then. A prince of Denmark, who travelled through Iceland some years before, had been there, but had returned without effecting his purpose.

Our road at first led us through beautiful fields, and then over plains of black sand enclosed on all sides by streams, hillocks, and mountains of piled-up lava. Closer and closer these fearful masses approach, and scarcely permit a passage through a narrow cleft; we had to climb over blocks and hills of lava, where it is difficult to find a firm resting-place for the foot. The lava rolled beside and behind us, and we had to proceed carefully not to fall or be hit by the rolling lava. But most dangerous were the chasms filled with snow over which we had to pass; the snow had been softened by the warmth of the season, so that we sank into it nearly every step, or, what was worse, slipped back more than we had advanced. I scarcely think there can be another mountain whose ascent offers so many difficulties.

After a labour of about three hours and a half we neared the summit of the mountain, where we were obliged to leave our horses. I should, indeed, have preferred to do so long before, as I was apprehensive of the poor animals falling as they climbed over these precipices--one might almost call them rolling mountains--but my guide would not permit it. Sometimes we came to spots where they were useful, and then he maintained that I must ride as far as possible to reserve my strength for the remaining difficulties. And he was right; I scarcely believe I should have been able to go through it on foot, for when I thought we were near the top, hills of lava again rose between us, and we seemed farther from our journey's end than before.

My guide told me that he had never taken any one so far on horseback, and I can believe it. Walking was bad enough--riding was fearful.

At every fresh declivity new scenes of deserted, melancholy districts were revealed to us; every thing was cold and dead, every where there was black burnt lava. It was a painful feeling to see so much, and behold nothing but a stony desert, an immeasurable chaos.

There were still two declivities before us,--the last, but the worst. We had to climb steep masses of lava, sharp and pointed, which covered the whole side of the mountain. I do not know how often I fell and cut my hands on the jagged points of the lava. It was a fearful journey!

The dazzling whiteness of the snow contrasted with the bright black lava beside it had an almost blinding effect. When crossing fields of snow I did not look at the lava; for having tried to do so once or twice, I could not see my way afterwards, and had nearly grown snow-blind.

After two hours' more labour we reached the summit of the mountain. I stood now on Mount Hecla, and eagerly sought the crater on the snowless top, but did not find it. I was the more surprised, as I had read detailed accounts of it in several descriptions of travel.

I traversed the whole summit of the mountain and climbed to the adjoining jokul, but did not perceive an opening, a fissure, a depressed space, nor any sign of a crater. Lower down in the sides of the mountain, but not in the real cone, I saw some clefts and fissures from which the streams of lava probably poured. The height of the mountain is said to be 4300 feet.

During the last hour of our ascent the sun had grown dim. Clouds of mist blown from the neighbouring glaciers enshrouded the hill-tops, and soon enveloped us so closely that we could scarcely see ten paces before us. At last they dissolved, fortunately not in rain but in snow, which profusely covered the black uneven lava. The snow remained on the ground, and the thermometer stood at one degree of cold.

In a little while the clear blue sky once more was visible, and the sun again shone over us. I remained on the top till the clouds had separated beneath us, and afforded me a better distant view over the country.

My pen is unfortunately too feeble to bring vividly before my readers the picture such as I beheld it here, and to describe to them the desolation, the extent and height of these lava-masses. I seemed to stand in a crater, and the whole country appeared only a burnt-out fire. Here lava was piled up in steep inaccessible mountains; there stony rivers, whose length and breadth seemed immeasurable, filled the once-verdant fields. Every thing was jumbled together, and yet the course of the last eruption could be distinctly traced.

I stood there, in the centre of horrible precipices, caves, streams, valleys, and mountains, and scarcely comprehended how it was possible to penetrate so far, and was overcome with terror at the thought which involuntarily obtruded itself--the possibility of never finding my way again out of these terrible labyrinths.

Here, from the top of Mount Hecla, I could see far into the uninhabited country, the picture of a petrified creation, dead and motionless, and yet magnificent,--a picture which once seen can never again fade from the memory, and which alone amply compensates for all the previous troubles and dangers. A whole world of glaciers, lava-mountains, snow and ice-fields, rivers and lakes, into which no human foot has ever ventured to penetrate. How nature must have laboured and raged till these forms were created! And is it over now? Has the destroying element exhausted itself; or does it only rest, like the hundred-headed Hydra, to break forth with renewed strength, and desolate those regions which, pushed to the verge of the sea-shore, encircle the sterile interior as a modest wreath? I thank God that he has permitted me to behold this chaos in his creation; but I thank him more heartily that he has placed me to dwell in regions where the sun does more than merely give light; where it inspires and fertilises animals and plants, and fills the human heart with joy and thankfulness towards its Creator. {43}

The Westmann Isles, which are said to be visible from the top of Hecla, I could not see; they were probably covered by clouds.

During the ascent of the Hecla I had frequently touched lava,--sometimes involuntarily, when I fell; sometimes voluntarily, to find a hot or at least a warm place. I was unfortunate enough only to find cold ones. The falling snow was therefore most welcome, and I looked anxiously around to see a place where the subterranean heat would melt it. I should then have hastened thither and found what I sought. But unfortunately the snow remained unmelted every where. I could neither see any clouds of smoke, although I gazed steadily at the mountain for hours, and could from my post survey it far down the sides.

As we descended we found the snow melting at a depth of 500 to 600 feet; lower down, the whole mountain smoked, which I thought was the consequence of the returning warmth of the sun, for my thermometer now stood at nine degrees of heat. I have noticed the same circumstance often on unvolcanic mountains. The spots from which the smoke rose were also cold.

The smooth jet-black, bright, and dense lava is only found on the mountain itself and in its immediate vicinity. But all lava is not the same: there is jagged, glassy, and porous lava; the former is black, and so is the sand which covers one side of Hecla. The farther the lava and sand are from the mountain, the more they lose this blackness, and their colour plays into iron-colour and even into light-grey; but the lighter-coloured lava generally retains the brightness and smoothness of the black lava.

After a troublesome descent, having spent twelve hours on this excursion, we arrived safely at Salsun; and I was on the point of returning to my lodging, somewhat annoyed at the prospect of spending another night in such a hole, when my guide surprised me agreeably by the proposition to return to Struvellir at once. The horses, he said, were sufficiently rested, and I could get a good room there in the priest's house. I soon packed, and in a short time we were again on horseback. The second time I came to the deep Rangaa, I rode across fearlessly, and needed no protection at any side. Such is man: danger only alarms him the first time; when he has safely surmounted it once, he scarcely thinks of it the second time, and wonders how he can have felt any fear.

I saw five little trees standing in a field near the stream. The stems of these, which, considering the scarcity of trees in Iceland, may be called remarkable phenomena, were crooked and knotty, but yet six or seven feet high, and about four or five inches in diameter.

As my guide had foretold, I found a very comfortable room and a good bed in the priest's house. Herr Horfuson is one of the best men I have ever met with. He eagerly sought opportunities for giving me pleasure, and to him I owe several fine minerals and an Icelandic book of the year 1601. May God reward his kindness and benevolence!

July 1st.

We retraced our steps as far as the river Huitha, over which we rowed, and then turned in another direction. Our journey led us through beautiful valleys, many of them producing abundance of grass; but unfortunately so much moss grew among it, that these large plains were not available for pastures, and only afforded comfort to travellers by their aspect of cheerfulness. They were quite dry.

The valley in which Hjalmholm, our resting-place for this night, was situated, is traversed by a stream of lava, which had, however, been modest enough not to fill up the whole valley, but to leave a space for the pretty stream Elvas, and for some fields and hillocks, on which many cottages stood. It was one of the most populous valleys I had seen in Iceland.

Hjalmholm is situated on a hill. In it lives the Sysselmann of the Rangaar district, in a large and beautiful house such as I saw no where in Iceland except in Reikjavik. He had gone to the capital of the island as member of the Allthing; but his daughters received me very hospitably and kindly.

We talked and chatted much; I tried to display my knowledge of the Danish language before them, and must often have made use of curious phrases, for the girls could not contain their laughter. But that did not abash me; I laughed with them, applied to my dictionary, which I carried with me, and chatted on. They seemed to gather no very high idea of the beauty of my countrywomen from my personal appearance; for which I humbly crave the forgiveness of my countrywomen, assuring them that no one regrets the fact more than I do. But dame Nature always treats people of my years very harshly, and sets a bad example to youth of the respect due to age. Instead of honouring us and giving us the preference, she patronises the young folks, and every maiden of sixteen can turn up her nose at us venerable matrons. Besides my natural disqualifications, the sharp air and the violent storms to which I had been subjected had disfigured my face very much. They had affected me more than the burning heat of the East. I was very brown, my lips were cracked, and my nose, alas, even began to rebel against its ugly colour. It seemed anxious to possess a new, dazzling white, tender skin, and was casting off the old one in little bits.

The only circumstance which reinstated me in the good opinion of the young girls was, that having brushed my hair unusually far out of my face, a white space became visible. The girls all cried out simultaneously, quite surprised and delighted: "Hun er quit" (she is white). I could not refrain from laughing, and bared my arm to prove to them that I did not belong to the Arab race.

A great surprise was destined me in this house; for, as I was ransacking the Sysselmann's book-case, I found Rotteck's Universal History, a German Lexicon, and several poems and writings of German poets.

July 2d.

The way from Kalmannstunga to Thingvalla leads over nothing but lava, and the one to-day went entirely through marshes. As soon as we had crossed one, another was before us. Lava seemed to form the soil here, for little portions of this mineral rose like islands out of the marshes.

The country already grew more open, and we gradually lost sight of the glaciers. The high mountains on the left seemed like hills in the distance, and the nearer ones were really hills. After riding about nine miles we crossed the large stream of Elvas in a boat, and then had to tread carefully across a very long, narrow bank, over a meadow which was quite under water. If a traveller had met us on this bank, I do not know what we should have done; to turn round would have been as dangerous as to sink into the morass. Fortunately one never meets any travellers in Iceland.

Beyond the dyke the road runs for some miles along the mountains and hills, which all consist of lava, and are of a very dark, nearly black colour. The stones on these hills were very loose; in the plain below many colossal pieces were lying, which must have fallen down; and many others threatened to fall every moment. We passed the dangerous spot safely, without having had to witness such a scene.

I often heard a hollow sound among these hills; I at first took it for distant thunder, and examined the horizon to discover the approaching storm. But when I saw neither clouds nor lightning, I perceived that I must seek the origin of the sounds nearer, and that they proceeded from the falling portions of rock.

The higher mountains to the left fade gradually more and more from view; but the river Elvas spreads in such a manner, and divides into so many branches, that one might mistake it for a lake with many islands. It flows into the neighbouring sea, whose expanse becomes visible after surmounting a few more small hills.

The vale of Reikum, which we now entered, is, like that of Reikholt, rich in hot springs, which are congregated partly in the plain, partly on or behind the hills, in a circumference of between two and three miles.

When we had reached the village of Reikum I sent my effects at once to the little church, took a guide, and proceeded to the boiling springs. I found very many, but only two remarkable ones; these, however, belong to the most noteworthy of their kind. The one is called the little Geyser, the other the Bogensprung.

The little Geyser has an inner basin of about three feet diameter. The water boils violently at a depth of from two to three feet, and remains within its bounds till it begins to spout, when it projects a beautiful voluminous steam of from 20 to 30 feet high.

At half-past eight in the evening I had the good fortune to see one of these eruptions, and needed not, as I had done at the great Geyser, to bivouac near it for days and nights. The eruption lasted some time, and was tolerably equable; only sometimes the column of water sank a little, to rise to its former height with re-newed force. After forty minutes it fell quite down into the basin again. The stones we threw in, it rejected at once, or in a few seconds, shivered into pieces, to a height of about 12 to 15 feet. Its bulk must have been 1 to 1.5 feet in diameter. My guide assured me that this spring generally plays only twice, rarely thrice, in twenty-four hours, and not, as I have seen it stated, every six minutes. I remained near it till midnight, but saw no other eruption.

This spring very much resembles the Strukker near the great Geyser, the only difference being that the water sinks much lower in the latter.

The second of the two remarkable springs, the arched spring, is situated near the little Geyser, on the declivity of a hill. I had never seen such a curious forma-tion for the bed of a spring as this is. It has no basin, but lies half open at your feet, in a little grotto, which is separated into various cavities and holes, and which is half-surrounded by a wall of rock bending over it slightly at a height of about 2 feet, and then rises 10 to 12 feet higher. This spring never is at rest more than a minute; then it begins to rise and boil quickly, and emits a voluminous column, which, striking against the projecting rock, is flattened by it, and rises thence like an arched fan. The height of this peculiarly-spread jet of water may be about 12 feet, the arch it describes 15 to 20 feet, and its breadth 3 to 8 feet. The time of eruption is often longer than that of repose. After an eruption the water always sinks a few feet into the cave, and for 15 or 20 seconds admits of a glance into this wonderful grotto. But it rises again immediately, fills the grotto and the basin, which is only a continua-tion of the grotto, and springs again.

I watched this miraculous play of nature for more than an hour, and could not tear myself from it. This spring, which is certainly the only one of its kind, gratified me much more than the little Geyser.

There is another spring called the roaring Geyser; but it is nothing more than a misshapen hole, in which one hears the water boil, but cannot see it. The noise is, also, not at all considerable.

July 3d.

Near Reikum we crossed a brook into which all the hot springs flow, and which has a pretty fall. We then ascended the adjoining mountain, and rode full two hours on the high plain. The plain itself was monotonous, as it was only covered with lava-stones and moss, but the prospect into the valley was varied and beautiful. Vale and sea were spread before me, and I saw the Westmann Islands, with their beautiful hills, which the envious clouds had concealed from me on the Hecla, lying in the distance. Below me stood some houses in the port-town, Eierbach, and near them the waters of the Elvas flow into the sea.

At the end of this mountain-level a valley was situated, which was also filled with lava, but with that jagged black lava which presents such a beautiful appearance. Immense streams crossed it from all sides, so that it almost resembled a black lake separated from the sea by a chain of equally black mountains.

We descended into this sombre vale through piles of lava and fields of snow, and went on through valleys and chasms, over fields of lava, plains of meadow-land, past dark mountains and hills, till we reached the chief station of my Icelandic journey, the town of Reikjavik.

The whole country between Reikum and Reikjavik, a distance of 45 to 50 miles, is, for the most part, uninhabited. Here and there, in the fields of lava, stand little pyramids of the same substance, which serve as landmarks; and there are two houses built for such persons as are obliged to travel during the winter. But we found much traffic on the road, and often overtook caravans of 15 to 20 horses. Being the beginning of August, it was the time of trade and traffic in Iceland. Then the country people travel to Reikjavik from considerable distances, to change their produce and manufactures, partly for money, partly for necessaries and luxuries. At this period the merchants and factors have not hands enough to barter the goods or close the accounts which the peasants wish to settle for the whole year.

At this season an unusual commotion reigns in Reikjavik. Numerous groups of men and horses fill the streets; goods are loaded and unloaded; friends who have not met for a year or more welcome each other, others take leave. On one spot curious tents {44} are erected, before which children play; on another drunken men stagger along, or gallop on horseback, so that one is terrified, and fears every moment to see them fall.

This unusual traffic unfortunately only lasts six or eight days. The peasant hastens home to his hay-harvest; the merchant must quickly regulate the produce and manufactures he has purchased, and load his ships with them, so that they may sail and reach their destination before the storms of the autumnal equinox.

	Miles.
From Reikjavik to Thingvalla is	45
From Thingvalla to the Geyser	36
From the Geyser to Skalholt	28
From Skalholt to Salsun	36
From Salsun to Struvellir	9
From Struvellir to Hjalmholm	28
From Hjalmholm to Reikum	32
From Reikum to Reikjavik	45
	259

CHAPTER VII

During my travels in Iceland I had of course the opportunity of becoming acquainted with its inhabitants, their manners and customs. I must confess that I had formed a higher estimate of the peasants. When we read in the history of that country that the first inhabitants had emigrated thither from civilised states; that they had brought knowledge and religion with them; when we hear of the simple good-hearted people, and their patriarchal mode of life in the accounts of former travellers, and which we know that nearly every peasant in Iceland can read and write, and that at least a Bible, but generally other religions books also, are found in every cot,--one feels inclined to consider this nation the best and most civilised in Europe. I deemed their morality sufficiently secured by the absence of foreign intercourse, by their isolated position, and the poverty of the country. No large town there affords opportunity for pomp or gaiety, or for the commission of smaller or greater sins. Rarely does a foreigner enter the island, whose remoteness, severe climate, inhospitality, and poverty, are uninviting. The grandeur and peculiarity of its natural formation alone makes it interesting, and that does not suffice for the masses.

I therefore expected to find Iceland a real Arcadia in regard to its inhabitants, and rejoiced at the anticipation of seeing such an Idyllic life realised. I felt so happy when I set foot on the island that I could have embraced humanity. But I was soon undeceived.

I have often been impatient at my want of enthusiasm, which must be great, as I see every thing in a more prosaic form than other travellers. I do not maintain that my view is *right*, but I at least possess the virtue of describing facts as I see them, and do not repeat them from the accounts of others.

I have already described the impoliteness and heartlessness of the so-called higher classes, and soon lost the good opinion I had formed of them. I now came to the working classes in the vicinity of Reikjavik. The saying often applied to the Swiss people, "No money, no Swiss," one may also apply to the Icelanders. And of this fact I can cite several examples.

Scarcely had they heard that I, a foreigner, had arrived, than they frequently came to me, and brought quite common objects, such as can be found any where in Iceland, and expected me to pay dearly for them. At first I purchased from charity, or to be rid of their importunities, and threw the things away again; but I was soon obliged to give this up, as I should else have been besieged from morning to night. Their anxiety to gain money without labour annoyed me less than the extortionate prices with which they tried to impose on a stranger. For a beetle, such as could be found under every stone, they asked 5 kr. (about 2d.); as much for a caterpillar, of which thousands were lying on the beach; and for a common bird's egg, 10 to 20 kr. (4d. to 8d.) Of course, when I declined buying, they reduced their demand, sometimes to less than half the original sum; but this was certainly not in consequence of their honesty. The baker in whose house I lodged also experienced the selfishness of these people. He had engaged a poor labourer to tar his house, who, when he had half finished his task, heard of other employment. He did not even take the trouble to ask the baker to excuse him for a few days; he went away, and did not return to finish the interrupted work for a whole week. This conduct was the more inexcusable as his children received bread, and even butter, twice a week from the baker.

I was fortunate enough to experience similar treatment. Herr Knudson had engaged a guide for me, with whom I was to take my departure in a few days. But it happened that the magistrate wished also to take a trip, and sent for my guide. The latter expected to be better paid by him, and went; he did not come to me to discharge himself, but merely sent me word on the eve of my departure, that he was ill, and could therefore not go with me. I could enumerate many more such examples, which do not much tend to give a high estimate of Icelandic morality.

I consoled myself with the hope of finding simplicity and honesty in the more retired districts, and therefore anticipated a twofold pleasure from my journey into the interior. I found many virtues, but unfortunately so many faults, that I am no longer inclined to exalt the Icelandic peasants as examples.

The best of their virtues is their honesty. I could leave my baggage unguarded any where for hours, and never missed the least article, for they did not even permit their children to touch any thing. In this point they are so conscientious, that if a peasant comes from a distance, and wishes to rest in a cottage, he never fails to knock at the door, even if it is open. If no one calls "come in," he does not enter. One might fearlessly sleep with open doors.

Crimes are of such rare occurrence here, that the prison of Reikjavik was changed into a dwelling-house for the chief warden many years since. Small crimes are punished summarily, either in Reikjavik or at the seat of the Sysselmann. Criminals of a deeper dye are sent to Copenhagen, and are sentenced and punished there.

My landlord at Reikjavik, the master-baker Bernhoft, told me that only one crime had been committed in Iceland during the thirteen years that he had resided there. This was the murder of an illegitimate child immediately after its birth. The most frequently occurring crime is cow-stealing.

I was much surprised to find that nearly all the Icelanders can read and write. The latter quality only was somewhat rarer with the women. Youths and men often wrote a firm, good hand. I also found books in every cottage, the Bible always, and frequently poems and stories, sometimes even in the Danish language.

They also comprehend very quickly; when I opened my map before them, they soon understood its use and application. Their quickness is doubly surprising, if we consider that every father instructs his own children, and sometimes the neighbouring orphans. This is of course only done in the winter; but as winter lasts eight months in Iceland, it is long enough.

There is only one school in the whole island, which originally was in Bessestadt, but has been removed to Reikjavik since 1846. In this school only youths who can read and write are received, and they are either educated for priests, and may complete their studies here, or for doctors, apothecaries, or judges, when they must complete their studies in Copenhagen.

Besides theology, geometry, geography, history, and several languages, such as Latin, Danish, and, since 1846, German and also French, are taught in the school of Reikjavik.

The chief occupation of the Icelandic peasants consists in fishing, which is most industriously pursued in February, March, and April. Then the inhabitants of the interior come to the coasting villages and hire themselves to the dwellers on the beach, the real fishermen, as assistants, taking a portion of the fish as their wages. Fishing is attended to at other times also, but then exclusively by the real fishermen. In the months of July and August many of the latter go into the interior and assist in the hay-harvest, for which they receive butter, sheep's wool, and salt lamb. Others ascend the mountains and gather the Iceland moss, of which they make a decoction, which they drink mixed with milk, or they grind it to flour, and bake flat cakes of it, which serve them in place of bread.

The work of the women consists in the preparation of the fish for drying, smoking, or salting; in tending the cattle, in knitting, sometimes in gathering moss. In winter both men and women knit and weave.

As regards the hospitality of the Icelanders, {45} I do not think one can give them so very much credit for it. It is true that priests and peasants gladly receive any European traveller, and treat him to every thing in their power; but they know well that the traveller who comes to their island is neither an adventurer nor a beggar, and will therefore pay them well. I did not meet one peasant or priest who did not accept the proffered gift without hesitation. But I must say of the priests that they were every where obliging and ready to serve me, and satisfied with the smallest gift; and their charges, when I required horses for my excursions, were always moderate. I only found the peasant less interested in districts where a traveller scarcely ever appeared; but in such places as were more visited, their charges were often exorbitant. For example, I had to pay 20 to 30 kr. (8d. to 1s.) for being ferried over a river; and then my guide and I only were rowed in the boat, and the horses had to swim. The guide who accompanied me on the Hecla also overcharged me; but he knew that I was forced to take him, as there is no choice of guides, and one does not give up the ascent for the sake of a little money.

This conduct shows that the character of the Icelanders does not belong to the best; and that they take advantage of travellers with as much shrewdness as the landlords and guides on the continent.

A besetting sin of the Icelanders is their drunkenness. Their poverty would probably not be so great if they were less devoted to brandy, and worked more industriously. It is dreadful to see what deep root this vice has taken. Not only on Sundays, but also on week-days, I met peasants who were so intoxicated that I was surprised how they could keep in their saddle. I am, however, happy to say that I never saw a woman in this degrading condition.

Another of their passions is snuff. They chew and snuff tobacco with the same infatuation as it is smoked in other countries. But their mode of taking it is very peculiar. Most of the peasants, and even many of the priests, have no proper snuff-box, but only a box turned of bone, shaped like a powder-flask. When they take snuff, they throw back their head, insert the point of the flask in their nose, and shake a dose of tobacco into it. They then, with the greatest amiability, offer it to their neighbour, he to his, and so it goes round till it reaches the owner again.

I think, indeed, that the Icelanders are second to no nation in uncleanliness; not even to the Greenlanders, Esquimaux, or Laplanders. If I were to describe a portion only of what I experienced, my readers would think me guilty of gross exaggeration; I prefer, therefore, to leave it to their imagination; merely saying that they cannot conceive any thing too dirty for Iceland delicacy.

Beside this very estimable quality, they are also insuperably lazy. Not far from the coast are immense meadows, so marshy that it is dangerous to cross them. The fault lies less in the soil than the people. If they would only make ditches, and thus dry the ground, they would have the most splendid grass. That this would grow abundantly is proved by the little elevations which rise from above the marshes, and which are thickly covered with grass, herbage, and wild clover. I also passed large districts covered with good soil, and some where the soil was mixed with sand.

I frequently debated with Herr Boge, who has lived in Iceland for forty years, and is well versed in farming matters, whether it would not be possible to produce important pasture-grounds and hay-fields with industry and perseverance. He agreed with me, and thought that even potato-fields might be reclaimed, if only the people were not so lazy, preferring to suffer hunger and resign all the comforts of cleanliness rather than to work. What nature voluntarily gives, they are satisfied with, and it never occurs to them to force more from her. If a few German peasants were transported hither, what a different appearance the country would soon have!

The best soil in Iceland is on the Norderland. There are a few potato-grounds there, and some little trees, which, without any cultivation, have reached a height of seven to eight feet. Herr Boge, established here for thirty years, had planted some mountain-ash and birch-trees, which had grown to a height of sixteen feet.

In the Norderland, and every where except on the coast, the people live by breeding cattle. Many a peasant there possesses from two to four hundred sheep, ten to fifteen cows, and ten to twelve horses. There are not many who are so rich, but at all events they are better off than the inhabitants of the sea-coast. The soil there is for the most part bad, and they are therefore nearly all compelled to have recourse to fishing.

Before quitting Iceland, I must relate a tradition told me by many Icelanders, not only by peasants, but also by people of the so-called higher classes, and who all implicitly believe it.

It is asserted that the inhospitable interior is likewise populated, but by a peculiar race of men, to whom alone the paths through these deserts are known. These savages have no intercourse with their fellow-countrymen during the whole year, and only come to one of the ports in the beginning of July, for one day at the utmost, to buy several necessaries, for which they pay in money. They then vanish suddenly, and no one knows in which direction they are gone. No one knows them; they never bring their wives or children with them, and never reply to the question whence they come. Their language, also, is said to be more difficult than that of the other inhabitants of Iceland.

One gentleman, whom I do not wish to name, expressed a wish to have the command of twenty to twenty-five well-armed soldiers, to search for these wild men.

The people who maintain that they have seen these children of nature, assert that they are taller and stronger than other Icelanders; that their horses' hoofs, instead of being shod earth iron, have shoes of horn; and that they have much money, which they can only have acquired by pillage. When I inquired what respectable inhabitants of Iceland had been robbed by these savages, and when and where, no one could give me an answer. For my part, I scarcely think that one man, certainly not a whole race, could live by pillage in Iceland.

DEPARTURE FROM ICELAND.--JOURNEY TO COPENHAGEN.

I had seen all there was to be seen in Iceland, had finished all my excursions, and awaited with inexpressible impatience the sailing of the vessel which was destined to bring me nearer my beloved home. But I had to stay four very long weeks in Reikjavik, my patience being more exhausted from day to day, and had after this long delay to be satisfied with the most wretched accommodation.

The delay was the more tantalising, as several ships left the port in the mean time, and Herr Knudson, with whom I had crossed over from Copenhagen, invited me to accompany him on his return; but all the vessels went to England or to Spain, and I did not wish to visit either of these countries. I was waiting for an opportunity to go to Scandinavia, to have at least a glance at these picturesque districts.

At last there were two sloops which intended to sail towards the end of July. The better of the two went to Altona; the destination of the other was Copenhagen. I had intended to travel in the former; but a merchant of Reikjavik had already engaged the only berth,--for there rarely is more than one in such a small vessel,--and I deemed myself lucky to obtain the one in the other ship. Herr Bernhoft thought, indeed, that the vessel might be too bad for such a long journey, and proposed to examine it, and report on its condition. But as I had quite determined to go to Denmark, I requested him to waive the examination, and agree with the captain about my passage. If, as I anticipated, he found the vessel too wretched, his warnings might have shaken my resolution, and I wished to avoid that contingency.

We heard, soon, that a young Danish girl, who had been in service in Iceland, wished to return by the same vessel. She had been suffering so much from homesickness, that she was determined, under any circumstances, to see her beloved fatherland again. If, thought I to myself, the home-sickness is powerful enough to make this girl indifferent to the danger, longing must take its place in my breast and effect the same result.

Our sloop bore the consolatory name of Haabet (hope), and belonged to the merchant Fromm, in Copenhagen.

Our departure had been fixed for the 26th of July, and after that day I scarcely dared to leave my house, being in constant expectation of a summons on board. Violent storms unfortunately prevented our departure, and I was not called till the 29th of July, when I had to bid farewell to Iceland.

This was comparatively easy. Although I had seen many wonderful views, many new and interesting natural phenomena, I yet longed for my accustomed fields, in which we do not find magnificent and overpowering scenes, but lovelier and more cheerful ones. The separation from Herr Knudson and the family of Bernhoft was more difficult. I owed all the kindness I had experienced in the island, every good advice and useful assistance in my travels, only to them. My gratitude to these kind and good people will not easily fade from my heart.

At noon I was already on board, and had leisure to admire all the gay flags and streamers with which the French frigate anchoring here had been decked, to celebrate the anniversary of the July revolution.

I endeavoured to turn my attention as much as possible to exterior objects, and not to look at our ship, for all that I had involuntarily seen had not impressed me very favourably. I determined also not to enter the cabin till we were in the open sea and the pilots had left our sloop, so that all possibility of return would be gone.

Our crew consisted of captain, steersman, two sailors, and a cabin-boy, who bore the title of cook; we added that of valet, as he was appointed to wait on us.

When the pilots had left us, I sought the entrance of the cabin,--the only, and therefore the common apartment. It consisted of a hole two feet broad, which gaped at my feet, and in which a perpendicular ladder of five steps was inserted. I stood before it puzzled to know which would be the best mode of descent, but knew no other way than to ask our host the captain. He shewed it me at once, by sitting at the entrance and letting his feet down. Let the reader imagine such a proceeding with our long dresses, and, above all, in bad weather, when the ship was pitched about by storms. But the thought that many other people are worse off, and can get on, was always the anchor of consolation to which I held; I argued with myself that I was made of the same stuff as other human beings, only spoiled and pampered, but that I could bear what they bore. In consequence of this self-arguing, I sat down at once, tried the new sliding-ladder, and arrived below in safety.

I had first to accustom my eyes to the darkness which reigned here, the hatches being constructed to admit the light very sparingly. I soon, however, saw too much; for all was raggedness, dirt, and disorder. But I will describe matters in the order in which they occurred to me; for, as I flatter myself that many of my countrywomen will in spirit make this journey with me, and as many of them probably never had the opportunity of being in such a vessel, I wish to describe it to them very accurately. All who are accustomed to the sea will testify that I have adhered strictly to the truth. But to return to the sloop. Its age emulated mine, she being a relic of the last century. At that time little regard was paid to the convenience of passengers, and the space was all made available for freight; a fact which cannot surprise us, as the seaman's life is passed on deck, and the ship was not built for travellers. The entire length of the cabin from one berth to the other was ten feet; the breadth was six feet. The latter space was made still narrower by a box on one side, and by a little table and two little seats on the other, so that only sufficient space remained to pass through.

At dinner or supper, the ladies--the Danish girl and myself--sat on the little benches, where we were so squeezed, that we could scarcely move; the two cavaliers--the captain and the steersman--were obliged to stand before the table, and eat their meals in that position. The table was so small that they were obliged to hold their plates in their hands. In short, every thing shewed the cabin was made only for the crew, not for the passengers.

The air in this enclosure was also not of the purest; for, besides that it formed our bed-room, dining-room, and drawing-room, it was also used as store-room, for in the side cupboards provisions of various kinds were stored, also oil-colours, and a variety of other matter. I preferred to sit on the deck, exposed to the cold and the storm, or to be bathed by a wave, than to be half stifled below. Sometimes, however, I was obliged to descend, either when rain and storms were too violent, or when the ship was so tossed by contrary winds that the deck was not safe. The rolling and pitching of our little vessel was often so terrible, that we ladies could neither sit nor stand, and were therefore obliged to lie down in the miserable berths for many a weary day. How I envied my companion! she could sleep day and night, which I could not. I was nearly always awake, much to my discomfort; for the hatches and the entrance were closed during the storm, and an Egyptian darkness, as well as a stifling atmosphere, filled the cabin.

In regard to food, all passengers, captain and crew, ate of the same dish. The morning meal consisted of miserable tea, or rather of nauseous water having the colour of tea. The sailors imbibed theirs without sugar, but the captain and the steersman took a small piece of candied sugar, which does not melt so quickly as the refined sugar, in their mouth, and poured down cup after cup of tea, and ate ship's biscuit and butter to it.

The dinner fare varied. The first day we had salt meat, which is soaked the evening before, and boiled the next day in sea-water. It was so salt, so hard, and so tough, that only a sailor's palate can possibly enjoy it. Instead of soup, vegetables, and pudding, we had pearl-barley boiled in water, without salt or butter; to which treacle and vinegar was added at the dinner-table. All the others considered this a delicacy, and marvelled at my depraved taste when I declared it to be unpalatable.

The second day brought a piece of bacon, boiled in sea-water, with the barley repeated. On the third we had cod-fish with peas. Although the latter were boiled hard and without butter, they were the most eatable of all the dishes. On the fourth day the bill of fare of the first was repeated, and the same course followed again. At the end of every dinner we had black coffee. The supper was like the breakfast,-- tea-water, ship's biscuit and butter.

I wished to have provided myself with some chickens, eggs, and potatoes in Reikjavik, but I could not obtain any of these luxuries. Very few chickens are kept- -only the higher officials or merchants have them; eggs of eider-ducks and other birds may often be had, but more are never collected than are wanted for the daily supply, and then only in spring; for potatoes the season was not advanced enough. My readers have now a picture of the luxurious life I led on board the ship. Had I been fortunate enough to voyage in a better vessel, where the passengers are more commodiously lodged and better fed, the seasickness would certainly not have at- tacked me; but in consequence of the stifling atmosphere of the cabin and the bad food, I suffered from it the first day. But on the second I was well again, regained my appetite, and ate salt meat, bacon, and peas as well as a sailor; the stockfish, the barley, and the coffee and tea, I left untouched.

A real sailor never drinks water; and this observation of mine was confirmed by our captain and steersman: instead of beer or wine, they took tea, and, except at meals, cold tea.

On Sunday evenings we had a grand supper, for the captain had eight eggs, which he had brought from Denmark, boiled for us four people. The crew had a few glasses of punch-essence mixed in their tea.

As my readers are now acquainted with the varied bill of fare in such a ship, I will say a few words of the table-linen. This consisted only of an old sailcloth, which was spread over the table, and looked so dirty and greasy that I thought it would be much better and more agreeable to leave the table uncovered. But I soon repented the unwise thought, and discovered how important this cloth was. One morning I saw our valet treating a piece of sailcloth quite outrageously: he had spread it upon the deck, stood upon it, and brushed it clean with the ship's broom. I recognised our tablecloth by the many spots of dirt and grease, and in the evening found the table bare. But what was the consequence? Scarcely had the tea-pot been placed on the table than it began to slip off; had not the watchful captain quickly caught it, it would have fallen to the ground and bathed our feet with its contents. Nothing could stand on the polished table, and I sincerely pitied the captain that he had not another tablecloth.

My readers will imagine that what I have described would have been quite sufficient to make my stay in the vessel any thing but agreeable; but I discovered another circumstance, which even made it alarming. This was nothing less than that our little vessel was constantly letting in a considerable quantity of water, which had to be pumped out every few hours. The captain tried to allay my uneasiness by asserting that every ship admitted water, and ours only leaked a little more because it was so old. I was obliged to be content with his explanation, as it was now too late to think of a change. Fortunately we did not meet with any storms, and therefore incurred less danger.

Our journey lasted twenty days, during twelve of which we saw no land; the wind drove us too far east to see the Feroe or the Shetland Isles. I should have cared less for this, had I seen some of the monsters of the deep instead, but we met with scarcely any of these amiable animals. I saw the ray of water which a whale emitted from his nostrils, and which exactly resembled a fountain; the animal itself was unfortunately too far from our ship for us to see its body. A shark came a little nearer; it swam round our vessel for a few moments, so that I could easily look at him: it must have been from sixteen to eighteen feet long.

The so-called flying-fish afforded a pretty sight. The sea was as calm as a mirror, the evening mild and moonlight; and so we remained on deck till late, watching the gambols of these animals. As far as we could see, the water was covered with them. We could recognise the younger fishes by their higher springs; they seemed to be three to four feet long, and rose five to six feet above the surface of the sea. Their leaping looked like an attempt at flying, but their gills did not do them good service in the trial, and they fell back immediately. The old fish did not seem to have the same elasticity; they only described a small arch like the dolphins, and only rose so far above the water that we could see the middle part of their body.

These fish are not caught; they have little oil, and an unpleasant taste.

On the thirteenth day we again saw land. We had entered the Skagerrak, and saw the peninsula of Jutland, with the town of Skaggen. The peninsula looks very dreary from this side; it is flat and covered with sand.

On the sixteenth day we entered the Cattegat. For some time past we had always either been becalmed or had had contrary winds, and had been tossed about in the Skagerrak, the Cattegat, and the Sound for nearly a week. On some days we scarcely made fifteen to twenty leagues a day. On such calm days I passed the time with fishing; but the fish were wise enough not to bite my hook. I was daily anticipating a dinner of mackerel, but caught only one.

The multitude of vessels sailing into the Cattegat afforded me more amusement; I counted above seventy. The nearer we approached the entrance of the Sound, the more imposing was the sight, and the more closely were the vessels crowded together. Fortunately we were favoured by a bright moonlight; in a dark or stormy night we should not with the greatest precaution and skill have been able to avoid a collision.

The inhabitants of more southern regions have no idea of the extraordinary clearness and brilliancy of a northern moonlight night; it seems almost as if the moon had borrowed a portion of the sun's lustre. I have seen splendid nights on the coast of Asia, on the Mediterranean; but here, on the shores of Scandinavia, they were lighter and brighter.

I remained on deck all night; for it pleased me to watch the forests of masts crowded together here, and endeavouring simultaneously to gain the entrance to the Sound. I should now be able to form a tolerable idea of a fleet, for this number of ships must surely resemble a merchant-fleet.

On the twentieth day of our journey we entered the port of Helsingor. The Sound dues have to be paid here, or, as the sailor calls it, the ship must be cleared. This is a very tedious interruption, and the stopping and restarting of the ship very incommodious. The sails have to be furled, the anchor cast, the boat lowered, and the captain proceeds on shore; hours sometimes elapse before he has finished. When he returns to the ship, the boat has to be hoisted again, the anchor raised, and the sails unfurled. Sometimes the wind has changed in the mean time; and in consequence of these formalities, the port of Copenhagen cannot be reached at the expected time.

If a ship is unfortunate enough to reach Helsingor on a dark night, she may not enter at all for fear of a collision. She has to anchor in the Cattegat, and thus suffer two interruptions. If she arrives at Helsingor in the night before four o'clock, she has to wait, as the custom-house is not opened till that time.

The skipper is, however, at liberty to proceed direct to Copenhagen, but this liberty costs five thalers (fifteen shillings). If, however, the toll may thus be paid in Copenhagen just as easily, the obligation to stop at Helsingor is only a trick to gain the higher toll; for if a captain is in haste, or the wind is too favourable to be lost, he forfeits the five thalers, and sails on to Copenhagen.

Our captain cared neither for time nor trouble; he cleared the ship here, and so we did not reach Copenhagen until two o'clock in the afternoon. After my long absence, it seemed so familiar, so beautiful and grand, as if I had seen nothing so beautiful in my whole life. My readers must bear in mind, however, where I came from, and how long I had been imprisoned in a vessel in which I scarcely had space to move. When I put foot on shore again, I could have imitated Columbus, and prostrated myself to kiss the earth.

DEPARTURE FROM COPENHAGEN.--CHRISTIANIA.

On the 19th August, the day after my arrival from Iceland, at two o'clock in the afternoon, I had already embarked again; this time in the fine royal Norwegian steamer *Christiania*, of 170 horsepower, bound for the town of Christiania, distant 304 sea-miles from Copenhagen. We had soon passed through the Sound and arrived safely in the Cattegat, in which we steered more to the right than on the journey to Iceland; for we not only intended to see Norway and Sweden, but to cast anchor on the coast.

We could plainly see the fine chain of mountains which bound the Cattegat on the right, and whose extreme point, the Kulm, runs into the sea like a long promontory. Lighthouses are erected here, and on the other numerous dangerous spots of the coast, and their lights shine all around in the dark night. Some of the lights are movable, and some stationary, and point out to the sailor which places to avoid.

August 20th.

Bad weather is one of the greatest torments of a traveller, and is more disagreeable when one passes through districts remarkable for beauty and originality. Both grievances were united to-day; it rained, almost incessantly; and yet the passage of the Swedish coast and of the little fiord to the port of Gottenburg was of peculiar interest. The sea here was more like a broad stream which is bounded by noble rocks, and interspersed by small and large rocks and shoals, over which the waters dashed finely. Near the harbour, some buildings lie partly on and partly between the rocks; these contain the celebrated royal Swedish iron-foundry, called the new foundry. Even numerous American ships were lying here to load this metal. {46}

The steamer remains more than four hours in the port of Gottenburg, and we had therefore time to go into the town, distant about two miles, and whose suburbs extend as far as the port. On the landing-quay a captain lives who has always a carriage and two horses ready to drive travellers into the town. There are also one-horse vehicles, and even an omnibus. The former were already engaged; the latter, we were told, drives so slowly, that nearly the whole time is lost on the road; so I and two travelling companions hired the captain's carriage. The rain poured in torrents on our heads; but this did not disturb us much. My two companions had business to transact, and curiosity attracted me. I did not at that time know that I should have occasion to visit this pretty little town again, and would not leave without seeing it.

The suburbs are built entirely of wood, and contain many pretty one-story houses, surrounded, for the most part, by little gardens. The situation of the suburbs is very peculiar. Rocks, or little fields and meadows, often lie between the houses; the rocks even now and then cross the streets, and had to be blasted to form a road. The view from one of the hills over which the road to the town lies is truly beautiful.

The town has two large squares: on the smaller one stands the large church; on the larger one the town-hall, the post-office, and many pretty houses. In the town every thing is built of bricks. The river Ham flows through the large square, and increases the traffic by the many ships and barks running into it from the sea, and bringing provisions, but principally fuel, to market. Several bridges cross it. A visit to the well-stocked fish-market is also an interesting feature in a short visit to this town.

I entered a Swedish house for the first time here. I remarked that the floor was strewed over with the fine points of the fir-trees, which had an agreeable odour, a more healthy one probably than any artificial perfume. I found this custom prevalent all over Sweden and Norway, but only in hotels and in the dwellings of the poorer classes.

About eleven o'clock in the forenoon we continued our journey. We steered safely through the many rocks and shoals, and soon reached the open sea again. We did not stand out far from the shore, and saw several telegraphs erected on the rocks. We soon lost sight of Denmark on the left, and arrived at the fortress Friedrichsver towards evening, but could not see much of it. Here the so-called Scheren begin, which extend sixty leagues, and form the Christian's Sound. By what I could see in the dim twilight, the scene was beautiful. Numerous islands, some merely consisting of bare rocks, others overgrown with slender pines, surrounded us on all sides. But our pilot understood his business perfectly, and steered us safely through to Sandesund, spite of the dark night. Here we anchored, for it would have been too dangerous to proceed. We had to wait here for the steamer from Bergen, which exchanged passengers with us. The sea was very rough, and this exchange was therefore extremely difficult to effect. Neither of the steamers would lower a boat; at last our steamer gave way, after midnight, and the terrified and wailing passengers were lowered into it. I pitied them from my heart, but fortunately no accident happened.

August 21st

I could see the situation of Sandesund better by day; and found it to consist only of a few houses. The water is so hemmed in here that it scarcely attains the breadth of a stream; but it soon widens again, and increases in beauty and variety with every yard. We seemed to ride on a beautiful lake; for the islands lie so close to the mountains in the background, that they look like a continent, and the bays they form like the mouths of rivers. The next moment the scene changes to a succession of lakes, one coming close on the other; and when the ship appears to be hemmed in, a new opening is suddenly presented to the eye behind another island. The islands themselves are of a most varied character: some only consist of bare rocks, with now and then a pine; some are richly covered with fields and groves; and the shore presents so many fine scenes, that one hardly knows where to look in order not to miss any of the beauties of the scenery. Here are high mountains overgrown from the bottom to the summit with dark pine-groves; there again lovely hills, with verdant meadows, fertile fields, pretty farmsteads and yards; and on another side the mountains separate and form a beautiful perspective of precipices and valleys. Sometimes I could follow the bend of a bay till it mingled with the distant clouds; at others we passed the most beautiful valleys, dotted with little villages and towns. I cannot describe the beauties of the scenery in adequate terms: my words are too weak, and my knowledge too insignificant; and I can only give an idea of my emotions, but not describe them.

Near Walloe the country grows less beautiful; the mountains decrease into hills, and the water is not studded with islands. The little town itself is almost concealed behind the hills. A remarkable feature is the long row of wooden huts and houses adjoining, which all belong to a salt-work established there.

We entered one of the many little arms of the sea to reach the town of Moss. Its situation is beautiful, being built amphi-theatrically on a hillock which leans against a high mountain. A fine building on the sea-shore, whose portico rests upon pillars, is used for a bathing institution.

A dock-yard, in which men-of-war are built at the expense of the state, is situated near the town of Horten, which is also picturesquely placed. There does not seem to be much work doing here, for I only saw one ship lying at anchor, and none on the stocks. About eight leagues beyond Horten a mountain rises in the middle of the sea, and divides it into two streams, uniting again beyond it, and forming a pretty view.

We did not see Christiania till we were only ten leagues from it. The town, the suburbs, the fortress, the newly-erected royal palace, the freemasons' lodge, &c., lie in a semicircle round the port, and are bounded by fields, meadows, woods, and hills, forming a delightful ***coup-d'oeil***. It seems as if the sea could not part from such a lovely view, and runs in narrow streams, through hills and plains, to a great distance beyond the town.

Towards eleven o'clock in the forenoon we reached the port of Christiania. We had come from Sandesund in seven hours, and had stopped four times on the way; but the boats with new-comers, with merchandise and letters, had always been ready, had been received, and we had proceeded without any considerable delay.

CHAPTER VIII

My first care on arriving in this town was to find a countrywoman of mine who had been married to a lawyer here. It is said of the Viennese that they cannot live away from their Stephen's steeple; but here was a proof of the contrary, for there are few couples living so happily as these friends, and yet they were nearly one thousand miles from St. Stephen's steeple. {47}

I passed through the whole town on the way from the quay to the hotel, and thence to my friend. The town is not large, and not very pretty. The newly-built portion is the best, for it at least has broad, tolerably long streets, in which the houses are of brick, and sometimes large. In the by-streets I frequently found wooden barracks ready to fall. The square is large, but irregular; and as it is used as a general market-place, it is also very dirty.

[Picture: Christiania]

In the suburbs the houses are mostly built of wood. There are some rather pretty public buildings; the finest among them are the royal castle and the fortress. They are built on little elevations, and afford a beautiful view. The old royal palace is in the town, but not at all distinguishable from a common private house. The house in which the Storthing {48} assembles is large, and its portico rests on pillars; but the steps are of wood, as in all stone houses in Scandinavia. The theatre seemed large enough for the population; but I did not enter it. The freemasons' lodge is one of the most beautiful buildings in the town; it contains two large saloons, which are used for assemblies or festivities of various kinds, besides serving as the meeting-place of the freemasons. The university seemed almost too richly built; it is not finished yet, but is so beautiful that it would be an ornament to the largest capital. The butchers' market is also very pretty. It is of a semi-circular shape, and is surrounded by arched passages, in which the buyers stand, sheltered from the weather. The whole edifice is built of bricks, left in their natural state, neither stuccoed with mortar nor whitewashed. There are not many other palaces or fine public buildings, and most of the houses are one-storied.

One of the features of the place--a custom which is of great use to the traveller, and prevails in all Scandinavian towns--is, that the names of the streets are affixed at every corner, so that the passer-by always knows where he is, without the necessity of asking his way.

Open canals run through the town; and on such nights as the almanac announces a full or bright moon the streets are not lighted.

Wooden quays surround the harbour, on which several large warehouses, likewise built of wood, are situated; but, like most of the houses, they are roofed with tiles.

The arrangement and display of the stores are simple, and the wares very beautiful, though not of home manufacture. Very few factories exist here, and every thing has to be imported.

I was much shocked at the raggedly-clad people I met every where in the streets; the young men especially looked very ragged. They rarely begged; but I should not have been pleased to meet them alone in a retired street.

I was fortunate enough to be in Christiania at the time when the Storthing was sitting. This takes place every three years; the sessions commence in January or February, and usually last three months; but so much business had this time accumulated, that the king proposed to extend the length of the session. To this fortunate accident I owed the pleasure of witnessing some of the meetings. The king was expected to close the proceedings in September. {49}

The hall of meeting is long and large. Four rows of tapestried seats, one rising above the other, run lengthways along the hall, and afford room for eighty legislators. Opposite the benches a table stands on a raised platform, and at this table the president and secretary sit. A gallery, which is open to the public, runs round the upper portion of the hall.

Although I understood but little of the Norwegian language, I attended the meetings daily for an hour. I could at least distinguish whether long or short speeches were made, or whether the orator spoke fluently. Unfortunately, the speakers I heard spoke the few words they mustered courage to deliver so slowly and hesitatingly, that I could not form a very favourable idea of Norwegian eloquence. I was told that the Storthing only contained three or four good speakers, and they did not display their talents during my stay.

I have never seen such a variety of carriages as I met with here. The commonest and most incommodious are called Carriols. A carriol consists of a narrow, long, open box, resting between two immensely high wheels, and provided with a very small seat. You are squeezed into this contrivance, and have to stretch your feet forward. You are then buckled in with a leather apron as high as the hips, and must remain in this position, without moving a limb, from the beginning to the end of your ride. A board is hung on behind the box for the coachman; and from this perch he, in a kneeling or standing position, directs the horses, unless the temporary resident of the box should prefer to take the reins himself. As it is very unpleasant to hear the quivering of the reins on one side and the smacking of the whip on the other, every one, men and women, can drive. Besides these carriols, there are phaetons, droschkas, but no closed vehicles.

The carts which are used for the transport of beer are of a very peculiar construction. The consumption of beer in Christiania is very great, and it is at once bottled when made, and not sold in casks. The carts for the transport of these bottles consist of roomy covered boxes a foot and a half high, which are divided into partitions like a cellaret, in which many bottles can be easily and safely transported from one part to another.

Another species of basket, which the servants use to carry such articles as are damp or dirty, and which my readers will excuse my describing, is made of fine white tin, and provided with a handle. Straw baskets are only used for bread, and for dry and clean provisions.

There are no public gardens or assemblies in Christiania, but numerous promenades; indeed, every road from the town leads to the most beautiful scenery, and every hill in the neighbourhood affords the most delightful prospects.

Ladegardoen is the only spot which is often resorted to by the citizens by carriage or on foot. It affords many and splendid views of the sea and its islands, of the surrounding mountains, valleys, and pine and fir groves. The majority of the country-houses are built here. They are generally small, but pretty, and surrounded by flower-gardens and orchards. While there, I seemed to be far in the south, so green and verdant was the scenery. The corn-fields alone betrayed the north. Not that the corn was poor; on the contrary, I found many ears bending to the ground under their weight; but now, towards the end of August, most of it was standing uncut in the fields.

Near the town stands a pine-grove, from which one has splendid views; two monuments are raised in it, but neither of them are of importance: one is raised to the memory of a crown-prince of Sweden, Christian Augustus; the other to Count Hermann Wenel Jarlsberg.

JOURNEY TO DELEMARKEN.

All I had hitherto seen in Norway had gratified me so much, that I could not resist the temptation of a journey to the wildly romantic regions of Delemarken. I was indeed told that it would be a difficult undertaking for a female, alone and almost entirely ignorant of the language, to make her way through the peasantry. But I found no one to accompany me, and was determined to go; so I trusted to fate, and went alone.

According to the inquires I had instituted in respect to this journey, I anticipated that my greatest difficulties would arise from the absence of all institutions for the speedy and comfortable progress of travellers. One is forced to possess a carriage, and to hire horses at every station. It is sometimes possible to hire a vehicle, but this generally consists only of a miserable peasant's cart. I hired, therefore, a carriol for the whole journey, and a horse to the next station, the townlet of Drammen, distant about twenty-four miles.

On the 25th August, at three o'clock in the afternoon, I left Christiania, squeezed myself into my carriage, and, following the example of Norwegian dames, I seized the reins. I drove as if I had been used to it from infancy. I turned right and left, and my horse galloped and trotted gaily on.

The road to Drammen is exquisite, and would afford rich subjects for an artist.

All the beauties of nature are here combined in most perfect harmony. The richness and variety of the scenery are almost oppressive, and would be an inexhaustible subject for the painter. The vegetation is much richer than I had hoped to find it so far north; every hill, every rock, is shaded by verdant foliage; the green of the meadows was of incomparable freshness; the grass was intermingled with flowers and herbs, and the corn-fields bent under their golden weight.

I have been in many countries, and have seen beautiful districts; I have been in Switzerland, in Tyrol, in Italy, and in Salzburg; but I never saw such peculiarly beautiful scenery as I found here: the sea every where intruding and following us to Drammen; here forming a lovely lake on which boats were rocking, there a stream rushing through hills and meadows; and then again, the splendid expanse dotted with proud three-masters and with countless islets. After a five hours' ride through rich valleys and splendid groves, I reached the town of Drammen, which lies on the shores of the sea and the river Storri Elf, and whose vicinity was announced by the beautiful country-houses ornamenting the approach to it.

A long, well-built wooden bridge, furnished with beautiful iron palisadings, leads over the river. The town of Drammen has pretty streets and houses, and above 6000 inhabitants. The hotel where I lodged was pretty and clean. My bedroom was a large room, with which the most fastidious might have been contented. The supper which they provided for me was, however, most frugal, consisting only of soft-boiled eggs. They gave me neither salt nor bread with them, nor a spoon; nothing but a knife and fork. And it is a mystery to me how soft eggs can be eaten without bread, and with a knife and fork.

August 25th.

I hired a fresh horse here, with which I proceeded to Kongsberg, eighteen miles farther. The first seven miles afforded a repetition of the romantic scenery of the previous day, with the exception of the sea. But instead I had the beautiful river, until I had ascended a hill, from whose summit I overlooked a large and apparently populous valley, filled with groups of houses and single farms. It is strange that there are very few large towns in Norway; every peasant builds his house in the midst of his fields.

Beyond this hill the scenery grows more monotonous. The mountains are lower, the valley narrower, and the road is enclosed by wood or rocks. One peculiarity of Norwegian rocks is their humidity. The water penetrates through countless fissures, but only in such small quantities as to cover the stones with a kind of veil. When the sun shines on these wet surfaces of rock, of which there are many and large ones, they shine like mirrors.

Delemarken seems to be tolerably populous. I often met with solitary peasant-huts in the large gloomy forests, and they gave some life to the monotonous landscape. The industry of the Norwegian peasant is very great; for every spot of earth, even on the steepest precipices, bore potatoes, barley, or oats; their houses also look cheerful, and were painted for the most part of a brick-red colour.

I found the roads very good, especially the one from Christiania to Drammen; and the one from Drammen to Kongsberg was not very objectionable. There is such an abundance of wood in Norway, that the streets on each side are fenced by wooden enclosures; and every field and meadow is similarly protected against the intrusion of cattle, and the miserable roads through the woods are even covered with round trunks of trees.

The peasantry in this district have no peculiar costume; only the head-covering of the females is curious. They wear a lady's hat, such as was fashionable in the last century, ornamented with a bunch behind, and with an immense shade in front. They are made of any material, generally of the remains of old garments; and only on Sundays better ones, and sometimes even silk ones, make their appearance.

In the neighbourhood of Kongsberg this head-dress is no longer worn. There they wear little caps like the Suabian peasantry, petticoats commencing under the shoulders, and very short spencers: a very ugly costume, the whole figure being spoilt by the short waist.

The town of Kongsberg is rather extended, and is beautifully situated on a hill in the centre of a splendid wooded valley. It is, like all the towns in Norway except Christiania, built of wood; but it has many pretty, neat houses and some broad streets.

The stream Storri Elf flows past the town, and forms a small but very picturesque waterfall a little below the bridge. What pleased me most was the colour of the water as it surged over the rock. It was about noon as I drove across the bridge; the sun illuminated the whole country around, and the waves breaking against the rocks seemed by this light of a beautiful pale-yellow colour, so that they resembled thick masses of pure transparent amber.

Two remarkable sights claimed my attention at Kongsberg,--a rich silver-mine, and a splendid waterfall called the Labrafoss. But as my time was limited and I could only remain a few hours in Kongsberg, I preferred to see the waterfall and believe the accounts of the silver-mine; which were, that the deepest shaft was eight hundred feet below the surface, and that it was most difficult to remain there, as the cold, the smoke, and the powder-smell had a very noxious effect on the traveller accustomed to light and air.

I therefore hired a horse and drove to the fall, which is situated in a narrow pass about four miles from Kongsberg. The river collects in a quiet calm basin a little distance above the fall, and then rushes over the steep precipice with a sudden bound. The considerable depth of the fall and the quality of water make it a very imposing sight. This is increased by a gigantic rock planted like a wall in the lower basin, and opposing its body to the progress of the hurrying waters. The waves rebound from the rock, and, collecting in mighty masses, rush over it, forming several smaller waterfalls in their course.

I watched it from a high rock, and was nevertheless covered by the spray to such a degree, that I sometimes could scarcely open my eyes. My guide then took me to the lower part of the fall, so that I might have a view of it from all sides; and each view seemed different and more splendid. I perceived the same yellow transparent colour which I had remarked in the fall at Kongsberg in the waters which dashed over the rock and were illuminated by the sun. I imagine it arises from the rock, which is every where of a brownish-red colour, for the water itself was clear and pure.

At four o'clock in the afternoon I left Kongsberg, and drove to Bolkesoe, a distance of eighteen miles. It was by no means a beautiful or an agreeable drive; for the road was very bad, and took me through passes and valleys, across woods and over steep mountains, while the night was dark and unilluminated by the moon. The thought involuntarily entered my mind, how easily my guide, who sat close behind me on the vehicle, could put me out of the world by a gentle blow, and take possession of my effects. But I had confidence in the upright character of the Norwegians, and drove on quietly, devoting my attention entirely to the reins of my little steed, which I had to lead with a sure hand over hill and valley, over ruts and stones, and along precipices. I heard no sound but the rushing of the mountain-river, which leaped, close beside us, over the rocks, and was heard rushing in the far distance.

We did not arrive at Bolkesoe until ten o'clock at night. When we stopped before an insignificant-looking peasant's cot, and I remembered my Icelandic night-accommodations, whose exterior this resembled, my courage failed me; but I was agreeably disappointed when the peasant's wife led me up a broad staircase into a large clean chamber furnished with several good beds, some benches, a table, a box, and an iron stove. I found equal comforts on all the stations of my journey.

There are no proper hotels or posthouses on the little-frequented Norwegian roads; but the wealthy peasants undertake the duties of both. I would, however, advise every traveller to provide himself with bread and other provisions for the trip; for his peasant-host rarely can furnish him with these. His cows are on the hills during the summer; fowls are far too great a luxury for him; and his bread is scarcely eatable: it consists of large round cakes, scarcely half an inch thick, and very hard; or of equally large cakes scarcely as thick as a knife, and quite dry. The only eatables I found were fish and potatoes; and whenever I could stay for several hours, they fetched milk for me from the hills.

The travelling conveniences are still more unattainable; but these I will mention in a future chapter, when my experience will be a little more extensive.

August 26th.

I could not see the situation of the town of Bolkesoe till daylight to-day, for when I arrived the darkness of night concealed it. It is situated in a pretty wooded vale, on a little hill at whose foot lies a beautiful lake of the same name.

The road from here to Tindosoe, about sixteen miles, is not practicable for vehicles, and I therefore left my carriol here and proceeded on horseback. The country grows more quiet and uninhabited, and the valleys become real chasms. Two lakes of considerable size form an agreeable variety to the wildness of the scenery. The larger one, called the Foelsoe, is of a regular form, and above two miles in diameter; it is encircled by picturesque mountains. The effect of the shadows which the pine-covered mountain-tops throw on the lakes is particularly attractive. I rode along its shores for more than an hour, and had leisure to see and examine every thing very accurately, for the horses here travel at a very slow pace. The reason of this is partly that the guide has no horse, and walks beside you in a very sleepy manner; the horse knows its master's peculiarities by long experience, and is only too willing to encourage him in his slow, dull pace. I spent more than five hours in reaching Tindosoe. My next object of interest was the celebrated waterfall of Rykanfoss, to reach which we had to cross a large lake. Although it had rained incessantly for an hour, and the sky looked threatening, I at once hired a boat with two rowers to continue my journey without interruption; for I anticipated a storm, and then I should not have found a boatman who would have ventured a voyage of four or five hours on this dangerous lake. In two hours my boat was ready, and I started in the pouring rain, but rejoiced at least at the absence of fog, which would have concealed the beauties of nature which surrounded me. The lake is eighteen miles long, but in many parts only from two to three miles wide. It is surrounded by mountains, which rise in terraces without the least gap to admit a distant view. As the mountains are nearly all covered with dark fir-groves, and overshadow the whole breadth of the narrow lake, the water seems quite dark, and almost black. This lake is dangerous to navigate on account of the many rocks rising perpendicularly out of the water, which, in a storm, shatter a boat dashed against them to pieces, and the passengers would find an inevitable grave in the deep waters. We had a flesh and a favourable breeze, which blew us quickly to our destination. One of the rocks on the coast has a very loud echo.

An island about a mile long divides the lake into equal parts; and when we had passed it, the landscape became quite peculiar. The mountains seemed to push before each other, and try whose foot should extend farthest into the sea. This forms numerous lovely bays; but few of them are adapted for landing, as the dangerous rocks seem to project every where.

The little dots of field and meadow which seem to hang against the rock, and the modest cottages of the peasants, which are built on the points of the most dangerous precipices, and over which rocks and stones tower as mountains, present a very curious appearance. The most fearful rocks hang over the huts, and threaten to crush them by falling, which would inevitably carry cottage and field with them into the sea. It is difficult to say whether the boldness or the stupidity of the peasants induces them to choose such localities for their dwellings.

From the mountains many rivers flow into the lake, and form beautiful falls.

This might only have been the case at that time, because it was raining incessantly, and the water poured down from all sides, so that the mountains seemed embroidered with silver threads. It was a beautiful sight; but I would willingly have relinquished it for a day of sunshine. It is no trifle to be exposed to such a shower-bath from morning till night; I was wet through, and had no hope for better weather, as the sky was clouded all round. My perseverance was nearly exhausted; and I was on the point of relinquishing the purpose of my journey,--the sight of the highest Norwegian waterfall,--when it occurred to me that the bad weather was most favourable for my plan, as each drop of water would increase the splendour of the waterfall.

After three hours and a half's rowing we reached Haukaness-am-See, where it is usual to stop a night as there is a pretty farm here, and the distance from the fall is still considerable.

August 27th.

My first care in the morning was the weather; it was unchanged, and the experienced peasants prophesied that it would remain wet. As I would not return nor wait for better weather, I could only take to my boat again, put on my half-dried cloak, and row on boldly.

The termination of the lake, which we soon reached, was already sufficient to compensate for my perseverance. A high mountain advances into the lake, and divides it into two beautiful bays. We entered the left bay, and landed at Mael, which lies at the mouth of the river Rykaness. The distance from Haukaness is a little more than two miles. I had to mount a horse to reach the waterfall, which was yet eleven miles distant. The road runs through a narrow valley, which gradually narrows still more until it can only contain the river; and the traveller is obliged to ascend the heights and grope on along the sides of the mountains. Below in the vale he sees the foam of the waves surging against the rocks; they flow like a narrow band of silver in the deep chasm. Sometimes the path is so high that one neither sees nor hears the river. The last half mile has to be journeyed on foot, and goes past spots which are really dangerous; numerous waterfalls rush from the mountain-sides, and have to be crossed on paths of tree-trunks laid alongside each other; and roads scarcely a foot wide lead along giddy precipices. But the traveller may trust unhesitatingly to his guide's arm, who has hitherto led every one in safety to his destination.

The road from Haukaness to the waterfall must be the finest that can be imagined on a bright sunny day; for I was enchanted with the wildly-romantic scenery in spite of the incessant rain and my wet clothes, and would on no consideration have missed this sight. Unfortunately the bad weather increased, and thick fogs rolled down into the valleys. The water flowed down from the mountains, and transformed our narrow path into a brook, through which we had to wade ankle-deep in water. At last we reached the spot which afforded the best view of the fall. It was yet free from mist, and I could still admire the extraordinary beauty of the fall and its quantity of water. I saw the immense mountain-rock which closes the valley, the tremendous pillar of water which dashes over it, and rebounds from the rock projecting in the centre of the fall, filling the whole valley with clouds of spray, and concealing the depth to which it descends. I saw this, one of the rarest and of the most magnificent of natural beauties; but alas, I saw it only for a moment, and had scarcely time to recover from the surprise of the first view when I lost it for ever! I was not destined to see the single grandeurs of the fall and of the surrounding scenery, and was fain to be content with one look, one glance. Impenetrable mists rolled from all sides into the wild glen, and shrouded every thing in complete darkness; I sat on a piece of rock, and gazed for two hours stedfastly at the spot where a faint outline of the fall was scarcely distinguishable through the mist sometimes this faint trace even was lost, and I could perceive its vicinity only by the dreadful sounds of the fall, and by the trembling of the rock beneath my feet.

After I had gazed, and hoped, and raised my eyes entreatingly to heaven for a single ray of sunshine, all in vain, I had at last to determine on my return. I left my post almost with tears in my eyes, and turned my head more backwards than forwards as we left the spot. At the least indication of a clearing away of the fog I should have returned.

But I retired farther and farther from it till I reached Mael again, where I sadly entered my boat, and proceeded uninterruptedly to Tindosoe. I arrived there towards ten o'clock at night. The wet, the cold, the want of food, and, above all, the depressed and disappointed state of my mind, had so affected me, that I went to bed with a slight attack of fever, and feared that I should not be able to continue my journey on the following day. But my strong constitution triumphed over every thing, and at five o'clock in the morning I was ready to continue my journey to

Bolkesoe on horseback.

I was obliged to hurry for fear of missing the departure of the steamer from Christiania. The journey to Delemarken had been represented to me as much shorter than I found it in reality; for the constant waiting for horses, boats, guides, &c. takes up very much time.

August 28th.

I had ordered my horse to be ready at five o'clock, but was obliged to wait for it until seven o'clock.

Although I made only a short trip into the interior, I had sufficient opportunities for experiencing the extortions and inconveniences to which a traveller is liable in Norway. No country in Europe is so much in its infancy as regards all conveniences for locomotion. It is true that horses, carriages, boats, &c. can be had at every station, and the law has fixed the price of these commodities; but every thing is in the hands of the peasants and the publicans, and they are so skilled in tormenting the traveller by their intentional slowness, that he is compelled to pay the two-fold tax, in order to proceed a little more quickly. The stations are short, being rarely above five or six miles, and one is therefore constantly changing horses. Arrived at a station, it either happens that there is really no horse to be had, or that this is an ostensible excuse. The traveller is told that the horse has to be fetched from the mountain, and that he can be served in one and a half or two hours. Thus he rides one hour, and waits two. It is also necessary to keep the tariff, as every trifle, the saddle, the carriage, the harness, fetching the horse, the boat, &c., has to be paid for extra; and when the traveller does not know the fixed prices, he is certain to be dreadfully imposed upon. At every station a book lies, containing the legal prices; but it is written in the language of the district, and utterly unintelligible to the stranger. Into this book, which is examined by the judge of the district every month, one may enter complaints against the peasant or publican; but they do not seem to fear it, for the guide who accompanied me to the fall of Rykanfoss endeavoured to cheat me twice in the most barefaced manner, by charging me six-fold for the use of the saddles and the fetching of the horse. When I threatened to inscribe my complaint in the book, he seemed not to care, and insisted on his demand, till I was obliged to pay him. On my return to Mael, I kept my word, asked for the book, and entered my complaint, although I was alone with all the peasants. It was not so much the money which annoyed me, as the shameless imposition. I am of opinion that every one should complain when he is wronged; if it does not benefit him, it will make the matter more easy for his successor.

I must confess, in justice to the peasants, that they were very indignant when I told them of the dishonesty of their countryman, and did not attempt to prevent my complaint.

To conclude my journey, I need only remark that, although the rain had ceased, the sky was still covered with clouds, and the country shrouded in mist. I therefore took the shorter road to Christiania, by which I had come, although I thereby missed a beautiful district, where I should, as I was told, have seen the most splendid perspective views in Norway. This would have been on the road from Kongsberg over Kroxleben to Christiania. The finest part is near Kroxleben.

But the time was too short to take this round, and I returned by way of Drammen. In the village of Muni, about five miles from Kongsberg, where I arrived at seven o'clock in the evening, the amiable host wished to keep me waiting again two hours for a horse; and as this would probably have happened at every station, I was obliged to hire a horse for the whole distance to Christiania, at a threefold price. I slept here for a few hours, left in the night at one o'clock, and arrived at Christiania the following afternoon at two.

On this journey I found all those people very kind and obliging with whom I came into no sort of pecuniary relation; but the hosts, the boatmen, the drivers, the guides, were as selfish and grasping as in any other country. I believe that kindness and disinterestedness would only be found in any district by him who has the good fortune to be the first traveller.

This little excursion was very dear; and yet I think I could now travel cheaply even in this country, universally acknowledged to be dear. I would go with the steamer along the coast to Hammerfest, buy a little vehicle and a good horse there, and then travel pleasantly, and without annoyance, through the whole country. But for a family who wished to travel in a comfortable covered carriage, it would be incalculably dear, and in many parts impossible, on account of the bad roads.

The Norwegian peasantry are strong and robust, but their features are not the most comely, and they seemed neither wealthy nor cleanly. They were generally very poorly clad, and always barefooted. Their cottages, built of wood and covered with tiles, are more roomy than those of the Icelanders; but they are nevertheless dirty and wretched. A weakness of the Norwegians is their fondness for coffee, which they drink without milk or sugar. The old women, as well as the men, smoke their pipes morning and night.

	Miles.
From Christiania to Kongsberg is about	41
From Kongsberg to the waterfall Labrafoss	5
From Kongsberg to Bolkosoe	14
From Bolkosoe to Tindosoe	16
From Tindosoe across the lake to Mael	16
From Mael to the waterfall Rykanfoss	11
	103

CHAPTER IX

August 30th.

At seven o'clock this morning I left Christiania, accompanied by the good wishes of my countrywoman and her husband, and went back to Gottenburg by the same steamer which had brought me thence ten days before. I need only mention the splendid view of a portion of Christian's Sound--also called Fiord--which I lost on the former journey from the darkness of the night. We passed it in the afternoon. The situation of the little town of Lauervig is superb. It is built on a natural terrace, bordered in the background by beautiful mountains. In front, the fortress of Friedrichsver lies on a mountain surrounded by rocks, on which little watch-towers are erected; to the left lies the vast expanse of sea.

We were delayed an hour at Friedrichsver to transfer the travellers for Bergen {50} to a vessel waiting for them, as we had stopped on our previous journey at

Sandesund for the same purpose.

This is the last view in the fiord; for now we steered into the open sea, and in a few hours we had lost sight of land. We saw nothing but land and water till we arrived the next morning at the Scheren, and steered for Gottenburg.

August 31st.

The sea had been rough all night, and we therefore reached Gottenburg three hours later than usual. In this agitated sea, the surging of the breakers against the many rocks and islets near Gottenburg has a very curious effect.

The few travellers who could keep on their feet, who did not suffer from sea-sickness, and remained on deck, spoke much of the dangerous storm. I had frequently marvelled to hear people who had made a journey, if it were even only a short one of forty to sixty leagues, relate of some fearful storm they had witnessed. Now I comprehended the reason, when I heard the travellers beside me call the brisk breeze, which only occasioned what seamen call a little swell, a dreadful storm; and they will probably tell at home of the dangers they have passed. Storms are, fortunately, not so frequent. I have travelled many thousand leagues, and have often met with stormy weather, especially on the passage from Copenhagen to Iceland; but I only experienced one real storm, but a violent and dangerous one, as I was crossing the Black Sea to Constantinople in April 1842.

We arrived at Gottenburg at nine instead of at six o'clock in the morning. I landed at once, to make the celebrated trip through the locks, over the waterfalls of Trollhatta, with the next Stockholm steamer. By the junction of the river Gotha with some of the interior lakes, this great construction crosses the whole country, and connects the North Sea with the Baltic.

I found the town of Gottenburg very animated, on account of the presence of the king of Sweden, who was spending a few days here on his way to Christiania to prorogue the Storthing. I arrived on a Sunday, and the king, with his son, were in the church. The streets swarmed with human beings, all crowding towards the cathedral to catch a glimpse of his majesty on his departure. I, of course, mingled with the crowd, and was fortunate enough to see the king and prince come out of the church, enter their carriage, and drive away very near to me. Both were handsome, amiable-looking men. The people rushed after the carriage, and eagerly caught the friendly bows of the intelligent father and his hopeful son; they followed him to his palace, and stationed themselves in front of it, impatiently longing for the moment when the royal pair would appear at a window.

I could not have arrived at a more favourable time; for every one was in holiday attire, and the military, the clergy, the officials, citizens and people, were all exerting themselves to the utmost to do honour to their king.

I noticed two peasant-girls among the crowd who were peculiarly dressed. They wore black petticoats reaching half way down the calf of the leg, red stockings, red spensers, and white chemises, with long white sleeves; a kerchief was tied round the head. Some of the citizens' wives wore caps like the Suabian caps, covered by a little black, embroidered veil, which, however, left the face free.

Here, as in Copenhagen, I noticed boys of ten to twelve years of age among the drummers, and in the bands of the military.

The king remained this day and the next in Gottenburg, and continued his journey on the Tuesday. On the two evenings of his stay the windows in the town were ornamented with wreaths of fresh flowers, interspersed with lighted tapers. Some houses displayed transparencies, which, however, did not place the inventive powers of the amiable Gottenburgers in a very favourable light. They were all alike, consisting of a tremendous O (Oscar), surmounted by a royal crown.

I was detained four days in Gottenburg; and small consideration seems to be paid to the speedy transport of travellers in Sweden. The steamer for Stockholm started on the day I arrived from Christiania, but unfortunately at five o'clock in the morning; and as in the month of September only two steamers go in the week to Stockholm, I was compelled to wait till Thursday. The time hung heavily on my hands; for I had seen the town itself, and the splendid views on the hills between the suburbs, during my former visit to the town, and the other portions only consisted of bare rocks and cliffs, which were of no interest.

September 4th.

The press of travellers was so great this time, that two days before the departure the cabins were all engaged; several ladies and gentlemen who would not wait for the next steamer were compelled to be satisfied with the deck, and I was among them; for the probability of such a crowd of passengers had not occurred to me, and I applied for a place only two days before our departure. During the journey fresh passengers were taken in at every station, and the reader may conceive the misery of the poor citizens unused to such hardships. Every one sought a shelter for the night, and the little cabins of the engineer and steersman were given up to some, while others crept into the passages, or squatted down on the steps of the stairs leading to the cabins. A place was offered to me in the engineer's cabin; but as three or four other persons were to share the apartment calculated only for one person, I preferred to bivouac night and day upon deck. One of the gentlemen was kind enough to lend me a thick cloak, in which I could wrap myself; and so I slept much more comfortably under the high canopy of heaven than my companions did in their sweating-room.

The arrangements in the vessels navigating the Gotha canal are by no means the best. The first class is very comfortable, and the cabin-place is divided into pretty light divisions for two persons; but the second class is all the more uncomfortable: its cabin is used for a common dining-room by day, and by night hammocks are slung up in it for sleeping accommodation. The arrangements for the luggage are worse still. The canal-boats, having only a very small hold, trunks, boxes, portmanteaus, &c. are heaped up on the deck, not fastened at all, and very insufficiently protected against rain. The consequence of this carelessness on a journey of five or six days was, that the rain and the high waves of the lakes frequently put the after-deck several inches under water, and then the luggage was wetted through. It was worse still in a squall on the Wenner lake; for while the ship was rather roughly tossed about, many a trunk lost its equilibrium and fell from its high position, frequently endangering the safety of the passengers' heads. The fares are, however, very cheap, which seemed doubly strange, as the many locks must cause considerable expense.

And now for the journey itself. We started at five o'clock in the morning, and soon arrived in the river Gotha, whose shores for the first few miles are flat and bare. The valley itself is bounded by bare, rocky hills. After about nine miles we came to the town of Kongelf, which is said to have 1000 inhabitants. It is so situated among rocks, that it is almost hidden from view. On a rock opposite the town are the ruins of the fortress Bogus. Now the scenery begins to be a little more diversified, and forests are mingled with the bleak rocks; little valleys appear on both the shores; and the river itself, here divided by an islet, frequently expands to a considerable breadth. The peasants' cottages were larger and better than those in Norway; they are generally painted brick-red, and are often built in groups.

The first lock is at Lilla Edet: there are five here; and while the ship passes through them, the passengers have leisure to admire the contiguous low, but broad and voluminous fall of the Gotha.

This first batch of locks in the canal extends over some distance past the fall, and they are partly blasted out of the rock, or built of stone. The river past Akestron flows as through a beautiful park; the valley is hemmed in by fertile hills, and leaves space only for the stream and some picturesque paths winding along its shores, and through the pine-groves descending to its banks.

In the afternoon we arrived at the celebrated locks near Trollhatta. They are of gigantic construction, which the largest states would be honoured in completing, and which occasion surprise when found in a country ranking high neither in extent nor in influence. There are eleven locks here, which rise 112 feet in a space of 3500 feet. They are broad, deep, blasted out of the rock, and walled round with fine freestone. They resemble the single steps of a giant's staircase; and by this name they might fitly rank as one of the wonders of the world. Lock succeeds lock, mighty gates close them, and the large vessel rises miraculously to the giddy heights in a wildly romantic country.

Scarcely arrived at the locks, the traveller is surrounded by a crowd of boys, who offer their services as guides to the waterfalls near Trollhatta. There is abundance of time for this excursion; for the passage of the ship through the many locks occupies three to four hours, and the excursion can be made in half the time. Before starting, it is, however, advisable to climb the rock to which the locks ascend. A pavilion is erected on its summit, and the view from it down over all the locks is exceedingly fine.

Pretty paths hewn out of the wood lead to Trollhatta, which is charmingly situated in a lovely valley, surrounded by woods and hills, on the shore of a river, whose white foaming waves contrast strongly with the dark foliage of the overshadowing groves. The canal, which describes a large semicircle round the chief stream, glitters in the distance; but the highest locks are quite concealed behind rocks; we could neither observe the opening of the gates nor the rising of the water in them, and were therefore surprised when suddenly the masts and then the ship itself rose from the depth. An invisible hand seemed to raise it up between the rocks.

The falls of the river are less distinguished for their height than for their diversity and their volumes of water. The principal arm of the river is divided at the point of decline into two equal falls by a little island of rock. A long narrow suspension-bridge leads to this island, and hangs over the fall; but it is such a weak, frail construction, that one person only can cross it at a time. The owner of this dangerous path keeps it private, and imposes a toll of about 3.5d. on all passengers.

A peculiar sensation oppresses the traveller crossing the slender path. He sees the stream tearing onwards, breaking itself on the projecting rock, and fall surging into the abyss; he sees the boiling waves beneath, and feels the bridge vibrate at every footstep, and timidly hastens to reach the island, not taking breath to look around until he has found footing; on the firm island. A solid rock projects a little over the fall, and affords him a safe position, whence he sees not only the two falls on either side, but also several others formed above and below his point of view. The scene is so enchanting, that it is difficult to tear oneself away.

Beyond Trollhatta the river expands almost to a lake, and is separated into many arms by the numerous islands. The shores lose their beauty, being flat and uninteresting.

We unfortunately did not reach the splendid Wennersee, which is from forty-five to sixty-five miles long, and proportionally broad, until evening, when it was already too dark to admire the scenery. Our ship remained some hours before the insignificant village Wennersborg.

We had met six or seven steamers on our journey, which all belonged to Swedish or Norwegian merchants; and it afforded us a peculiarly interesting sight to see these ships ascend and descend in the high locks.

September 5th.

As we were leaving Wennersborg late on the previous night, and were cruising about the sea, a contrary wind, or rather a squall, arose, which would have signified little to a good vessel, but to which our small ship was not equal. The poor captain tried in vain to navigate the steamer across the lake; he was at last compelled to give up the attempt, to return and to cast anchor. We lost our boat during this storm; a high wave dashed over the deck and swept it away: it had probably been as well fastened as our boxes and trunks.

Though it was but nine o'clock in the morning, our captain declared that he could not proceed during the day, but that if the weather became more favourable, he would start again about midnight. Fortunately a fishing-boat ventured to come alongside, and some of the passengers landed. I was among them, and made use of this opportunity to visit some cottages lying at the edge of a wood near the lake. They were very small, but consisted of two chambers, which contained several beds and other furniture; the people were also somewhat better clad than the Norwegians. Their food too was not so unpalatable; they boiled a thick mess of coarse black flour, which was eaten with sweet milk.

September 6th.

We raised anchor at one o'clock in the morning, and in about five hours arrived at the island Eken, which consists entirely of rock, and is surrounded by a multitude of smaller islets and cliffs. This is one of the most important stations in the lake. A large wooden warehouse stands on the shore, and in it is stored the merchandise of the vicinity intended for export; and in return it receives the cargo from the ships. There are always several vessels lying at anchor here.

We had now to wind through a cluster of islands, till we again reached the open lake, which, however, was only remarkable for its size. Its shores are bare and monotonous, and only dotted here and there with woods or low hills; the distant view even is not at all noteworthy. One of the finest views is the tolerably large castle of Leko, which lies on a rock, and is surrounded by fertile groves.

Further off rises the Kinne Kulle, {51} to which the traveller's attention is directed, because it is said to afford an extended view, not only over the lake, but far into the country. A curious grotto is said to exist in this hill; but unfortunately one loses these sights since the establishment of steamers, for we fly past every object of interest, and the longest journey will soon be described in a few words.

A large glass-factory is established at Bromoe, which fabricates window-glass exclusively. We stopped a short time, and took a considerable cargo of the brittle material on board.

The factory and the little dwellings attached to it are prettily situated on the undulating ground.

Near Sjotorp we entered the river again through several locks. The passage of the Wennersee is calculated at about ten or eleven hours.

The river at first winds through woods; and while the ship slowly passes through the locks, it is pleasanter to walk a portion of the distance in their shade.

Farther on it flows through broad valleys, which, however, present no very attractive features.

September 7th.

Early in the morning we crossed the pretty Vikensee, which distinguishes itself, like all Swedish lakes, by the multitude of its islands, cliffs, and rocks. These islands are frequently covered with trees, which make the view more interesting.

The lake is 306 feet above the level of the North Sea, and is the highest point of the journey; from thence the locks begin to descend. The number of ascending and descending locks amounts to seventy-two.

A short canal leads into the Boltensee, which is comparatively free from islands. The passage across this little lake is very charming; the shores are diversified by hills, woods, meadows, and fields. After it comes the Weltersee, which can be easily defended by the beautiful fortress of Karlsborg. This lake has two peculiarities: one being the extraordinary purity and transparency of its waters; the other, the number of storms which prevail in it. I was told that it frequently raged and stormed on the lake while the surrounding country remained calm and free. The storm sometimes overtakes the ship so suddenly and violently, that escape is impossible; and the sagas and fables told of the deceitful tricks of these waves are innumerable.

We fortunately escaped, and crossed its surface cheerfully and merrily. On its shores are situated the beautiful ladies' pensionary, Wadstena, and the celebrated mountain Omberg, at whose foot a battle was fought.

The next canal is short, and leads through a lovely wood into the little lake of Norbysee. It is customary to walk this distance, and inspect the simple monument of Count Platen, who made the plans for the locks and canals,--a lasting, colossal undertaking. The monument is surrounded by an iron railing, and consists of a slab bearing an inscription, simply stating in Swedish his name, the date of his death, &c. Nearly opposite the monument, on the other side of the canal, is the town of Motala, distinguished principally for its large iron factories, in which the spacious work-rooms are especially remarkable.

Fifteen locks lead from the Norbysee into the Roxersee, which is a descent of 116 feet. The canal winds gracefully through woods and meadows, crossed by pretty roads, and studded with elegant little houses and larger edifices. Distant church-steeples point out the village of Norby, which sometimes peeps forth behind little forests, and then vanishes again from the view of the traveller. When the sun shines on the waters of this canal, it has a beautiful, transparent, pea-green colour, like the purest chrysolite.

The view from the hill which rises immediately before the lake of Roxen is exceedingly fine. It looks down upon an immense valley, covered with the most beautiful woods and rocks, and upon the broad lake, whose arm flows far in land. The evening sun shed its last rays over a little town on the lake-shore, and its newly-painted tiles shone brightly in its light beams.

While the ship descended through the many locks, we visited the neighbouring church of the village of Vretakloster, which contains the skeletons of several kings in beautifully-made metal coffins.

We then crossed the lake, which is from four to five miles broad, and remained all night before the entrance of the canal leading into a bay of the Baltic.

September 8th.

This canal is one of the longest; its environs are very pretty, and the valley through which it runs is one of the largest we had passed. The town of Soderkoping is situated at the foot of high, picturesque groups of rocks, which extend to a considerable distance.

Every valley and every spot of soil in Sweden are carefully cultivated.

The people in general are well dressed, and inhabit small but very pretty houses, whose windows are frequently decorated with clean white draperies. I visited several of these houses, as we had abundance of time for such excursions while the ship was going through the locks. I think one might walk the whole distance from Gottenburg to Stockholm in the same time that the ship takes for the journey. We lose some hours daily with the locks, and are obliged to lie still at night on their account. The distance is calculated at from 180 to 250 miles, and the journey takes five days.

In the evening we approached the Baltic, which has the same character as the Scheren of the North Sea. The ship threads its way through a shoal of islands and islets, of rocks and cliffs; and it is as difficult to imagine here as there how it is possible to avoid all the projecting cliffs, and guide the ship so safely through them. The sea divides itself into innumerable arms and bays, into small and large lakes, which are formed between the islands and rocks, and are hemmed in by beautiful hills. But nothing can exceed the beauty of the view of the castle Storry Husby, which lies on a high mountain, in a bay. In front of the mountain a beautiful meadow-lawn reaches to the shores of the sea, while the back is surrounded in the distance by a splendid pine-forest. Near this picturesque castle a steeple rises on a neighbouring island, which is all that remains of the ancient castle of Stegeborg. Nothing can be more romantic than the scenery here, and on the whole journey over the fiord; for it presents itself in ever-varying pictures to the traveller's notice.

But gradually the hills become lower, the islands more rare; the sea supersedes every thing, and seems jealously anxious to exclude other objects from the traveller's attention, as if it wished to monopolise it. Now we were in the open sea, and saw only water and sky; and then again we were so hemmed in by the rocks and cliffs, that it would be impossible to extricate the ship without the assistance of an experienced pilot.

September 9th.

We left the sea, and entered another lake, the Malarsee, celebrated for its numerous islands, by a short canal. The town of Sotulje lies at its entrance, charmingly situated in a narrow valley at the foot of a rather steep hill. This lake at first resembles a broad river, but widens at every step, and soon shews itself in its whole expanse. The passage of the Malarsee takes four hours, and is one of the most charming excursions that can be made. It is said to contain about a thousand islets of various sizes; and it may be imagined how varied in form and feature the scenery must be, and, like the fiord of the Baltic, what a constant succession of new scenes it must present.

The shores also are very beautiful: in some spots hills descend sharply to the water's edge, the steep rocks forming dangerous points; on others dark, sombre pine-forests grow; and again there are gay valleys and meadows, with villages or single cottages. Many travellers assert that this lake is, after all, very monotonous; but I cannot agree with their opinion. I found it so attractive, that I could repeat the journey many times without wearying of this lovely sameness. It certainly has not the majestic backgrounds of the Swiss lakes; but this profusion of small islands is a pleasing peculiarity which can be found on no other lake.

On the summit of a steep precipice of the shore the hat of the unfortunate Eric is hoisted, fastened to a long pole. History tells that this king fled from the enemy in a battle; that one of his soldiers pursued him, and reproached him for his cowardice, whereupon Eric, filled with shame and despair, gave spurs to his horse and leaped into the fearful abyss. At his fall his hat was blown from his head, and was left on this spot.

Not far from this point the suburbs of Stockholm make their appearance, being spread round one of the broad arms of the lake. With increasing curiosity we gazed towards the town as we gradually approached it. Many of the pretty villas, which are situated in the valleys or on the sides of the hills as forerunners of the town, come into view, and the suburbs rise amphi-theatrically on the steep shores. The town itself closes the prospect by occupying the whole upper shore of the lake, and is flanked by the suburbs at either side. The Ritterholm church, with its cast-iron perforated towers, and the truly grand royal palace, which is built entirely in the Italian style, can be seen and admired from this distance.

We had scarcely cast anchor in the port of Stockholm, when a number of Herculean women came and offered us their services as porters. They were Delekarliers, {52} who frequently come to Stockholm to earn a livelihood as porters, water-carriers, boatwomen, &c. They easily find employment, because they possess two excellent qualities: they are said to be exceedingly honest and hard-working, and, at the same time, have the strength and perseverance of men.

Their dress consists of black petticoats, which come half way over the calf of the leg, red bodices, white chemises with long sleeves, short narrow aprons of two colours, red stockings, and shoes with wooden soles an inch thick. They twist a handkerchief round their head, or put on a little close black cap, which fits close on the back part of the head.

In Stockholm there are entire houses, as well as single rooms, which, as in a hotel, are let by the day. They are much cheaper than hotels, and are therefore more in demand. I at once hired one of these rooms, which was very clean and bright, and for which, with breakfast, I only paid one riksdaler, which is about one shilling.

CHAPTER X

As my journey was ostensibly only to Iceland, and as I only paid a flying visit to this portion of Scandinavia, my readers will pardon me if I treat it briefly. This portion of Europe has been so frequently and so excellently described by other travellers, that my observations would be of little importance.

I remained in Stockholm six days, and made as good use of my time as I could. The town is situated on the shores of the Baltic Sea and the Malar lake. These two waters are connected by a short canal, on whose shores the most delightful houses are erected.

My first visit was to the beautiful church of Ritterholm, which is used more for a cemetery and an armory than for a place of worship. The vaults serve as burial-places for the kings, and their monuments are erected in the side-chapels. On each side of the nave of the church are placed effigies of armed knights on horseback, whose armour belonged to the former kings of Sweden. The walls and angles of the church are profusely decorated with flags and standards, said to number five thousand. In addition to this, the keys of conquered towns and fortresses hang along the side-walls, and drums are piled upon the floor; trophies taken from different nations with which Sweden has been at war.

Besides these curiosities, several coats of armour and garments of Swedish regents are displayed behind glass-cases in the side-chapels. Among them, the dress which Charles XII. wore on the day of his death, and his hat perforated by a ball, interested me most. His riding-boots stand on the ground beside it. The modern dress and hat, embroidered with gold and ornamented with feathers, of the last king, the founder of the new dynasty, is not less interesting, partly perhaps from the great contrast.

The church of St. Nicholas stands on the same side of the canal, and is one of the finest Protestant churches I had seen; it is very evident that it was built in Catholic times, and that its former decorations have been allowed to remain. It contains several large and small oil-paintings, some ancient and some modern monuments, and a profusion of gilding. The organ is fine and large; flanking the entrance of the church are beautiful reliefs, hewn in stone; and above it, carved in wood, a statue of the archangel Michael, larger than life, sitting on horseback on a bridge, in the act of killing the dragon.

Near the church is situated the royal palace, which needs a more fluent pen than mine to describe it. It would fill a volume were I to enumerate and describe the treasures, curiosities, and beauties of its construction, or its interior arrangement; I can only say that I never saw any thing to equal it, except the royal palace of Naples. Such an edifice is the more surprising in the north, and in a country which has never been overstocked with wealth.

The church of Shifferholm is remarkable only for its position and its temple-like form; it stands on the ledge of a rock facing the royal palace, on the opposite shore of the same indentation of the Baltic. A long bridge of boats leads from the one to the other.

The church of St. Catharine is large and beautiful. In an outer angle of the church is shewn the stone on which one of the brothers Sturre was beheaded. {53}

On the Ritterplatz stands the Ritterhouse, a very fine palace; also the old royal palace, and several other royal and private mansions; but they are not nearly so numerous nor so fine as in Copenhagen, and the streets and squares also cannot be compared with those of the capital of Denmark.

The finest prospect is from a hill in one of the suburbs called the Great Mosbecken; it affords a magnificent view of the sea and the lake, of the town and its suburbs, as far as the points of the mountains, and of the lovely country-houses which border the shores of lake and sea. The town and its environs are so interspersed with islets and rocks, that these seem to be part of the town; and this gives Stockholm such a curious appearance, that I can compare it to no other city I have seen. Wooded hills and naked rocks prolong the view, and their ridges extend into the far distance; while level fields and lawns take up but a very small proportion of the magnificent scenery.

On descending from this hill the traveller should not fail to go to Sodermalm, and to inspect the immense iron-stores, where iron is heaped up in countless bars. The corn-market of Stockholm is insignificant. The principal buildings besides those already enumerated are, the bank, the mint, the guard-house, the palace of the crown-prince, the theatre, &c. The latter is interesting, partly because Gustavus

III. was shot in it. He fell on the stage, while a grand masquerade was taking place, for which the theatre had been changed into a ball-room. The king was shot by a mask, and died in a few hours.

There is not a representation in the theatre every night; and on the one evening of performance during my visit a festival was to be celebrated in the hall of antiquities. The esteemed artist Vogelberg, a native of Sweden, had beautifully sculptured the three heathen gods, Thor, Balder, and Odin, in colossal size, and brought them over from Rome. The statues had only been lately placed, and a large company had been invited to meet in the illuminated saloon, and do honour to the artist. Solemn hymns were to be sung at the uncovering of the statues, beside other festivities. I was fortunate enough to receive an invitation to this festival, which was to commence a little past seven. Before that I went to the theatre, which, I was told, would open at half-past six. I intended to remain there half an hour, and then drive to the palace, where my friends would meet me to accompany me to the festival. I went to the theatre at six, and anxiously waited half an hour for the commencement of the overture; it was after half-past six, and no signs of the commencement. I looked again at the bill, and saw, to my annoyance, that the opera did not begin till seven. But as I would not leave until I had seen the stage, I spent the time in looking at the theatre itself. It is tolerably large, and has five tiers of boxes, but is neither tastefully nor richly decorated. I was most surprised at the exorbitant price and the variety of seats. I counted twenty-six different kinds; it seems that every row has a different price, else I don't understand how they could make such a variety.

At last the overture began; I listened to it, saw the curtain rise, looked at the fatal spot, and left after the first air. The door-keeper followed me, took my arm, and wished to give me a return-ticket; and when I told him that I did not require one, as I did not intend to return, he said that it had only just commenced, and that I ought to stop, and not have spent all the money for nothing. I was unfortunately too little acquainted with the Swedish language to explain the reason of my departure, so I could give him no answer, but went away. I, however, heard him say to some one, "I never met with such a woman before; she sat an hour looking at the curtain, and goes away as soon as it rises." I looked round and saw how he shook his head thoughtfully, and pointed with his forefinger to his forehead. I could not refrain from smiling, and enjoyed the scene as much as I should have done the second act of Mozart's **Don Giovanni**.

I called for my friends at the royal palace, and spent the evening very agreeably in the brilliantly-illuminated galleries of antiquities and of pictures. I had the pleasure also of being introduced to Herr Vogelberg. His modest, unpretending manners must inspire every one with respect, even if one does not know what distinguished talent he possesses.

The royal park is one of the finest sights in the neighbourhood of Stockholm, and is one of the best of its kind. It is a fine large natural park, with an infinity of groves, meadows, hills, and rocks; here and there lies a country-house with its fragrant flower-garden, or tasteful coffee and refreshment houses, which on fine Sundays are filled with visitors from the town. Good roads are made through the park, and commodious paths lead to the finest points of view over sea and land.

The bust of the popular poet Bellmann stands on an open sunny spot, and an annual festival is given here in his honour.

Deeper in the park lies the so-called Rosenthal (Rose valley), a real Eden. The late king was so partial to this spot, that he spent many hours in the little royal country-house here, which is built on a retired spot in the midst of groves and flower-beds. In front of the palace stands a splendid vase made of a single piece of porphyry. I was told that it was the largest in Europe, but I consider the one in the Museum of Naples much larger.

I spent the last hours of my visit to Stockholm in this spot, with the amiable family of Herr Boje from Finnland, whose acquaintance I had made on the journey from Gottenburg to Stockholm. I shall therefore never forget this beautiful park and the agreeable associations connected with it.

I made a very agreeable excursion also to the royal palace of Haga, to the large cemetery, and to the military school Karlberg.

The royal castle of Haga is surrounded by a magnificent park, which owes little to art; it contains some of the finest trees, with here and there a hill, and is crossed by majestic alleys and well-kept roads for driving and walking. The palace itself is so small, that I could not but admire the moderation of the royal family; but I was informed that this is the smallest of their summer palaces.

Nearly opposite to this park is the great cemetery; but as it has only existed for about seventeen years, the trees in it are yet rather young. This would be of little consequence in other countries, but in Sweden the cemeteries serve as promenades, and are crossed by alleys, ornamented with groves, and provided with seats for the accommodation of visitors. This cemetery is surrounded by a dark pine-forest, and really seems quite shut off from the outer world. It is the only burial-place out of the town; the others all lie between the churches and the neighbouring houses, whose fronts often form the immediate boundary. Burials take place there constantly, so that the inhabitants are quite familiar with the aspect of death.

From the great cemetery a road leads to the neighbouring Karlberg, which is the academy for military and naval cadets. The extensive buildings attached to this seminary are built on the slope of a mountain, which is washed on one side by the waters of the lake, and surrounded on the other by the beautiful park-plantations.

Before leaving Stockholm I had the honour of being introduced to her majesty the Queen of Sweden. She had heard of my travels, and took a particular interest in my account of Palestine. In consequence of this favour, I received the special permission to inspect the whole interior of the palace. Although it was inhabited, I was conducted, not only through the state-rooms, but through all the private rooms of the court. It would be impossible to describe the splendour which reigns here, the treasures of art, the magnificent appointments, and the evident taste every where displayed. I was delighted with all the treasures and splendour, but still more with the warm interest with which her majesty conversed with me about Palestine. This interview will ever dwell on my memory as the bright salient point of my northern expedition.

EXCURSION TO THE OLD ROYAL CASTLE OF GRIPTHOLM ON THE MALARSEE

Every Sunday morning, at eight o'clock, a little steamer leaves Stockholm for this castle; the distance is about forty-five miles, and is passed in four hours; four hours more are allowed for the stay, and in the evening the steamer returns to Stockholm. This excursion is very interesting, although we pass the greater part of the time on that portion of the lake which we had seen on our arrival, but for the last few miles the ship turned into a pretty bay, at whose apex the castle is situated. It is distinguished for its size, its architecture, and its colossal turrets. It is unfortunately, however, painted with the favourite brick-red colour of the Swedes.

Two immense cannons, which the Swedes once gained in battle from the Russians, stand in the courtyard. The apartments in the castle, which are kept in good condition, display neither splendour nor profusion of appointments, indeed almost the contrary. The pretty theatre is, however, an exception: for its walls are inlaid from top to bottom with mirrors, its pillars are gilt, and the royal box tapestried with rich red velvet. There has been no performance here since the death of Gustavus III.

The immensely massive walls are a remarkable feature of this palace, and must measure about three yards in thickness in the lower stories.

The upper apartments are all large and high, and afford a splendid view of the lake from their windows. But it is impossible to enjoy these beautiful scenes when one thinks of the sad events which have taken place here.

Two kings, John III. and Eric XIV., the latter with four of his ministers, who were subsequently beheaded, were imprisoned here for many years. The captivity of John III. would not have been so bad, if captivity were not bad enough in itself. He was confined in a large splendid saloon, but which he was not permitted to quit, and which he would therefore probably have gladly exchanged for the poorest hut and liberty. His wife inhabited two smaller apartments adjoining; she was not treated as a prisoner, and could leave the castle at will. His son Sigismund was born here in the year 1566, and the room and bed in which he was born are still shewn as curiosities.

Eric's fate was much more unfortunate, for he was kept in narrow and dark confinement. A small rudely-furnished apartment, with narrow, iron-barred windows, in one of the little turrets was his prison. The entrance was closed by a solid oaken door, in which a small opening had been made, through which his food was given him. For greater security this oaken door was covered by an iron one. Round the outside of the apartment a narrow gallery had been made, on which the guards were posted, and could at all times see their prisoner through the barred windows. The spot is still shewn at one of the windows where the king sat for hours looking into the distance, his head leaning on his hand. What must have been his feelings as he gazed on the bright sky, the verdant turf, and the smiling lake! How many sighs must have been echoed from these walls, how many sleepless nights must he have passed during those two long years in anxious expectation of the future!

The guide who took us round the castle maintained that the floor was more

worn on this spot than any where else, and that the window-sash had been hol-
lowed by the elbow of the miserable king; but I could not perceive any difference. Eric was kept imprisoned here for two years, and was then taken to another
prison.

There is a large picture-gallery in this castle; but it contains principally portraits of kings, not only of Sweden, but of other countries, from the Middle Ages
down to the present time; also portraits of ministers, generals, painters, poets, and
learned men; of celebrated Swedish females, who have sacrificed themselves for
their country, and of the most celebrated female beauties. The name and date of
birth of each person are affixed to his or her portrait, so that each visitor may find
his favourite without guide or catalogue. In many of them the colouring and draw-
ing are wretched enough, but we will hope that the resemblance is all the more
striking.

On our return several gentlemen were kind enough to direct my attention to
the most interesting points of the lake. Among these I must mention Kakeholm,
its broadest point; the island of Esmoi, on which a Swedish female gained a battle;
Norsberg, also celebrated for a battle which took place there; and Sturrehof, the
property of a great Swedish family. Near Bjarkesoe a simple cross is erected, ostensibly on the spot where Christianity was first introduced. Indeed the Malarsee has
so many historical associations, in addition to the attractions of its scenery, that it is
one of the most interesting seas not only of Sweden but of Europe.

JOURNEY FROM STOCKHOLM TO UPSALA AND TO THE IRON-MINES
OF DANEMORA

September 12th.

The intercourse between Stockholm and Upsala is very considerable. A steamer leaves both places every day except Sunday, and traverses the distance in six
hours.

Tempted by this convenient opportunity of easily and quickly reaching the celebrated town of Upsala, and by the unusually fine weather, I took my passage one
evening, and was greatly disappointed when, on the following morning, the rain
poured down in torrents. But if travellers paid much attention to the weather, they
would not go far; so I nevertheless embarked at half-past seven, and arrived safely
in Upsala. I remained in the cabin during the passage, and could not even enjoy the

prospect from the cabin-windows, for the rain beat on them from the outside, while inside they were obscured by the heat. But I did not venture on deck, hoping to be favoured by better weather on my return.

At last, about three o'clock, when I had been in Upsala more than an hour, the weather cleared up, and I sallied out to see the sights.

First I visited the cathedral. I entered, and stood still with astonishment at the chief portal, on looking up at the high roof resting on two rows of pillars, and covering the whole church. It is formed in one beautiful straight line, unbroken by a single arch. The church itself is simple: behind the grand altar a handsome chapel is erected, the ceiling of which is painted azure blue, embossed with golden stars. In this chapel Gustavus I. is interred between his two wives. The monument which covers the grave is large, and made of marble, but clumsy and void of taste. It represents a sarcophagus, on which three bodies, the size of life, are laid; a marble canopy is raised over them. The walls of the chapel are covered with pretty frescoes, representing the most remarkable scenes in the life of this monarch. The most interesting among them are, one in which he enters a peasant's hut in peasant's attire, at the same moment that his pursuers are eagerly inquiring after him in front of the hut; the other, when he stands on a barrel, also dressed as a peasant, and harangues his people. Two large tablets in a broad gold frame contain in Swedish, and not in the Latin language, the explanation of the different pictures, so that every Swede may easily learn the monarch's history.

Several other monuments are erected in the side-chapels; those of Catharine Magelone, John III., Gustavus Erichson, who was beheaded, and of the two brothers Sturre, who were murdered. The monument of Archbishop Menander, in white marble, is a tasteful and artistic modern production. The great Linnaeus is buried under a simple marble slab in this church; but his monument is in one of the side-chapels, and not over his grave, and consists of a beautiful dark-brown porphyry slab, on which his portrait is sculptured in relief.

The splendid organ, which reaches nearly to the roof of the church, also deserves special attention. The treasure-chamber does not contain great treasures; the blood-stained and dagger-torn garments of the unfortunate brothers Sturre are kept in a glass case here; and here also stands a wooden statue of the heathen god Thor. This wooden affair seems to have originally been an Ecce Homo, which was perhaps the ornament of some village church, then carried off by some unbeliever, and made more shapeless than its creator, not proficient in art, had made it. It has a greater resemblance now to a frightful scarecrow than to any thing else.

The churchyard near the church is distinguished for its size and beauty. It is surrounded by a wall of stone two feet high, surmounted by an iron palisading of equal height, broken by stone pillars. On several sides, steps are made into the burying-ground over this partition. In this cemetery, as in the one of Stockholm, one seems to be in a lovely garden, laid out with alleys, arbours, lawns, &c.; but it is more beautiful than the other, because it is older. The graves are half concealed by arbours; many were ornamented with flowers and wreaths, or hedged by rose-bushes. The whole aspect of this cemetery, or rather of this garden, seems equally adapted for the amusement of the living or the repose of the dead.

The monuments are in no way distinguished; only two are rather remarkable, for they consist of tremendous pieces of rock in their natural condition, standing upright on the graves. One of these monuments resembles a mountain; it covers the ashes of a general, and is large enough to have covered his whole army; his relatives probably took the graves of Troy as a specimen for their monument. It is moreover inscribed by very peculiar signs, which seemed to me to be runic characters. The good people have united in this monument two characteristics of the ancients of two entirely distinct empires.

The university or library building in Upsala is large and beautiful; it is situated on a little hill, with a fine front facing the town. The park, which is, however, still somewhat young, forms the background. {54}

Near this building, on the same hill, stands a royal palace, conspicuous for its brick-red colour. It is very large, and the two wings are finished by massive round towers.

In the centre of the courtyard, behind the castle, is placed a colossal bust of Gustavus I., and a few paces from it two artificial hills serve as bastions, on which cannons are planted. This being the highest point of the town, affords the best view over it, and over the surrounding country.

The town itself is built half of wood and half of stone, and is very pretty, being crossed by broad streets, and ornamented with tastefully laid-out gardens. It has one disadvantage, which is the dark brownish-red colour of the houses, which has a peculiarly sombre appearance in the setting sun.

An immense and fertile plain, diversified by dark forests contrasting with the bright green meadows and the yellow stubble-fields, surrounds the town, and in the distance the silvery river Fyris flows towards the sea. Forests close the distant view with their dark shadows. I saw but few villages; they may, however, have been hidden by the trees, for that they exist seems to be indicated by the well-kept high roads crossing the plain in all directions.

Before quitting my position on the bastions of the royal palace I cast a glance on the castle-gardens, which were lying lower down the hill, and are separated from the castle by a road; they do not seem to be large, but are very pretty.

I should have wished to be able to visit the botanic garden near the town, which was the favourite resort of Linnaeus, whose splendidly-sculptured bust is said to be its chief ornament; but the sun was setting behind the mountains, and I repaired to my chamber, to prepare for my journey to Danemora.

September 13th.

I left Upsala at four o'clock in the morning, to proceed to the far-famed iron-mines of Danemora, upwards of thirty miles distant, and where I wished to arrive before twelve, as the blasting takes place at that hour, after which the pits are closed. As I had been informed how slowly travelling is done in this country, and how tedious the delays are when the horses are changed, I determined to allow time enough for all interruptions, and yet arrive at the appointed hour.

A few miles behind Upsala lies Old Upsala (Gamla Upsala). I saw the old church and the grave-hills in passing; three of the latter are remarkably large, the others smaller. It is presumed that the higher ones cover the graves of kings. I saw similar tumuli during my journey to Greece, on the spot where Troy is said to have stood. The church is not honoured as a ruin; it has yet to do service; and it grieved me to see the venerable building propped up and covered with fresh mortar on many a time-worn spot.

Half way between Upsala and Danemora we passed a large castle, not distinguished for its architecture, its situation, or any thing else. Then we neared the river Fyris, and the long lake of Danemora; both are quite overgrown with reeds and grass, and have flat uninteresting shores; indeed the whole journey offers little variety, as the road lies through a plain, only diversified by woods, fields, and pieces of rock. These are interesting features, because one cannot imagine how they came there, the mountains being at a great distance, and the soil by no means rocky.

The little town of Danemora lies in the midst of a wood, and only consists of a church and a few large and small detached houses. The vicinity of the mines is indicated before arriving at the place by immense heaps of stones, which are brought by horse-gins from the pits, and which cover a considerable space.

I had fortunately arrived in time to see the blastings. Those in the great pit are the most interesting; for its mouth is so very large, that it is not necessary to descend in order to see the pit-men work; all is visible from above. This is a very peculiar and interesting sight. The pit, 480 feet deep, with its colossal doors and entrances leading into the galleries, looks like a picture of the lower world, from which bridges of rocks, projections, arches and caverns formed in the walls, ascend to the upper world. The men look like pigmies, and one cannot follow their movements until the eye has accustomed itself to the depth and to the darkness prevailing below. But the darkness is not very dense; I could distinguish most of the ladders, which seemed to me like children's toys.

It was nearly twelve, and the workmen left the pits, with the exception of those in charge of the mines. They ascended by means of little tubs hanging by ropes, and were raised by a windlass. It is a terrible sight to see the men soaring up on the little machine, especially when two or three ascend at once; for then one man stands in the centre, while the other two ride on the edge of the tub.

[Picture: Mines of Danemora]

I should have liked to descend into the great pit, but it was too late on this day, and I would not wait another. I should not have feared the descent, as I was familiar with such adventures, having explored the salt-mines of Wieliczka and Bochnia, in Gallicia, some years before, in which I had had to let myself down by a rope, which is a much more dangerous method than the tub.

With the stroke of twelve, four blasting trains in the large pit were fired. The man whose business it was to apply the match ran away in great haste, and sheltered himself behind a wall of rock. In a few moments the powder flashed, some stones fell, and then a fearful crash was heard all around, followed by the rolling and falling of the blasted masses. Repeated echoes announced the fearful explosion in the interior of the pits: the whole left a terrible impression on me. Scarcely had one mine ceased to rage, when the second began, then the third, and so on. These blastings take place daily in different mines.

The other pits are deeper, the deepest being 600 feet; but the mouths are smaller, and the shafts not perpendicular, so that the eye is lost in darkness, which is a still more unpleasant sensation. I gazed with oppressed chest into the dark space, vainly endeavouring to distinguish something. I should not like to be a miner; I could not endure life without the light of day; and when I turned from the dark pits, I cast my eyes thankfully on the cheerful landscape basking in the sun.

I returned to Upsala on the same day, having made this little journey by post. I can merely narrate the facts, without giving an opinion on the good or bad conveniences for locomotion, as this was more a pleasure-trip than a journey.

As I had hired no carriage, I had a different vehicle at every station, and these vehicles consisted of ordinary two-wheeled wooden carts. My seat was a truss of hay covered with the horse-cloth. If the roads had not been so extremely good, these carts would have shaken terribly; but as it was, I must say that I rode more comfortably than in the carriols of the Norwegians, although they were painted and vanished; for in them I had to be squeezed in with my feet stretched out, and could not change my position.

The stations are unequal,--sometimes long, sometimes short. The post-horses are provided here, as in Norway, by wealthy peasants, called Dschns-peasants. These have to collect a certain number of horses every evening for forwarding the travellers the next morning. At every post-house a book is kept, in which the traveller can see how many horses the peasant has, how many have already been hired, and how many are left in the stable. He must then inscribe his name, the hour of his departure, and the number of horses he requires. By this arrangement deception and extortion are prevented, as every thing is open, and the prices fixed. {55}

Patience is also required here, though not so much as in Norway. I had always to wait from fifteen to twenty minutes before the carriage was brought and the horses and harness prepared, but never longer; and I must admit that the Swedish post-masters hurried as much as possible, and never demanded double fare, although they must have known that I was in haste. The pace of the horse depends on the will of the coachman and the powers of his steed; but in no other country did I see such consideration paid to the strength of the horses. It is quite ridiculous to see what small loads of corn, bricks, or wood, are allotted to two horses, and how slowly and sleepily they draw their burdens.

The number of wooden gates, which divide the roads into as many parts as there are common grounds on it, are a terrible nuisance to travellers. The coachman has often to dismount six or eight times in an hour to open and close these gates. I was told that these delectable gates even exist on the great high road, only not quite in such profusion as on the by-roads.

Wood must be as abundant here as in Norway, for every thing is enclosed; even fields which seem so barren as not to be worth the labour or the wood.

The villages through which I passed were generally pretty and cheerful, and I found the cottages, which I entered while the horses were changed, neatly and comfortably furnished.

The peasants of this district wear a peculiar costume. The men, and frequently also the boys, wear long dark-blue cloth surtouts, and cloth caps on their heads; so that, at a distance, they look like gentlemen in travelling dress. It seems curious to a foreigner to see these apparent gentlemen following the plough or cutting grass. At a nearer view, of course the aspect changes, and the rents and dirt appear, or the leathern apron worn beneath the coat, like carpenters in Austria, becomes visible. The female costume was peculiar only in so far that it was poor and ragged. In dress and shoes the Norwegian and Swedes are behind the Icelanders, but they surpass them in the comfort of their dwellings.

September 14th.

To-day I returned to Stockholm on the Malarsee, and the weather being more favourable than on my former passage, I could remain on deck the whole time. I saw now that we sailed for several miles on the river Fyris, which flows through woods and fields into the lake.

The large plain on which old and new Upsala lie was soon out of sight, and after passing two bridges, we turned into the Malar. At first there are no islands on its flat expanse, and its shores are studded with low tree-covered hills; but we soon, however, arrived at the region of islands, where the passage becomes more interesting, and the beauty of the shores increases. The first fine view we saw was the pretty estate Krusenberg, whose castle is romantically situated on a fertile hill. But much more beautiful and surprising is the splendid castle of Skukloster, a large, beautiful, and regular pile, ornamented with four immense round turrets at the four corners, and with gardens stretching down to the water's edge.

From this place the scenery is full of beauty and variety; every moment presents another and a more lovely view. Sometimes the waters expand, sometimes they are hemmed in by islands, and become as narrow as canals. I was most charmed with those spots where the islands lie so close together that no outlet seems possible, till another turn shews an opening between them, with a glimpse of the lake beyond. The hills on the shores are higher, and the promontories larger, the farther the ship advances; and the islands appear to be merely projections of the continent, till a nearer approach dispels the illusion.

The village of Sixtuna lies in a picturesque and charming little valley, filled with ruins, principally of round towers, which are said to be the remains of the Roman town of Sixtum; the name being retained by the new town with a slight modification.

After this follow cliffs and rocks rising perpendicularly from the sea, and whose vicinity would be by no means desirable in a storm. Of the castle of Rouse only three beautiful domes rise above the trees; a frowning bleak hill conceals the rest from the eye. Then comes a palace, the property of a private individual, only re-markable for its size. The last of the notabilities is the Rokeby bridge, said to be one of the longest in Sweden. It unites the firm land with the island on which the royal castle of Drottingholm stands. The town of Stockholm now becomes visible; we turn into the portion of the lake on which it lies, and arrive there again at two o'clock in the afternoon.

FROM STOCKHOLM TO TRAVEMUNDE AND HAMBURGH

I bade farewell to Stockholm on the 18th September, and embarked in the steamer *Svithiold*, of 100-horse power, at twelve o'clock at noon, to go to Trave-munde.

Few passages can be more expensive than this one is. The distance is five hun-dred leagues, and the journey generally occupies two and a half to three days; for this the fare, without food, is four pounds. The food is also exorbitantly dear; in addition to which the captain is the purveyor; so that there is no appeal for the grossest extortion or insufficiency.

It pained me much when one of the poorer travellers, who suffered greatly from sea-sickness, having applied for some soup to the steward, who referred him to the amiable captain, to hear him declare he would make no exception, and that a basin of soup would be charged the whole price of a complete dinner. The poor man was to do without the soup, of which he stood so much in need, or scrape every farthing together to pay a few shillings daily for his dinner. Fortunately for him some benevolent persons on deck paid for his meals. Some of the gentlemen brought their own wine with them, for which they had to pay as much duty to the captain as the wine was worth.

To these pleasures of travelling must be added the fact, that a Swedish vessel does not advance at all if the weather is unfavourable. Most of the passengers considered that the engines were inefficient. However this may be, we were delayed twenty-four hours at the first half of our journey, from Stockholm to Calmar, although we had only a slight breeze against us and a rather high sea, but no storm. In Calmar we cast anchor, and waited for more favourable wind. Several gentlemen, whose business in Lubeck was pressing, left the steamer, and continued their journey by land.

At first the Baltic very much resembles the Malarsee; for islands, rocks, and a variety of scenery make it interesting. To the right we saw the immensely long wooden bridge of Lindenborg, which unites one of the larger islands with the continent.

At the end of one of the turns of the sea lies the town of Wachsholm; and opposite to it, upon a little rocky island, a splendid fortress with a colossal round tower. Judging by the number of cannons planted along the walls, this fortress must be of great importance. A few hours later we passed a similar fortress, Friedrichsborg; it is not in such an open situation as the other, but is more surrounded by forests. We passed at a considerable distance, and could not see much of it, nor of the castle lying on the opposite side, which seems to be very magnificent, and is also surrounded by woods.

The boundaries of the right shore now disappear, but then again appear as a terrible heap of naked rocks, at whose extreme edge is situated the fine fortress Dolero. Near it groups of houses are built on the bare rocks projecting into the sea, and form an extensive town.

September 19th.

To-day we were on the open, somewhat stormy sea. Towards noon we arrived at the Calmar Sound, formed by the flat, uniform shores of the long island Oland on the left, and on the right by Schmoland. In front rose the mountain-island the Jungfrau, to which every Swede points with self-satisfied pride. Its height is only remarkable compared with the flatness around; beside the proud giant-mountain of the same name in Switzerland it would seem like a little hill.

September 20th.

On account of the contrary wind, we had cast anchor here last night, and this morning continued the journey to Calmar, where we arrived about two in the fore-noon. The town is situated on an immense plain, and is not very interesting. A few hours may be agreeably spent here in visiting the beautiful church and the antiquated castle, and we had more than enough leisure for it. Wind and weather seemed to have conspired against us, and the captain announced an indefinite stay at this place. At first we could not land, as the waves were too high; but at last one of the larger boats came alongside, and the more curious among us ventured to row to the land in the unsteady vessel.

The exterior of the church resembles a fine antiquated castle from its four cor-ner towers and the lowness of its dome, which rises very little above the building, and also because the other turrets here and there erected for ornament are scarcely perceptible. The interior of the church is remarkable for its size, its height, and a particularly fine echo. The tones of the organ are said to produce a most strik-ing effect. We sent for the organist, but he was nowhere to be found; so we had to content ourselves with the echo of our own voices. We went from this place to the old royal castle built by Queen Margaret in the sixteenth century. The castle is so dilapidated inside that a tarrying in the upper chambers is scarcely advisable. The lower rooms of the castle have been repaired, and are used as prisons; and as we passed, arms were stretched forth from some of the barred windows, and plaintive voices entreated the passers-by to bestow some trifle upon the poor inmates. Up-wards of 140 prisoners are said to be confined here. {56}

About three o'clock in the afternoon the wind abated, and we continued our journey. The passage is very uniform, and we saw only flat, bare shores; a group of trees even was a rarity.

September 21st.

When I came on deck this morning the Sound was far behind us. To the left we had the open sea; on the right, instead of the bleak Schmoland, we had the bleaker Schonen, which was so barren, that we hardly saw a paltry fishing-village between the low sterile hills.

At nine o'clock in the morning we anchored in the port of Ystadt. The town is pretty, and has a large square, in which stand the house of the governor, the theatre, and the town-hall. The streets are broad, and the houses partly of wood and partly of stone. The most interesting feature is the ancient church, and in it a much-damaged wooden altar-piece, which is kept in the vestry. Though the figures are coarse and disproportionate, one must admire the composition and the carving. The reliefs on the pulpit, and a beautiful monument to the right of the altar, also deserve admiration. These are all carved in wood.

In the afternoon we passed the Danish island Malmo.

At last, after having been nearly four days on the sea instead of two days and a half, we arrived safely in the harbour of Travemunde on the 22d September at two o'clock in the morning. And now my sea-journeys were over; I parted sorrowfully from the salt waters, for it is so delightful to see the water's expanse all around, and traverse its mirror-like surface. The sea presents a beautiful picture, even when it storms and rages, when waves tower upon waves, and threaten to dash the vessel to pieces or to engulf it--when the ship alternately dances on their points, or shoots into the abyss; and I frequently crept for hours in a corner, or held fast to the sides of the ship, and let the waves dash over me. I had overcome the terrible sea-sickness during my numerous journeys, and could therefore freely admire these fearfully beautiful scenes of excited nature, and adore God in His grandest works.

We had scarcely cast anchor in the port when a whole array of coachmen surrounded us, volunteering to drive us overland to Hamburgh, a journey of thirty-six miles, which it takes eight hours to accomplish.

Travemunde is a pretty spot, which really consists of only one street, in which the majority of the houses are hotels. The country from here to Lubeck, a distance of ten miles, is very pretty. A splendid road, on which the carriages roll smoothly along, runs through a charming wood past a cemetery, whose beauty exceeds that of Upsala; but for the monuments, one might take it for one of the most splendid parks or gardens.

I regretted nothing so much as being unable to spend a day in Lubeck, for I felt very much attracted by this old Hanse town, with its pyramidically-built houses, its venerable dome, and other beautiful churches, its spacious squares, &c.; but I was obliged to proceed, and could only gaze at and admire it as I hurried through. The pavement of the streets is better than I had seen it in any northern town; and on the streets, in front of the houses, I saw many wooden benches, on which the inhabitants probably spend their summer evenings. I saw here for the first time again the gay-looking street-mirrors used in Hamburgh. The Trave, which flows between Travemunde and Lubeck, has to be crossed by boat. Near Oldesloe are the salt-factories, with large buildings and immensely high chimneys; an old romantic castle, entirely surrounded by water, lies near Arensburg.

Past Arensburg the country begins to be uninteresting, and remains so as far as Hamburgh; but it seems to be very fertile, as there is an abundance of green fields and fine meadows.

The little journey from Lubeck to Hamburgh is rather dear, on account of the almost incredible number of tolls and dues the poor coachmen have to pay. They have first to procure a license to drive from Lubeck into Hamburgh territory, which costs about 1*s.* 3*d.*; then mine had to pay twice a double toll of 8*d.*, because we passed through before five o'clock in the morning, and the gates, which are not opened till five o'clock, were unfastened especially for us; besides these, there was a penny toll on nearly every mile.

This dreadful annoyance of the constant stopping and the toll-bars is unknown in Norway and in Sweden. There, an annual tax is paid for every horse, and the owner can then drive freely through the whole country, as no toll-bars are erected.

The farm-houses here are very large and far-spread, but the reason is, that stable, barn, and shippen are under the same roof: the walls of the houses are of wood filled in with bricks.

After passing Arensburg, we saw the steeples of Wandsbeck and Hamburgh in the distance; the two towns seem to be one, and are, in fact, only separated by pretty country-houses. But Wandsbeck compared to Hamburgh is a village, not a town.

I arrived in Hamburgh about two o'clock in the afternoon; and my relatives were so astonished at my arrival, that they almost took me for a ghost. I was at first startled by their reception, but soon understood the reason of it.

At the time I left Iceland another vessel went to Altona, by which I sent a box of minerals and curiosities to my cousin in Hamburgh. The sailor who brought the box gave such a description of the wretched vessel in which I had gone to Copenhagen, that, after having heard nothing of me for two months, he thought I must have gone to the bottom of the sea with the ship. I had indeed written from Copenhagen, but the letter had been lost; and hence their surprise and delight at my arrival.

CHAPTER XI

I had not much time to spare, so that I could only stay a few days with my relatives in Hamburgh; on the 26th September, I went in a little steamer from Hamburgh to Harburg, where we arrived in three quarters of an hour. From thence I proceeded in a stage-carriage to Celle, about sixty-five miles.

The country is not very interesting; it consists for the most part of plains, which degenerate into heaths and marshes; but there are a few fertile spots peeping out here and there.

September 27th.

We arrived at Celle in the night. From here to Lehrte, a distance of about seven miles, I had to hire a private conveyance, but from Lehrte the railway goes direct to Berlin. {57} Many larger and smaller towns are passed on this road; but we saw little of them, as the stations all lie at some distance, and the railway-train only stops a few minutes.

The first town we passed was Brunswick. Immediately beyond the town lies the pretty ducal palace, built in the Gothic style, in the centre of a fine park. Wolfenbuttel seems to be a considerable town, judging by the quantity of houses and church-steeples. A pretty wooden bridge, with an elegantly-made iron balustrade, is built here across the Ocker. From the town, a beautiful lane leads to a gentle hill, on whose top stands a lovely building, used as a coffee-house.

As soon as one has passed the Hanoverian domains the country, though it is not richer in natural curiosities, is less abundant in marshes and heaths, and is very well-cultivated land. Many villages are spread around, and many a charming town excites the wish to travel through at a slower pace.

We passed Schepenstadt, Jersheim, and Wegersleben, which latter town already belongs to Prussia. In Ashersleben and in Magdeburg we changed carriages. Near Salze we saw some fine buildings which belong to the extensive saltworks existing here. Jernaudau is a colony of Moravians. I should have wished to visit the town of Kotten,--for nothing can be more charming than the situation of the town in the midst of fragrant gardens,--but we unfortunately only stopped there a few minutes. The town of Dessau is also surrounded by pretty scenery: several bridges cross the various arms of the Elbe; that over the river itself rests on solid stone columns. Of Wittenberg we only saw house tops and church-steeples; the same of Juterbog, which looks as if it were newly built. Near Lukewalde the regions of sand begin, and the uniformity is only broken by a little ridge of wooded hills near Trebbin; but when these are past, the railway passes on to Berlin through a melancholy, unmitigated desert of sand.

I had travelled from six o'clock this morning until seven in the evening, over a distance of about two hundred and twenty miles, during which time we had frequently changed carriages.

The number of passengers we had taken up on the road was very great, on account of the Leipzic fairs; sometimes the train had thirty-five to forty carriages, three locomotives, and seven to eight hundred passengers; and yet the greatest order had prevailed. It is a great convenience that one can take a ticket from Lehrte to Berlin, although the railway passes through so many different states, because then one needs not look after the luggage or any thing else. The officials on the railway are all very civil. As soon as the train stopped, the guards announced with a loud voice the time allowed, however long or short it might be; so that the passengers could act accordingly, and take refreshments in the neighbouring hotels. The arrangements for alighting are very convenient: the carriages run into deep rails at the stations, so that the ground is level with the carriages, and the entrance and exit easy. The carriages are like broad coaches; two seats ran breadthwise across them, with a large door at each side. The first and second class contain eight persons in each division, the third class ten. The carriages are all numbered, so that every passenger can easily find his seat.

By these simple arrangements the traveller may descend and walk about a little, even though the train should only stop two minutes, or even purchase some refreshments, without any confusion or crowding.

These conveniences are, of course, impossible when the carriages have the length of a house, and contain sixty or seventy persons within locked doors, and where the doors are opened by the guards, who only call out the name of the station without announcing how long the stay is. In such railways it is not advisable for travellers to leave their seats; for before they can pass from one end of the carriage to the other, through the narrow door and down the steep steps, the horn is sounded, and at the same time the train moves on; the sound being the signal for the engine-driver, the passengers having none.

In these states there was also not the least trouble with the passport and the intolerable pass-tickets. No officious police-soldier comes to the carriage, and prevents the passengers alighting before they have answered all his questions. If passports had to be inspected on this journey, it would take a few days, for they must always be taken to the passport-office, as they are never examined on the spot.

Such annoying interruptions often occur several times in the same state. And one need not even come from abroad to experience them, as a journey from a provincial to a capital town affords enough scope for annoyance.

I had no reason to complain of such annoyances in any of the countries through which I had hitherto passed. My passport was only demanded in my hotel in the capitals of the countries, if I intended to remain several days. In Stockholm, however, I found a curious arrangement; every foreigner there is obliged to procure a Swedish passport, and pay half-a-crown for it, if he only remains a few hours in the town. This is, in reality, only a polite way of taking half-a-crown from the strangers, as they probably do not like to charge so much for a simple *vise*!

STAY IN BERLIN--RETURN TO VIENNA

I have never seen a town more beautifully or regularly built than Berlin,--I mean, the town of Berlin itself,--only the finest streets, palaces, and squares of Copenhagen would bear a comparison with it.

I spent but a few days here, and had therefore scarcely time to see the most remarkable and interesting sights.

The splendid royal palace, the extensive buildings for the picture-gallery and museums, the great dome--all these are situated very near each other.

The Dome church is large and regularly built; a chapel, surrounded by an iron enclosure, stands at each side of the entrance. Several kings are buried here, and antiquated sarcophagi cover their remains, known as the kings' graves. Near them stands a fine cast-iron monument, beneath which Count Brandenburg lies.

The Catholic church is built in the style of the Rotunda in Rome; but, unlike it, the light falls from windows made around the walls, and not from above. Beautiful statues and a simple but tasteful altar are the only ornaments of this church. The portico is ornamented by beautiful reliefs.

The Werder church is a modern erection, built in the Gothic style, and its turrets are ornamented by beautiful bronze reliefs. The walls inside are inlaid with coloured wood up to the galleries, where they terminate in Gothic scroll-work. The organ has a full, clear tone; in front of it stands a painting which, at first sight, resembles a scene from heathen mythology more than a sacred subject. A number of cupids soar among wreaths of flowers, and surround three beautiful female figures.

The mint and the architectural college stand near this church. The former is covered with fine sculptures; the latter is square, of a brick-red colour, without any architectural embellishment, and perfectly resembling an unusually large private house. The ground-floor is turned into fine shops.

Near the palace lies the Opera Square, in which stand the celebrated opera-house, the arsenal, the university, the library, the academy, the guardhouse, and several royal palaces. Three statues ornament the square: those of General Count Bulov, General Count Scharnhorst, and General Prince Blucher. They are all three beautifully sculptured, but the drapery did not please me; it consisted of the long military cloth cloak, which, opening in front, afforded a glimpse of the splendid uniforms.

The arsenal is one of the finest buildings in Berlin, and forms a square; at the time of my stay some repairs were being made, so that it was closed. I had to be content with glimpses through the windows of the first floor, which showed me immense saloons filled by tremendous cannons, ranged in rows.

The guardhouse is contiguous, and resembles a pretty temple, with its portico of columns.

The opera-house forms a long detached square. It would have a much better effect if the entrances were not so wretched. The one at the grand portal looks like a narrow, miserable church-door, low and gloomy. The other entrances are worse still, and one would not suppose that they could lead to such a splendid interior, whose appointments are indescribably luxurious and commodious. The pit is filled by rows of comfortably-cushioned chairs with cushioned backs, numbered, but not barred. The boxes are divided by very low partitions, so that the aristocratic world seems to sit on a tribune. The seats in the pit and the first and second tiers are covered with dark-red silk damask; the royal box is a splendid saloon, the floor of which is covered with the finest carpets. Beautiful oil-paintings, in tasteful gold frames, ornament the plafond; but the magnificent chandelier is the greatest curiosity. It looks so massively worked in bronze, that it is painful to see the heavy mass hang so loosely over the heads of the spectators. But it is only a delusion; for it is made of paste-board, and bronzed over. Innumerable lamps light the place; but one thing which I miss in such elegant modern theatres is a clock, which has a place in nearly every Italian theatre.

The other buildings on this square are also distinguished for their size and the beauty of their architecture.

An unusually broad stone bridge, with a finely-made iron balustrade, is built over a little arm of the Spree, and unites the square of the opera with that on which the palace stands.

The royal museum is one of the finest architectural piles, and its high portal is covered with beautiful frescoes. The picture-gallery contains many *chefs-d'oeuvre*; and I regretted that I had not more time to examine it and the hall of antiquities, having only three hours for the two.

From the academy runs a long street lined with lime-trees, and which is therefore called Under-the-limes (*unter den Linden*). This alley forms a cheerful walk to the Brandenburg-gate, beyond which the pleasure-gardens are situated. The longest and finest streets which run into the lime-alley are the Friedrichs Street and the Wilhelms Street. The Leipziger Street also belongs to the finest, but does not run into this promenade.

The Gens-d'arme Square is distinguished by the French and German churches, at least by their exterior,--by their high domes, columns, and porticoes. The interiors are small and insignificant. On this square stands also the royal theatre, a tasteful pile of great beauty, with many pillars, and statues of muses and deities.

I ascended the tower on which the telegraph works, on account of the view over the town and the flat neighbourhood. A very civil official was polite enough to explain the signs of the telegraph to me, and to permit me to look at the other telegraphs through his telescope.

The Konigstadt, situated on the opposite shore of the Spree, not far from the royal palace, contains nothing remarkable. Its chief street, the Konigsstrasse, is long, but narrow and dirty. Indeed it forms a great contrast to the town of Berlin in every thing; the streets are narrow, short, and winding. The post-office and the theatres are the most remarkable buildings.

The luxury displayed in the shop-windows is very great. Many a mirror and many a plate-glass window reminded me of Hamburgh's splendour, which surpasses that of Berlin considerably.

There are not many excursions round Berlin, as the country is flat and sandy. The most interesting are to the pleasure-gardens, Charlottenburg, and, since the opening of the railway, to Potsdam.

The park or pleasure-garden is outside the Brandenburg-gate; it is divided into several parts, one of which reminded me of our fine Prater in Vienna. The beautiful alleys were filled with carriages, riders, and pedestrians; pretty coffee-houses enlivened the woody portions, and merry children gambolled on the green lawns. I felt so much reminded of my beloved Prater, that I expected every moment to see a well-known face, or receive a friendly greeting. Kroll's Casino, sometimes called the Winter-garden, is built on this side of the park. I do not know how to describe this building; it is quite a fairy palace. All the splendour which fancy can invent in furniture, gilding, painting, or tapestry, is here united in the splendid halls, saloons, temples, galleries, and boxes. The dining-room, which will dine 1800 persons, is not lighted by windows, but by a glass roof vaulted over it. Rows of pillars support the galleries, or separate the larger and smaller saloons. In the niches, and in the corners, round the pillars, abound fragrant flowers, and plants in chaste vases or pots, which transform this place into a magical garden in winter. Concerts and *reunions* take place here every Sunday, and the press of visitors is extraordinary, although smoking is prohibited. This place will accommodate 5000 persons.

That side of the park which lies in the direction of the Potsdam-gate resembles an ornamental garden, with its well-kept alleys, flower-beds, terraces, islets, and gold-fish ponds. A handsome monument to the memory of Queen Louise is erected on the Louise island here.

On this side, the coffee-house Odeon is the best, but cannot be compared to Kroll's casino. Here also are rows of very elegant country-houses, most of which are built in the Italian style.

CHARLOTTENBURG

This place is about half an hour's distance from the Brandenburg-gate, where the omnibuses that depart every minute are stationed. The road leads through the park, beyond which lies a pretty village, and adjoining it is the royal country-palace of Charlottenburg. The palace is built in two stories, of which the upper one is very low, and is probably only used for the domestics. The palace is more broad than deep; the roof is terrace-shaped, and in its centre rises a pretty dome. The garden is simple, and not very large, but contains a considerable orangery. In a dark grove stands a little building, the mausoleum in which the image of Queen Louise has been excellently executed by the famed artist Rauch. Here also rest the ashes of the late king. There is also an island with statues in the midst of a large pond, on which some swans float proudly. It is a pity that dirt does not stick to these white-feathered animals, else they would soon be black swans; for the pond or river surrounding the island is one of the dirtiest ditches I have ever seen.

Fatigue would be very intolerable in this park, for there are very few benches, but an immense quantity of gnats.

POTSDAM.

The distance from Berlin to Potsdam is eighteen miles, which is passed by the railroad in three-quarters of an hour. The railway is very conveniently arranged; the carriages are marked with the names of the station, and the traveller enters the carriage on which the place of his destination is marked. Thus, the passengers are never annoyed by the entrance or exit of passengers, as all occupying the same carriage descend at the same time.

The road is very uninteresting; but this is compensated for by Potsdam itself, for which a day is scarcely sufficient.

Immediately in front of the town flows the river Havel, crossed by a long, beautiful bridge, whose pillars are of stone, and the rest of the bridge of iron. The large royal palace lies on the opposite shore, and is surrounded by a garden. The garden is not very extensive, but large enough for the town, and is open to the public. The palace is built in a splendid style, but is unfortunately quite useless, as the court has beautiful summer-palaces in the neighbourhood of Potsdam, and spends the winter in Berlin.

The castle square is not very good; it is neither large nor regular, and not even level. On it stands the large church, which is not yet completed, but promises to be a fine structure. The town is tolerably large, and has many fine houses. The streets, especially the Nauner Street, are wide and long, but badly paved; the stones are laid with the pointed side upwards, and for foot-passengers there is a stone pavement two feet broad on one side of the street only. The promenade of the townspeople is called Am Kanal (beside the canal), and is a fine square, through which the canal flows, and is ornamented with trees.

Of the royal pleasure-palaces I visited that of Sans Souci first. It is surrounded by a pretty park, and lies on a hill, which is divided into six terraces. Large conservatories stand on each side of these; and in front of them are long alleys of orange and lemon-trees.

The palace has only a ground floor, and is surrounded by arbours, trees, and vines, so that it is almost concealed from view. I could not inspect the interior, as the royal family was living there.

A side-path leads from here to the Ruinenberg, on which the ruins of a larger and a smaller temple, raised by the hand of art, are tastefully disposed. The top of the hill is taken up by a reservoir of water. From this point one can see the back of the palace of Sans Souci, and the so-called new palace, separated from the former by a small park, and distant only about a quarter of an hour.

The new palace, built by Frederick the Great, is as splendid as one can imagine. It forms a lengthened square, with arabesques and flat columns, and has a flat roof, which is surrounded by a stone balustrade, and ornamented by statues.

The apartments are high and large, and splendidly painted, tapestried, and furnished. Oil-paintings, many of them very good, cover the walls. One might fill a volume with the description of all the wonders of this place, which is, however, not inhabited.

Behind the palace, and separated from it by a large court, are two beautiful little palaces, connected by a crescent-shaped hall of pillars; broad stone steps lead to the balconies surrounding the first story of the edifices. They are used as barracks, and are, as such, the most beautiful I have ever seen.

From here a pleasant walk leads to the lovely palace of Charlottenburg. Coming from the large new palace it seemed too small for the dwelling even of the crown-prince. I should have taken it for a splendid pavilion attached to the new palace, to which the royal family sometimes walked, and perhaps remained there to take refreshment. But when I had inspected it more closely, and seen all the comfortable little rooms, furnished with such tasteful luxury, I felt that the crown-prince could not have made a better choice.

Beautiful fountains play on the terraces; the walls of the corridors and ante-rooms are covered with splendid frescoes, in imitation of those found in Pompeii. The rooms abound in excellent engravings, paintings, and other works of art; and the greatest taste and splendour is displayed even in the minor arrangements.

A pretty Chinese chiosque, filled with good statues, which have been unfortunately much damaged and broken, stands near the palace.

These three beautiful royal residences are situated in parks, which are so united that they seem only as one. The parks are filled with fine trees, and verdant fields crossed by well-kept paths and drives; but I saw very few flower-beds in them.

When I had contemplated every thing at leisure, I returned to the palace of Sans Souci, to see the beautiful fountains, which play twice a week, on Tuesday and Friday, from noon till evening. The columns projected from the basin in front of the castle are so voluminous, and rise with such force, that I gazed in amazement at the artifice. It is real pleasure to be near the basin when the sun shines in its full splendour, forming the most beautiful rainbows in the falling shower of drops. Equally beautiful is a fountain rising from a high vase, enwreathed by living flowers, and falling over it, so that it forms a quick, brisk fountain, transparent, and pure as the finest crystal. The lid of the vase, also enwreathed with growing flowers, rises above the fountain. The Neptune's grotto is of no great beauty; the water falls from an urn placed over it, and forms little waterfalls as it flows over nautilus-shells.

The marble palace lies on the other side of Potsdam, and is half an hour's distance from these palaces; but I had time enough to visit it.

Entering the park belonging to this palace, a row of neat peasants' cottages is seen on the left; they are all alike, but separated by fruit, flower, or kitchen-gardens. The palace lies at the extreme end of the park, on a pretty lake formed by the river Havel. It certainly has some right to the name of marble palace; but it seems presumption to call it so when compared to the marble palaces of Venice, or the marble mosques of Constantinople.

The walls of the building are of brick left in its natural colour. The lower and upper frame-work, the window-sashes, and the portals, are all of marble. The palace is partly surrounded by a gallery supported on marble columns. The stairs are of fine white marble, and many of the apartments are laid with this mineral. The interior is not nearly so luxurious as the other palaces.

This was the last of the sights I saw in Potsdam or the environs of Berlin; for I continued my journey to Vienna on the following day.

Before quitting Berlin, I must mention an arrangement which is particularly convenient for strangers--namely, the fares for hackney-carriages. One need ask no questions, but merely enter the carriage, tell the coachman where to drive, and pay him six-pence. This moderate fare is for the whole town, which is somewhat extensive. At all the railway stations there are numbers of these vehicles, which will drive to any hotel, however far it may be from the station, for the same moderate fare. If only all cab-drivers were so accommodating!

October 1st.

The railway goes through Leipzic to Dresden, where I took the mail-coach for Prague at eight o'clock the same evening, and arrived there in eighteen hours.

As it was night when we passed, we did not enjoy the beautiful views of the Nollendorf mountain. In the morning we passed two handsome monuments, one of them, a pyramid fifty-four feet high, to the memory of Count Colloredo, the other to the memory of the Russian troops who had fallen here; both have been erected since the wars of Napoleon.

On we went through charming districts to the famed bathing-place Teplitz, which is surrounded by the most beautiful scenery; and can bear comparison with the finest bathing-places of the world.

Further on we passed a solitary basaltic rock, Boren, which deserves attention for its beauty and as a natural curiosity. We unfortunately hurried past it, as we wished to reach Prague before six o'clock, so that we might not miss the train to Vienna.

My readers may imagine our disappointment on arriving at the gates of Prague, when our passports were taken from us and not returned. In vain we referred to the *vise* of the boundary-town Peterswalde; in vain we spoke of our haste. The answer always was, "That is nothing to us; you can have your papers back to-morrow at the police-office." Thus we were put off, and lost twenty-four hours.

I must mention a little joke I had on the ride from Dresden to Prague. Two gentlemen and a lady beside myself occupied the mail-coach; the lady happened to have read my diary of Palestine, and asked me, when she heard my name, if I were that traveller. When I had acknowledged I was that same person, our conversation turned on that and on my present journey. One of the gentlemen, Herr Katze, was very intelligent, and conversed in a most interesting manner on countries, nationalities, and scientific subjects. The other gentleman was probably equally well informed, but he made less use of his acquirements. Herr Katze remained in Teplitz, and the other gentleman proceeded with us to Vienna. Before arriving at our destination, he asked me if Herr Katze had not requested me to mention his name in my next book, and added, that if I would promise to do the same, he would tell me his name. I could not refrain from smiling, but assured him that Herr Katze had not thought of such a thing, and begged him not to communicate his name to me, so that he might see that we females were not so curious as we are said to be. But the poor man could not refrain from giving me his name--Nicholas B.--before we parted. I do not insert it for two reasons: first, because I did not promise to name him; and secondly, because I do not think it would do him any service.

The railway from Prague to Vienna goes over Olmutz, and makes such a considerable round, that the distance is now nearly 320 miles, and the arrangements on the railway are very imperfect.

There were no hotels erected on the road, and we had to be content with fruit, beer, bread, and butter, &c. the whole time. And these provisions were not easily obtained, as we could not venture to leave the carriages. The conductor called out at every station that we should go on directly, although the train frequently stood upwards of half an hour; but as we did not know that before, we were obliged to remain on our seats. The conductors were not of the most amiable character, which may perhaps be ascribed to the climate; for when we approached the boundary of the Austrian states at Peterswalde, the inspector received us very gruffly. We wished him good evening twice, but he took no notice of it, and demanded our papers in a loud and peremptory tone; he probably thought us as deaf as we thought him. At Ganserndorf, twenty-five miles from Vienna, they took our papers from us in a very uncivil, uncourteous manner.

On the 4th of October, 1845, after an absence of six months, I arrived again in sight of the dear Stephen's steeple, as most of my countrywomen would say.

I had suffered many hardships; but my love of travelling would not have been abated, nor would my courage have failed me, had they been ten times greater. I had been amply compensated for all. I had seen things which never occur in our common life, and had met with people as they are rarely met with--in their natural state. And I brought back with me the recollections of my travels, which will always remain, and which will afford me renewed pleasure for years.

And now I take leave of my dear readers, requesting them to accept with indulgence my descriptions, which are always true, though they may not be amusing. If I have, as I can scarcely hope, afforded them some amusement, I trust they will in return grant me a small corner in their memories.

In conclusion, I beg to add an Appendix, which may not be uninteresting to many of my readers, namely:

1. A document which I procured in Reikjavik, giving the salaries of the royal Danish officials, and the sources from whence they are paid.

2. A list of Icelandic insects, butterflies, flowers, and plants, which I collected and brought home with me.

APPENDIX A

Salaries of the Royal Danish Officials in Iceland, which they receive
from the Icelandic land-revenues.

Florins {58}

The Governor of Iceland   2000
   Office expenses   600
The deputy for the western   1586
district
   Office expenses   400
   Rent   200
The deputy for the northern and   1286
eastern districts
   Office expenses   400
The bishop of Iceland, who draws   800
his salary from the
school-revenues, has paid him
from this treasury
The members of the Supreme Court:
   One judge   1184
   First assessor   890
   Second assessor   740
The land-bailiff of Iceland   600
   Office expenses   200
   Rent   150
The town-bailiff of Reikjavik   300
The first police-officer of   200
Reikjavik, who is at the same
time gaoler, and therefore has 50
fl. more than the second
officer
The second police-officer   150
The mayor of Reikjavik only draws   150
from this treasury his
house-rent, which is
The sysselman of the Westmanns   296
Islands
The other sysselmen, each   230

Medical department and midwifery:

The physician	900
House-rent	150
Apothecary of Reikjavik	185
House-rent	150
The second apothecary at Sikkisholm	90
Six surgeons in the country, each	300
House-rent for some	30
For others	25
A medical practitioner on the Northland	110
Reikjavik has two midwives, each receives	50
The other midwives in Iceland, amounting to thirty, each receives	100

These midwives are instructed and examined by the land physician, who has the charge of paying them annually.

Organist of Reikjavik	100

From the school-revenues

The bishop receives	1200

The teachers at the high school:

The teacher of theology	800
The head assistant, besides free lodging	500
The second assistant	500
House-rent	50
The third assistant	500

House-rent   50
The resident at the school   170

LIST OF INVERTEBRATED ANIMALS collected in Iceland

1. CRUSTACEA.

Pagarus Bernhardus, *Linnaeus*.

2. INSECTA.

a. *Coleoptera*. Nebria rubripes, *Dejean*. Patrobus hyperboreus. Calathus melanocephalus, *Fabr*. Notiophilus aquaticus. Amara vulgaris, *Duftsihm*. Ptinus fur, *Linn*. Aphodius Lapponum, *Schh*. Otiorhynchus laevigatus, *Dhl*. Otiorhynchus Pinastri, *Fabr*. Otiorhynchus ovatus. Staphylinus maxillosus. Byrrhus pillula.

b. *Neuroptera*. Limnophilus lineola, *Schrank*.

c. *Hymenoptera*. Pimpla instigator, *Gravh*. Bombus subterraneus, *Linn*.

d. *Lepidoptera*. Geometra russata, Hub. Geom. alche millata. Geom. spec. nov.

e. *Diptera*. Tipula lunata, *Meig*. Scatophaga stercoraria. Musca vomitaria. Musca mortuorum. Helomyza serrata. Lecogaster islandicus, *Scheff*. {59} Anthomyia decolor, *Fallin*.

LIST OF ICELANDIC PLANTS collected by Ida Pfeiffer in the Summer of the year 1845

Felices. Cystopteris fragilis.

Equisetaceae. Equisetum Teltamegra.

Graminae. Festuca uniglumis.

Cyperaceae. Carea filiformis. Carea caespitosa. Eriophorum caespitosum.

Juncaceae. Luzula spicata. Luzula campestris.

Salicineae. Salix polaris.

Polygoneae. Remux arifolus. Oxyria reniformes.

Plumbagineae. Armeria alpina (in the interior mountainous districts).

Compositae. Chrysanthemum maritimum (on the sea-shore, and on marshy fields). Hieracium alpinum (on grassy plains). Taraxacum alpinum. Erigeron uniflorum (west of Havenfiord, on rocky soil).

Rubiaceae. Gallium pusillum. Gallium verum.

Labiatae. Thynus serpyllum.

Asperifoliae. Myosotis alpestris. Myosotis scorpioicles.

Scrophularineae. Bartsia alpina (in the interior north-western valleys). Rhinanthus alpestris.

Utricularieae. Pinguicula alpina. Pinguicula vulgaris.

Umbelliferae. Archangelica officinalis (Havenfiord).

Saxifrageae. Saxifraga caespitosa (the real Linnaean plant: on rocks round Hecla).

Ranunculaceae. Ranunculus auricomus. Ranunculus nivalis. Thalictrum alpinum (growing between lava, near Reikjavik). Caltha palustris.

Cruciferae. Draba verna. Cardamine pratensis.

Violariceae. Viola hirta.

Caryophylleae. Sagina stricta. Cerastium semidecandrum. Lepigonum rubrum. Silene maritima. Lychnis alpina (on the mountain-fields round Reikjavik).

Empetreae. Empetrum nigrum.

Geraniaceae. Geranium sylvaticum (in pits near Thingvalla).

Troseaceae. Parnassia palustris.

OEnothereae. Epilobium latifolium (in clefts of the mountain at the foot of Hecla). Epilobium alpinum (in Reiker valley, west of Havenfiord).

Rosaceae. Rubus arcticus. Potentilla anserina. Potentilla gronlandica (on rocks near Kallmanstunga and Kollismola). Alchemilla montana. Sanguisorba officinalis. Geum rivale. Dryas octopela (near Havenfiord).

Papilionaceae. Trifolium repens.

FOOTNOTES:

{1} In this Gutenberg eText only Madame Pfeiffer's work appears--DP.

{2} Madame Pfeiffer's first journey was to the Holy Land in 1842; and on her return from Iceland she started in 1846 on a "Journey round the World," from which she returned in the end of 1848. This adventurous lady is now (1853) travelling among the islands of the Eastern Archipelago.

{3} A florin is worth about 2*s*. 1*d*.; sixty kreutzers go to a florin.

{4} At Kuttenberg the first silver groschens were coined, in the year 1300. The silver mines are now exhausted, though other mines, of copper, zinc, &c. are wrought in the neighbourhood. The population is only half of what it once was. --ED.

{5} The expression of Madame Pfeiffer's about Frederick "paying his score to the Austrians," is somewhat vague. The facts are these. In 1757 Frederick the Great of Prussia invaded Bohemia, and laid siege to Prague. Before this city an Austrian army lay, who were attacked with great impetuosity by Frederick, and completely defeated. But the town was defended with great valour; and during the time thus gained the Austrian general Daun raised fresh troops, with which he took the field at Collin. Here he was attacked by Frederick, who was routed, and all his baggage and cannon captured. This loss was "paying his score;" and the defeat was so complete, that the great monarch sat down by the side of a fountain, and tracing figures in the sand, was lost for a long time in meditation on the means to be adopted to retrieve his fortune.

{6} I mention this little incident to warn the traveller against parting with his effects.

{7} The true version of this affair is as follows. John of Nepomuk was a priest serving under the Archbishop of Prague. The king, Wenceslaus, was a hasty, cruel tyrant, who was detested by all his subjects, and hated by the rest of Germany. Two priests were guilty of some crime, and one of the court chamberlains, acting under royal orders, caused the priests to be put to death. The archbishop, indignant at this, placed the chamberlain under an interdict. This so roused the king that he attempted to seize the archbishop, who took refuge in flight. John of Nepomuk, however, and another priest, were seized and put to the torture to confess what were the designs of the archbishop. The king seems to have suspected that the queen was in some way connected with the line of conduct pursued by the archbishop. John of Nepomuk, however, refused, even though the King with his own hand burned him with a torch. Irritated by his obstinate silence, the king caused the poor monk to be cast over the bridge into the Moldau. This monk was afterwards canonised, and made the patron saint of bridges.--ED.

{8} Albert von Wallenstein (or Waldstein), the famous Duke of Friedland, is celebrated as one of the ablest commanders of the imperial forces during the protracted religious contest known in German history as the "Thirty Years' War." During its earlier period Wallenstein greatly distinguished himself, and was created by the Emperor Ferdinand Duke of Friedland and generalissimo of the imperial forces. In the course of a few months Wallenstein raised an army of forty thousand men in the Emperor's service. The strictest discipline was preserved *within* his camp, but his troops supported themselves by a system of rapine and plunder unprecedented even in those days of military license. Merit was rewarded with princely munificence, and the highest offices were within the reach of every common soldier who distinguished himself;--trivial breaches of discipline were punished with death. The dark and ambitious spirit of Wallenstein would not allow him to rest satisfied with the rewards and dignities heaped upon him by his imperial master. He temporised and entered into negotiations with the enemy; and during an interview with a Swedish general (Arnheim), is even said to have proposed an alliance to "hunt the Emperor to the devil." It is supposed that he aspired to the sovereignty of Bohemia. Ferdinand was informed of the ambitious designs of his general, and at length determined that Wallenstein should die. He despatched one of his generals, Gallas, to the commander-in-chief, with a mandate depriving him of his dignity of generalissimo, and nominating Gallas as his successor. Surprised before his plans were ripe, and deserted by many on whose support he had relied, Wallenstein retired hastily upon Egra. During a banquet in the castle, three of his generals who remained faithful to their leader were murdered in the dead of night. Roused by the noise, Wallenstein leapt from his bed, and encountered three soldiers who had been hired to despatch him. Speechless with astonishment and indignation, he stretched forth his arms, and receiving in his breast the stroke of a halbert, fell dead without a groan, in the fifty-first year of his age.

The following anecdote, curiously illustrative of the state of affairs in Wallenstein's camp, is related by Schiller in his ***History of the Thirty Years' War***, a work containing a full account of the life and actions of this extraordinary man. "The extortions of Wallenstein's soldiers from the peasants had at one period reached such a pitch, that severe penalties were denounced against all marauders; and every soldier who should be convicted of theft was threatened with a halter. Shortly afterwards, it chanced that Wallenstein himself met a soldier straying in the field, whom he caused to be seized, as having violated the law, and condemned to the gallows without a trial, by his usual word of doom: "Let the rascal be hung!" The soldier protested, and proved his innocence. "Then let them hang the innocent," cried the inhuman Wallenstein; "and the guilty will tremble the more." The preparations for carrying this sentence into effect had already commenced, when the soldier, who saw himself lost without remedy, formed the desperate resolution that he would not die unrevenged. Rushing furiously upon his leader, he was seized and disarmed by the bystanders before he could carry his intention into effect. "Now let him go," said Wallenstein; "it will excite terror enough.""--ED.

{9} Poniatowski was the commander of the Polish legion in the armies of Napoleon, by whom he was highly respected. At the battle of Leipzig, fought in October 1813, Poniatowski and Marshal MacDonald were appointed to command the rear of Napoleon's army, which, after two days hard fighting, was compelled to retreat before the Allies. These generals defended the retreat of the army so gallantly, that all the French troops, except those under their immediate command, had evacuated the town. The rear-guard was preparing to follow, when the only bridge over the

Elster that remained open to them was destroyed, through some mistake. This effectually barred the escape of the rear of Napoleon's army. A few, among whom was Marshal MacDonald, succeeded in swimming across; but Poniatowski, after making a brave resistance, and refusing to surrender, was drowned in making the same attempt.--ED.

{10} Leipzig has long been famous as the chief book-mart of Germany. At the great Easter meetings, publishers from all the different states assemble at the "Buchhandler Borse," and a large amount of business is done. The fairs of Leipzig have done much towards establishing the position of this city as one of the first trading towns in Germany. They take place three times annually: at New-year, at Easter, and at Michaelmas; but the Easter fair is by far the most important. These commercial meetings last about three weeks, and during this time the town presents a most animated appearance, as the streets are thronged with the costumes of almost every nation, the smart dress of the Tyrolese contrasting gaily with the sombre garb of the Polish Jews. The amount of business transacted at these fairs is very considerable; on several occasions, above twenty thousand dealers have assembled. The trade is principally in woollen cloths; but lighter wares, and even ornaments of every description, are sold to a large extent. The manner in which every available place is taken advantage of is very curious: archways, cellars, passages, and courtyards are alike filled with merchandise, and the streets are at times so crowded as to be almost impassable. When the three weeks have passed, the wooden booths which have been erected in the market-place and the principal streets are taken down, the buyers and sellers vanish together, and the visitor would scarcely recognise in the quiet streets around him the bustling busy city of a few days ago.--ED.

{11} The fire broke out on 4th May 1842, and raged with the utmost fury for three days. Whole streets were destroyed, and at least 2000 houses burned to the ground. Nearly half a million of money was raised in foreign countries to assist in rebuilding the city, of which about a tenth was contributed by Britain. Such awful fires, fearful though they are at the time, seem absolutely necessary to great towns, as they cause needful improvements to be made, which the indolence or selfishness of the inhabitants would otherwise prevent. There is not a great city that has not at one time or another suffered severely from fire, and has risen out of the ruins greater than before.--ED.

{12} There are no docks at Hamburgh, consequently all the vessels lie in the river Elbe, and both receive and discharge their cargoes there. Madame Pfeiffer, however, is mistaken in supposing that only London could show a picture of so many ships and so much commercial activity surpassing that of Hamburgh. Such a picture, more impressive even than that seen in the Elbe, is exhibited every day in the Mersey or the Hudson.--ED.

{13} Kiel, however, is a place of considerable trade; and doubtless the reason why Madame Pfeiffer saw so few vessels at it was precisely the same reason why she saw so many at Hamburgh. Kiel contains an excellent university.--ED.

{14} At sea I calculate by sea-miles, of which sixty go to a degree.

{15} This great Danish sculptor was born of poor parents at Copenhagen, on the 19th November, 1770; his father was an Icelander, and earned his living by carving figure-heads for ships. Albert, or "Bertel," as he is more generally called, was accustomed during his youth to assist his father in his labours on the wharf. At an early age he visited the Academy at Copenhagen, where his genius soon began to make itself conspicuous. At the age of sixteen he had won a silver, and at twenty a gold medal. Two years later he carried off the "great" gold medal, and was sent to study abroad at the expense of the Academy. In 1797 we find him practising his art at Rome under the eye of Zoega the Dane, who does not, however, seem to have discovered indications of extraordinary genius in the labours of his young country-man. But a work was soon to appear which should set all questions as to Thorwaldsen's talent for ever at rest. In 1801 he produced his celebrated statue of "Jason," which was at once pronounced by the great Canova to be "a work in a new and a grand style." After this period the path of fame lay open before the young sculptor; his bas-reliefs of "Summer" and "Autumn," the "Dance of the Muses," "Cupid and Psyche," and numerous other works, followed each other in rapid succession; and at length, in 1812, Thorwaldsen produced his extraordinary work, "The Triumph of Alexander." In 1819 Thorwaldsen returned rich and famous to the city he had quitted as a youth twenty-three years before; he was received with great honour, and many feasts and rejoicings were held to celebrate his arrival. After a sojourn of a year Thorwaldsen again visited Rome, where he continued his labours until 1838, when, wealthy and independent, he resolved to rest in his native country. This time his welcome to Copenhagen was even more enthusiastic than in 1819.

The whole shore was lined with spectators, and amid thundering acclamations the horses were unharnessed from his carriage, and the sculptor was drawn in triumph by the people to his ***atelier***. During the remainder of his life Thorwaldsen passed much of his time on the island of Nyso, where most of his latest works were executed. On Sunday, March 9th, 1842, he had been conversing with a circle of friends in perfect health. Halm's tragedy of ***Griselda*** was announced for the evening, and Thorwaldsen proceeded to the theatre to witness the performance. During the overture he rose to allow a stranger to pass, then resumed his seat, and a moment afterwards his head sunk on his breast--he was dead!

His funeral was most sumptuous. Rich and poor united to do honour to the memory of the great man, who had endeared himself to them by his virtues as by his genius. The crown-prince followed the coffin, and the people of Copenhagen stood in two long rows, and uncovered their heads as the coffin of the sculptor was carried past. The king himself took part in the solemnity. At the time of his decease Thorwaldsen had completed his seventy-second year.--ED.

{16} Tycho de Brahe was a distinguished astronomer, who lived between 1546 and 1601. He was a native of Denmark. His whole life may be said to have been devoted to astronomy. A small work that he published when a young man brought him under the notice of the King of Denmark, with whose assistance he constructed, on the small island of Hulln, a few miles north of Copenhagen, the celebrated Observatory of Uranienburg. Here, seated in "the ancient chair" referred to in the text, and surrounded by numerous assistants, he directed for seventeen years a series of observations, that have been found extremely accurate and useful. On the death of his patron he retired to Prague in Bohemia, where he was employed by Rodolph II. then Emperor of Germany. Here he was assisted by the great Kepler, who, on Tycho's death in 1601, succeeded him.--ED.

{17} The fisheries of Iceland have been very valuable, and indeed the chief source of the commerce of the country ever since it was discovered. The fish chiefly caught are cod and the tusk or cat-fish. They are exported in large quantities, cured in various ways. Since the discovery of Newfoundland, however, the fisheries of Iceland have lost much of their importance. So early as 1415, the English sent fishing vessels to the Icelandic coast, and the sailors who were on board, it would appear, behaved so badly to the natives that Henry V. had to make some compensation to the King of Denmark for their conduct. The greatest number of fishing vessels from England that ever visited Iceland was during the reign of James I., whose marriage with the sister of the Danish king might probably make England at the time the most favoured nation. It was in his time that an English pirate, "Gentleman John," as he was called, committed great ravages in Iceland, for which James had afterwards to make compensation. The chief markets for the fish are in the Catholic countries of Europe. In the seventeenth century, a great traffic in fish was carried on between Iceland and Spain.--ED.

{18} The dues charged by the Danish Government on all vessels passing through the Sound have been levied since 1348, and therefore enjoy a prescriptive right of more than five hundred years. They bring to the Danish Government a yearly revenue of about a quarter of a million; and, in consideration of the dues, the Government has to support certain lighthouses, and otherwise to render safe and easy the navigation of this great entrance to the Baltic. Sound-dues were first paid in the palmy commercial days of the Hanseatic League. That powerful combination of merchants had suffered severely from the ravages of Danish pirates, royal and otherwise; but ultimately they became so powerful that the rich merchant could beat the royal buccaneer, and tame his ferocity so effectually as to induce him to build and maintain those beacon-lights on the shores of the Sound, for whose use they and all nations and merchants after them have agreed to pay certain duties.--ED.

{19} The Feroe Islands consist of a great many islets, some of them mere rocks, lying about halfway between the north coast of Scotland and Iceland. At one time they belonged to Norway, but came into the possession of Denmark at the same time as Iceland. They are exceedingly mountainous, some of the mountains attaining an elevation of about 2800 feet. The largest town or village does not contain more than 1500 or 1600 inhabitants. The population live chiefly on the produce of their large flocks of sheep, and on the down procured, often at great risk to human life, from the eider-duck and other birds by which the island is frequented.--ED.

{20} I should be truly sorry if, in this description of our "life aboard ship," I had said any thing which could give offence to my kind friend Herr Knudson. I have, however, presumed that every one is aware that the mode of life at sea is different to life in families. I have only to add, that Herr Knudson lived most agreeably not only in Copenhagen, but what is far more remarkable, in Iceland also, and was provided with every comfort procurable in the largest European towns.

{21} It is not only at sea that ingenious excuses for drinking are invented. The lovers of good or bad liquor on land find these reasons as "plenty as blackberries," and apply them with a marvellous want of stint or scruple. In warm climates the liquor is drank to keep the drinker cool, in cold to keep him warm; in health to prevent him from being sick, in sickness to bring him back to health. Very seldom is the real reason, "because I like it," given; and all these excuses and reasons must be regarded as implying some lingering sense of shame at the act, and as forming part of "the homage that vice always pays to virtue."--ED.

{22} The sailors call those waves "Spanish" which, coming from the west, distinguish themselves by their size.

{23} These islands form a rocky group, only one of which is inhabited, lying about fifteen miles from the coast. They are said to derive their name from some natives of Ireland, called West-men, who visited Iceland shortly after its discovery by the Norwegians. In this there is nothing improbable, for we know that during the ninth and tenth centuries the Danes and Normans, called Easterlings, made many descents on the Irish coast; and one Norwegian chief is reported to have assumed sovereign power in Ireland about the year 866, though he was afterwards deposed, and flung into a lough, where he was drowned: rather an ignominious death for a "sea-king."--ED.

{24} This work, which Madame Pfeiffer does not praise too highly, was first published in 1810. After passing through two editions, it was reprinted in 1841, at a cheap price, in the valuable people's editions of standard works, published by Messrs. Chambers of Edinburgh.

{25} It is related of Ingold that he carried with him on his voyage the door of his former house in Ireland, and that when he approached the coast he cast it into the sea, watching the point of land which it touched; and on that land he fixed his future home. This land is the same on which the town of Reikjavik now stands. These old sea-kings, like the men of Athens, were "in all things too superstitious."--ED.

{26} These sea-rovers, that were to the nations of Europe during the middle ages what the Danes, Norwegians, and other northmen were at an earlier period, enjoyed at this time the full flow of their lawless prosperity. Their insolence and power were so great that many nations, our own included, were glad to purchase, by a yearly payment, exemption from the attacks of these sea-rovers. The Americans paid this tribute so late as 1815. The unfortunate Icelanders who were carried off in the seventeenth century nearly all died as captives in Algiers. At the end of ten years they were liberated; but of the four hundred only thirty-seven were alive when the joyful intelligence reached the place of their captivity; and of these twenty-four died before rejoining their native land.--ED.

{27} This town, the capital of Iceland, and the seat of government, is built on an arm of the sea called the Faxefiord, in the south-west part of the island. The resident population does not exceed 500, but this is greatly increased during the annual fairs. It consists mainly of two streets at right angles to each other. It contains a large church built of stone, roofed with tiles; an observatory; the residences of the governor and the bishop, and the prison, which is perhaps the most conspicuous building in the town.--ED.

{28} As Madame Pfeiffer had thus no opportunity of attending a ball in Iceland, the following description of one given by Sir George Mackenzie may be interesting to the reader.

"We gave a ball to the ladies of Reikjavik and the neighbourhood. The company began to assemble about nine o'clock. We were shewn into a small low-roofed room, in which were a number of men, but to my surprise I saw no females. We soon found them, however, in one adjoining, where it is the custom for them to wait till their partners go to hand them out. On entering this apartment, I felt considerable disappointment at not observing a single woman dressed in the Icelandic costume. The dresses had some resemblance to those of English chambermaids, but were not so smart. An old lady, the wife of the man who kept the tavern, was habited like the pictures of our great-grandmothers. Some time after the dancing commenced, the bishop's lady, and two others, appeared in the proper dress of the country.

"We found ourselves extremely awkward in dancing what the ladies were pleased to call English country dances. The music, which came from a solitary ill-scraped fiddle, accompanied by the rumbling of the same half-rotten drum that had summoned the high court of justice, and by the jingling of a rusty triangle, was to me utterly unintelligible. The extreme rapidity with which it was necessary to go through many complicated evolutions in proper time, completely bewildered us; and our mistakes, and frequent collisions with our neighbours, afforded much amusement to our fair partners, who found it for a long time impracticable to keep us in the right track. When allowed to breathe a little, we had an opportunity of remarking some singularities in the state of society and manners among the Danes of Reikjavik. While unengaged in the dance, the men drink punch, and walk about with tobacco-pipes in their mouths, spitting plentifully on the floor. The unrestrained evacuation of saliva seems to be a fashion all over Iceland; but whether the natives learned it from the Danes, or the Danes from the natives, we did not ascertain. Several ladies whose virtue could not bear a very strict scrutiny were pointed out to us.

"During the dances, tea and coffee were handed about; and negus and punch were ready for those who chose to partake of them. A cold supper was provided, consisting of hams, beef, cheese, &c., and wine. While at table, several of the ladies sang, and acquitted themselves tolerably well. But I could not enjoy the performance, on account of the incessant talking, which was as fashionable a rudeness in Iceland as it is now in Britain. This, however, was not considered as in the least unpolite. One of the songs was in praise of the donors of the entertainment; and, during the chorus, the ceremony of touching each other's glasses was performed. After supper, waltzes were danced, in a style that reminded me of soldiers marching in cadence to the dead march in Saul. Though there was no need of artificial light, a number of candles were placed in the rooms. When the company broke up, about three o'clock, the sun was high above the horizon."

{29} A man of eighty years of age is seldom seen on the island.--*Kerguelen*.

{30} Kerguelen (writing in 1768) says: "They live during the summer principally on cod's heads. A common family make a meal of three or four cods' heads boiled in sea-water."--ED.

{31} This bakehouse is the only one in Iceland, and produces as good bread and biscuit as any that can be procured in Denmark. [In Kerguelen's time (1768) bread was very uncommon in Iceland. It was brought from Copenhagen, and consisted of broad thin cakes, or sea-biscuits, made of rye-flour, and extremely black.--ED.]

{32} In all high latitudes fat oily substances are consumed to a vast extent by the natives. The desire seems to be instinctive, not acquired. A different mode of living would undoubtedly render them more susceptible to the cold of these inclement regions. Many interesting anecdotes are related of the fondness of these hyperborean races for a kind of food from which we would turn in disgust. Before gas was introduced into Edinburgh, and the city was lighted by oil-lamps, several Russian noblemen visited that metropolis; and it is said that their longing for the luxury of train-oil became one evening so intense, that, unable to procure the delicacy in any other way, they emptied the oil-lamps. Parry relates that when he was wintering in the Arctic regions, one of the seamen, who had been smitten with the charms of an Esquimaux lady, wished to make her a present, and knowing the taste peculiar to those regions, he gave her with all due honours a pound of candles, six to the pound! The present was so acceptable to the lady, that she eagerly devoured the lot in the presence of her wondering admirer.--ED.

{33} An American travelling in Iceland in 1852 thus describes, in a letter to the **Boston Post**, the mode of travelling:--"All travel is on horseback. Immense numbers of horses are raised in the country, and they are exceedingly cheap. As for travelling on foot, even short journeys, no one ever thinks of it. The roads are so bad for walking, and generally so good for riding that shoe-leather, to say nothing of fatigue, would cost nearly as much as horse-flesh. Their horses are small, compact, hardy little animals, a size larger than Shetland ponies, but rarely exceeding from 12 or 13.5 hands high. A stranger in travelling must always have a 'guide,' and if he does go equipped for a good journey and intends to make good speed, he wants as many as six horses; one for himself, one for the guide, one for the luggage, and three relay horses. Then when one set of horses are tired the saddles are exchanged to the others. The relay horses are tied together and are either led or driven before the others. A tent is often carried, unless a traveller chooses to chance it for his lodgings. Such an article as an hotel is not kept in Iceland out of the capital. You must also carry your provisions with you, as you will be able to get but little on your route. Plenty of milk can be had, and some fresh-water fish. The luggage is carried in trunks that are hung on each side of the horse, on a rude frame that serves as a pack-saddle. Under this, broad pieces of turf are placed to prevent galling the horse's back."

{34} The down of the eider-duck forms a most important and valuable article of Icelandic commerce. It is said that the weight of down procurable from each nest is about half a pound, which is reduced one-half by cleansing. The down is sold at about twelve shillings per pound, so that the produce of each nest is about three shillings. The eider-duck is nearly as large as the common goose; and some have been found on the Fern Islands, off the coast of Northumberland.--ED.

{35} The same remark applies with equal force to many people who are not Icelanders. It was once the habit among a portion of the population of Lancashire, on returning from market, to carry their goods in a bag attached to one end of a string slung over their shoulders, which was balanced by a bag containing a stone at the other. Some time ago, it was pointed out to a worthy man thus returning from market, that it would be easier for him to throw away the stone, and make half of his load balance the other half, but the advice was rejected with disdain; the plan he had adopted was that of his forefathers, and he would on no account depart from it.--ED.

{36} The description of the Wolf's Hollow occurs in the second act of *Der Freyschutz*, when Rodolph sings:

"How horrid, dark, and wild, and drear,
Doth this gaping gulf appear!
It seems the hue of hell to wear.
The bellowing thunder bursts yon clouds,
The moon with blood has stained her light!
What forms are those in misty shrouds,
That stalk before my sight?
And now, hush! hush!
The owl is hooting in yon bush;
How yonder oak-tree's blasted arms
Upon me seem to frown!
My heart recoils, but all alarms
Are vain: fate calls, I must down, down."

{37} The reader must bear in mind that, during the season of which I speak, there is no twilight, much less night, in Iceland.

{38} The springs of Carlsbad are said to have been unknown until about five hundred years ago, when a hunting-dog belonging to one of the emperors of Germany fell in, and by his howling attracted the hunters to the spot. The temperature of the chief spring is 165 degrees.--ED.

{39} History tells of this great Icelandic poet, that owing to his treachery the free island of Iceland came beneath the Norwegian sceptre. For this reason he could never appear in Iceland without a strong guard, and therefore visited the Allthing under the protection of a small army of 600 men. Being at length surprised by his enemies in his house at Reikiadal, he fell beneath their blows, after a short and ineffectual resistance. [Snorri Sturluson, the most distinguished name of which Iceland can boast, was born, in 1178, at Hoam. In his early years he was remarkably fortunate in his worldly affairs. The fortune he derived from his father was small, but by means of a rich marriage, and by inheritance, he soon became proprietor of large estates in Iceland. Some writers say that his guard of 600 men, during his visit to the Allthing, was intended not as a defence, as indicated in Madame Pfeiffer's note, but for the purposes of display, and to impress the inhabitants with forcible ideas of his influence and power. He was invited to the court of the Norwegian king, and there he either promised or was bribed to bring Iceland under the Norwegian power. For this he has been greatly blamed, and stigmatised as a traitor; though it would appear from some historians that he only undertook to do by peaceable means what otherwise the Norwegian kings would have effected by force, and thus saved his country from a foreign invasion. But be this as it may, it is quite clear that he sunk in the estimation of his countrymen, and the feeling against him became so strong, that he was obliged to fly to Norway. He returned, however, in 1239, and in two years afterwards he was assassinated by his own son-in-law. The work by which he is chiefly known is the **Heimskringla**, or Chronicle of the Sea-Kings of Norway, one of the most valuable pieces of northern history, which has been admirably translated into English by Mr. Samuel Laing. This curious name of Heimskringla was given to the work because it contains the words with which begins, and means literally *the circle of the world*.--ED.]

{40} A translation of this poem will be found in the Appendix. [Not included in this Gutenberg eText--DP]

{41} In Iceland, as in Denmark, it is the custom to keep the dead a week above ground. It may be readily imagined that to a non-Icelandic sense of smell, it is an irksome task to be present at a burial from beginning to end, and especially in summer. But I will not deny that the continued sensation may have partly proceeded from imagination.

{42} Every one in Iceland rides.

{43} I cannot forbear mentioning a curious circumstance here. When I was at the foot of Mount Etna in 1842, the fiery element was calmed; some months after my departure it flamed with renewed force. When, on my return from Hecla, I came to Reikjavik, I said jocularly that it would be most strange if this Etna of the north should also have an eruption now. Scarcely had I left Iceland more than five weeks when an eruption, more violent than the former one, really took place. This circumstance is the more remarkable, as it had been in repose for eighty years, and was already looked upon as a burnt-out volcano. If I were to return to Iceland now, I should be looked upon as a prophetess of evil, and my life would scarcely be safe.

{44} Every peasant in tolerably good circumstances carries a little tent with him when he leaves home for a few days. These tents are, at the utmost, three feet high, five or six feet long, and three broad.

{45} "Though their poverty disables them from imitating the hospitality of their ancestors in all respects, yet the desire of doing it still exists: they cheerfully give away the little they have to spare, and express the utmost joy and satisfaction if you are pleased with the gift." *Uno von Troil*, 1772.--ED.

{46} The presence of American ships in the port of Gottenburg is not to be wondered at, seeing that nearly three-fourths of all the iron exported from Gottenburg is to America.--ED.

{47} "St. Stephen's steeple" is 450 feet high, being about 40 feet higher than St. Paul's, and forms part of St. Stephen's Cathedral in Vienna, a magnificent Gothic building, that dates as far back as the twelfth century. It has a great bell, that weighs about eighteen tons, being more than double the weight of the bell in St. Peter's at Rome, and four times the weight of the "Great Tom of Lincoln." The metal used consisted of cannons taken from the Turks during their memorable sieges of Vienna. The cathedral is 350 feet long and 200 wide, being less than St. Paul's in London, which is 510 feet long and 282 wide.--ED.

{48} The *Storthing* is the name given to the Norwegian parliament, which assembles once every three years at Christiania. The time and place of meeting are fixed by law, and the king has no power to prevent or postpone its assembly. It consists of about a hundred members, who divide themselves into two houses. The members must not be under thirty years of age, and must have lived for ten years in Norway. The electors are required to be twenty-five years of age, and to be either burgesses of a town, or to possess property of the annual value of 30*l.* The members must possess the same qualification. The members of the Storthing are usually plain-spoken, sensible men, who have no desire to shine as orators, but who despatch with great native sagacity the business brought before them. This Storthing is the most independent legislative assembly in Europe; for not only has the king no power to prevent its meeting at the appointed time, but should he refuse to assent to any laws that are passed, these laws come into force without his assent, provided they are passed by three successive parliaments.--ED.

{49} The present king of Sweden and Norway is Oscar, one of the few fortunate scions of those lowly families that were raised to royal power and dignity by Napoleon. His father, Bernadotte, was the son of an advocate, and entered the French army as a common soldier; in that service he rose to the rank of marshal, and then became crown-prince, and ultimately king of Sweden. He died in 1844. The mother of Oscar was Desiree Clary, a sister of Julie Clary, wife of Joseph Bonaparte, the elder brother of Napoleon. This lady was asked in marriage by Napoleon himself, but her father refused his assent; and instead of becoming an unfortunate empress of France, she became a fortunate queen of Sweden and Norway. Oscar was born at Paris in 1799, and received his education chiefly in Hanover. He accompanied his father to Sweden in 1810, and ascended the throne on his father's death in 1844. In 1824 he married Josephine Beauharnois, daughter of Prince Eugene, and granddaughter of the brilliant and fascinating Josephine, the first and best wife of Napoleon. Oscar is much beloved by his subjects; his administration is mild, just, and equable; and his personal abilities and acquirements are far beyond the average of crowned heads.--ED.

{50} Bergen is a town of about twenty-five thousand inhabitants, situated near the Kons Fiord, on the west coast of Norway, and distant about 350 miles from Christiania. It is the seat of a bishopric, and a place of very considerable trade, its exports being chiefly fish. It has given its name to a county and a township in the state of New Jersey. There are three other Bergens,--one in the island of Rugen, one in the Netherlands, and another in the electorate of Hesse.

{51} *Kulle* is the Swedish for hill.

{52} Delekarlien is a Swedish province, situated ninety or one hundred miles north of Stockholm.

{53} The family of Sturre was one of the most distinguished in Sweden. Sten Sturre introduced printing into Sweden, founded the University of Upsala, and induced many learned men to come over. He was mortally wounded in a battle against the Danes, and died in 1520.

His successors as governors, Suante, Nilson Sturre, and his son, Sten Sturre the younger, still live in the memory of the Swedish nation, and are honoured for their patriotism and valour.

{54} The University of Upsala is the most celebrated in the north. It owes its origin to Sten Sturre, the regent of the kingdom, by whom it was founded in 1476, on the same plan as the University of Paris. Through the influence of the Jesuits, who wished to establish a new academy in Stockholm, it was dissolved in 1583, but re-established in 1598. Gustavus Vasa, who was educated at Upsala, gave it many privileges, and much encouragement; and Gustavus Adolphus reconstituted it, and give it very liberal endowments. There are twenty-four professors, and the number of students is between four and five hundred.--ED.

{55} See novel of *Ivar*, *the Skjuts Boy*, by Miss Emilie Carlen.

{56} At Calmar was concluded, in 1397, the famous treaty which bears its name, by which Denmark, Sweden, and Norway were united under one crown, that crown placed nominally on the head of Eric Duke of Pomerania, but virtually on that of his aunt Margaret, who has received the name of "the Semiramis of the North." --ED.

{57} There is now a railway direct from Hamburgh to Berlin.--ED.

{58} A florin is about two shillings sterling.-- *Tr.*

{59} Herr T. Scheffer of Modling, near Vienna, gives the following characteristic of this new dipteral animal, which belongs to the family muscidae, and resembles the species borborus:

Antennae deflexae, breves, triarticulatae, articulo ultimo phoereco; seda nuda.

Hypoctoma subprominulum, fronte lata, setosa. *Oculi* rotundi, remoti. Abdomen quinque annulatum, dorso nudo. *Tarsi* simplices. *Alae* incumbentes, abdomine longiores, nervo primo simplici.

Niger, abdomine nitido, antennis pedibusque rufopiceis.

www.bookjungle.com *email: sales@bookjungle.com fax: 630-214-0564 mail: Book Jungle PO Box 2226 Champaign, IL 61825*

The Codes Of Hammurabi And Moses
W. W. Davies

QTY

The discovery of the Hammurabi Code is one of the greatest achievements of archaeology, and is of paramount interest, not only to the student of the Bible, but also to all those interested in ancient history...

Religion   **ISBN:** *1-59462-338-4*   **Pages:132**
MSRP $12.95

The Theory of Moral Sentiments
Adam Smith

QTY

This work from 1749. contains original theories of conscience amd moral judgment and it is the foundation for systemof morals.

Philosophy **ISBN:** *1-59462-777-0*   **Pages:536**
MSRP $19.95

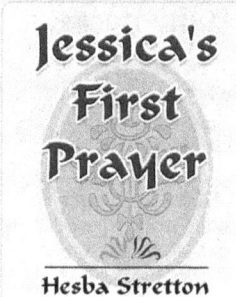

Jessica's First Prayer
Hesba Stretton

QTY

In a screened and secluded corner of one of the many railway-bridges which span the streets of London there could be seen a few years ago, from five o'clock every morning until half past eight, a tidily set-out coffee-stall, consisting of a trestle and board, upon which stood two large tin cans, with a small fire of charcoal burning under each so as to keep the coffee boiling during the early hours of the morning when the work-people were thronging into the city on their way to their daily toil...

Pages:84

Childrens   **ISBN:** *1-59462-373-2*   *MSRP $9.95*

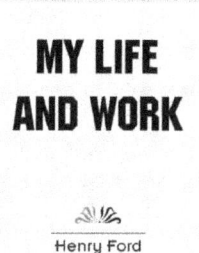

My Life and Work
Henry Ford

QTY

Henry Ford revolutionized the world with his implementation of mass production for the Model T automobile. Gain valuable business insight into his life and work with his own auto-biography... "We have only started on our development of our country we have not as yet, with all our talk of wonderful progress, done more than scratch the surface. The progress has been wonderful enough but..."

Pages:300

Biographies/   **ISBN:** *1-59462-198-5*   *MSRP $21.95*

The Art of Cross-Examination
Francis Wellman

QTY

I presume it is the experience of every author, after his first book is published upon an important subject, to be almost overwhelmed with a wealth of ideas and illustrations which could readily have been included in his book, and which to his own mind, at least, seem to make a second edition inevitable. Such certainly was the case with me; and when the first edition had reached its sixth impression in five months, I rejoiced to learn that it seemed to my publishers that the book had met with a sufficiently favorable reception to justify a second and considerably enlarged edition. ..

Pages:412

Reference   ISBN: *1-59462-647-2*   *MSRP $19.95*

On the Duty of Civil Disobedience
Henry David Thoreau

QTY

Thoreau wrote his famous essay, On the Duty of Civil Disobedience, as a protest against an unjust but popular war and the immoral but popular institution of slave-owning. He did more than write—he declined to pay his taxes, and was hauled off to gaol in consequence. Who can say how much this refusal of his hastened the end of the war and of slavery ?

Pages:48

Law   ISBN: *1-59462-747-9*   **Pages:48**

MSRP $7.45

Dream Psychology
Psychoanalysis for Beginners

Sigmund Freud

Dream Psychology Psychoanalysis for Beginners
Sigmund Freud

QTY

Sigmund Freud, born Sigismund Schlomo Freud (May 6, 1856 - September 23, 1939), was a Jewish-Austrian neurologist and psychiatrist who co-founded the psychoanalytic school of psychology. Freud is best known for his theories of the unconscious mind, especially involving the mechanism of repression; his redefinition of sexual desire as mobile and directed towards a wide variety of objects; and his therapeutic techniques, especially his understanding of transference in the therapeutic relationship and the presumed value of dreams as sources of insight into unconscious desires.

Pages:196

Psychology   ISBN: *1-59462-905-6*   *MSRP $15.45*

The Miracle of Right Thought
Orison Swett Marden

QTY

Believe with all of your heart that you will do what you were made to do. When the mind has once formed the habit of holding cheerful, happy, prosperous pictures, it will not be easy to form the opposite habit. It does not matter how improbable or how far away this realization may see, or how dark the prospects may be, if we visualize them as best we can, as vividly as possible, hold tenaciously to them and vigorously struggle to attain them, they will gradually become actualized, realized in the life. But a desire, a longing without endeavor, a yearning abandoned or held indifferently will vanish without realization.

Pages:360

Self Help   ISBN: *1-59462-644-8*   *MSRP $25.45*

QTY

The Rosicrucian Cosmo-Conception Mystic Christianity *by Max Heindel*   ISBN: *1-59462-188-8* **$38.95**
The Rosicrucian Cosmo-conception is not dogmatic, neither does it appeal to any other authority than the reason of the student. It is: not controversial, but is: sent forth in the, hope that it may help to clear...   New Age/Religion Pages 646

Abandonment To Divine Providence *by Jean-Pierre de Caussade*   ISBN: *1-59462-228-0* **$25.95**
"The Rev. Jean Pierre de Caussade was one of the most remarkable spiritual writers of the Society of Jesus in France in the 18th Century. His death took place at Toulouse in 1751. His works have gone through many editions and have been republished...   Inspirational/Religion Pages 400

Mental Chemistry *by Charles Haanel*   ISBN: *1-59462-192-6* **$23.95**
Mental Chemistry allows the change of material conditions by combining and appropriately utilizing the power of the mind. Much like applied chemistry creates something new and unique out of careful combinations of chemicals the mastery of mental chemistry...   New Age/Business Pages 422

The Letters of Robert Browning and Elizabeth Barret Barrett 1845-1846 vol II   ISBN: *1-59462-193-4* **$35.95**
by Robert Browning and Elizabeth Barrett   Biographies Pages 596

Gleanings In Genesis (volume I) *by Arthur W. Pink*   ISBN: *1-59462-130-6* **$27.45**
Appropriately has Genesis been termed "the seed plot of the Bible" for in it we have, in germ form, almost all of the great doctrines which are afterwards fully developed in the books of Scripture which follow...   Religion/Inspirational Pages 420

The Master Key *by L. W. de Laurence*   ISBN: *1-59462-001-6* **$30.95**
In no branch of human knowledge has there been a more lively increase of the spirit of research during the past few years than in the study of Psychology, Concentration and Mental Discipline. The requests for authentic lessons in Thought Control, Mental Discipline and...   New Age/Religion Pages 422

The Lesser Key Of Solomon Goetia *by L. W. de Laurence*   ISBN: *1-59462-092-X* **$9.95**
This translation of the first book of the "Lernegton" which is now for the first time made accessible to students of Talismanic Magic was done, after careful collation and edition, from numerous Ancient Manuscripts in Hebrew, Latin, and French...   New Age/Occult Pages 92

Rubaiyat Of Omar Khayyam *by Edward Fitzgerald*   ISBN:*1-59462-332-5* **$13.95**
Edward Fitzgerald, whom the world has already learned, in spite of his own efforts to remain within the shadow of anonymity, to look upon as one of the rarest poets of the century, was born at Bredfield, in Suffolk, on the 31st of March, 1809. He was the third son of John Purcell...   Music Pages 172

Ancient Law *by Henry Maine*   ISBN: *1-59462-128-4* **$29.95**
The chief object of the following pages is to indicate some of the earliest ideas of mankind, as they are reflected in Ancient Law, and to point out the relation of those ideas to modern thought.   Religion/History Pages 452

Far-Away Stories *by William J. Locke*   ISBN: *1-59462-129-2* **$19.45**
"Good wine needs no bush, but a collection of mixed vintages does. And this book is just such a collection. Some of the stories I do not want to remain buried for ever in the museum files of dead magazine-numbers an author's not unpardonable vanity..."   Fiction Pages 272

Life of David Crockett *by David Crockett*   ISBN: *1-59462-250-7* **$27.45**
"Colonel David Crockett was one of the most remarkable men of the times in which he lived. Born in humble life, but gifted with a strong will, an indomitable courage, and unremitting perseverance...   Biographies/New Age Pages 424

Lip-Reading *by Edward Nitchie*   ISBN: *1-59462-206-X* **$25.95**
Edward B. Nitchie, founder of the New York School for the Hard of Hearing, now the Nitchie School of Lip-Reading, Inc, wrote "LIP-READING Principles and Practice". The development and perfecting of this meritorious work on lip-reading was an undertaking...   How-to Pages 400

A Handbook of Suggestive Therapeutics, Applied Hypnotism, Psychic Science   ISBN: *1-59462-214-0* **$24.95**
by Henry Munro   Health/New Age/Health/Self-help Pages 376

A Doll's House: and Two Other Plays *by Henrik Ibsen*   ISBN: *1-59462-112-8* **$19.95**
Henrik Ibsen created this classic when in revolutionary 1848 Rome. Introducing some striking concepts in playwriting for the realist genre, this play has been studied the world over.   Fiction/Classics/Plays 308

The Light of Asia *by sir Edwin Arnold*   ISBN: *1-59462-204-3* **$13.95**
In this poetic masterpiece, Edwin Arnold describes the life and teachings of Buddha. The man who was to become known as Buddha to the world was born as Prince Gautama of India but he rejected the worldly riches and abandoned the reigns of power when...   Religion/History/Biographies Pages 170

The Complete Works of Guy de Maupassant *by Guy de Maupassant*   ISBN: *1-59462-157-8* **$16.95**
"For days and days, nights and nights, I had dreamed of that first kiss which was to consecrate our engagement, and I knew not on what spot I should put my lips..."   Fiction/Classics Pages 240

The Art of Cross-Examination *by Francis L. Wellman*   ISBN: *1-59462-309-0* **$26.95**
Written by a renowned trial lawyer, Wellman imparts his experience and uses case studies to explain how to use psychology to extract desired information through questioning.   How-to/Science/Reference Pages 408

Answered or Unanswered? *by Louisa Vaughan*   ISBN: *1-59462-248-5* **$10.95**
Miracles of Faith in China   Religion Pages 112

The Edinburgh Lectures on Mental Science (1909) *by Thomas*   ISBN: *1-59462-008-3* **$11.95**
This book contains the substance of a course of lectures recently given by the writer in the Queen Street Hall, Edinburgh. Its purpose is to indicate the Natural Principles governing the relation between Mental Action and Material Conditions...   New Age/Psychology Pages 148

Ayesha *by H. Rider Haggard*   ISBN: *1-59462-301-5* **$24.95**
Verily and indeed it is the unexpected that happens! Probably if there was one person upon the earth from whom the Editor of this, and of a certain previous history, did not expect to hear again...   Classics Pages 380

Ayala's Angel *by Anthony Trollope*   ISBN: *1-59462-352-X* **$29.95**
The two girls were both pretty, but Lucy who was twenty-one who supposed to be simple and comparatively unattractive, whereas Ayala was credited, as her Bombwhat romantic name might show, with poetic charm and a taste for romance. Ayala when her father died was nineteen...   Fiction Pages 484

The American Commonwealth *by James Bryce*   ISBN: *1-59462-286-8* **$34.45**
An interpretation of American democratic political theory. It examines political mechanics and society from the perspective of Scotsman James Bryce   Politics Pages 572

Stories of the Pilgrims *by Margaret P. Pumphrey*   ISBN: *1-59462-116-0* **$17.95**
This book explores pilgrims religious oppression in England as well as their escape to Holland and eventual crossing to America on the Mayflower, and their early days in New England...   History Pages 268

QTY

The Fasting Cure *by Sinclair Upton*   ISBN: *1-59462-222-1*   **$13.95**
In the Cosmopolitan Magazine for May, 1910, and in the Contemporary Review (London) for April, 1910, I published an article dealing with my experiences in fasting. I have written a great many magazine articles, but never one which attracted so much attention... New Age/Self Help/Health Pages 164

Hebrew Astrology *by Sepharial*   ISBN: *1-59462-308-2*   **$13.45**
In these days of advanced thinking it is a matter of common observation that we have left many of the old landmarks behind and that we are now pressing forward to greater heights and to a wider horizon than that which represented the mind-content of our progenitors... Astrology Pages 144

Thought Vibration or The Law of Attraction in the Thought World   ISBN: *1-59462-127-6*   **$12.95**
by William Walker Atkinson   Psychology/Religion Pages 144

Optimism *by Helen Keller*   ISBN: *1-59462-108-X*   **$15.95**
Helen Keller was blind, deaf, and mute since 19 months old, yet famously learned how to overcome these handicaps, communicate with the world, and spread her lectures promoting optimism. An inspiring read for everyone... Biographies/Inspirational Pages 84

Sara Crewe *by Frances Burnett*   ISBN: *1-59462-360-0*   **$9.45**
In the first place, Miss Minchin lived in London. Her home was a large, dull, tall one, in a large, dull square, where all the houses were alike, and all the sparrows were alike, and where all the door-knockers made the same heavy sound... Childrens/Classic Pages 88

The Autobiography of Benjamin Franklin *by Benjamin Franklin*   ISBN: *1-59462-135-7*   **$24.95**
The Autobiography of Benjamin Franklin has probably been more extensively read than any other American historical work, and no other book of its kind has had such ups and downs of fortune. Franklin lived for many years in England, where he was agent... Biographies/History Pages 332

Name	
Email	
Telephone	
Address	
City, State ZIP	

☐ **Credit Card**   ☐ **Check / Money Order**

Credit Card Number	
Expiration Date	
Signature	

Please Mail to: Book Jungle
PO Box 2226
Champaign, IL 61825
or Fax to: 630-214-0564

ORDERING INFORMATION

web: *www.bookjungle.com*
email: *sales@bookjungle.com*
fax: *630-214-0564*
mail: *Book Jungle PO Box 2226 Champaign, IL 61825*
or PayPal *to sales@bookjungle.com*

Please contact us for bulk discounts

DIRECT-ORDER TERMS

20% Discount if You Order Two or More Books
Free Domestic Shipping!
Accepted: Master Card, Visa, Discover, American Express

www.ingramcontent.com/pod-product-compliance
Lightning Source LLC
Chambersburg PA
CBHW080903020726

47502CB00008B/2333